T.

THE DEAL

by
Tony Drury

The Deal
Copyright ©2012 Tony Drury
Published in 2012 by City Fiction

Edited by Laura Keeling

City Fiction
c/o
Sue Richardson Associates Ltd
Minerva Mill Innovation Centre
Station Road
Alcester
Warwickshire B49 5ET
T: 01789 761345
www.cityfiction.com

A CIP record for this book is available from the British Library.

ISBN 978-0-9572017-2-9

Printed and bound in Great Britain by TJ International, Padstow,
Cornwall

The Deal is set mainly in London in 2011.

Also by Tony Drury

Megan's Game (2012)

"...she is my mistress and my queen. Her beauty transcends all the united charms of her whole sex; even those chimerical perfections, which the hyperbolical imaginations of poets in love have assigned to their mistresses, cease to be incredible descriptions when applied to her, in whom all those miraculous endowments are most divinely centred. The curling locks of her bright flowing hair are purest gold; her smooth forehead the Elysian Plain; her brows are two celestial bows; her eyes two glorious suns; her cheeks two beds of roses; her lips are coral; her teeth are pearl; her neck is alabaster; her breasts marble; her hands ivory; and snow would lose its whiteness near her bosom. Then, for the parts that modesty has veiled, my imagination, not to wrong them, chooses to lose itself in silent admiration; for nature boasts nothing that may give an idea of their incomparable worth."

Don Quixote by Cervantes

PART ONE

The terms

Chapter One

Ascent... yes, ascent, he pondered, as he quietly replayed the melody in his mind.

Oliver Chatham was sitting in the Polo Bar of The Westbury hotel, waiting for his companion to bring their drinks. Amanda Wavering had become impatient with the non-arrival of the somewhat flustered waitress and had gone over to the counter to place her order.

The music he was trying to recall had started with a strong piano introduction. Da- (long) de- (short) da- (long) which was repeated, da-de-da, before being joined by the strings of the orchestra, da-de-da, da-de-da, and then up an octave, repeating da-de-da several times. There was then an ascending piano and strings interplay, octave by octave, and crescendoing as the trumpets joined in. The violins then came in again, da-de-da, da-de-da, and the highest notes were reached with a crash of drums – dum! dum! dum! dum!

He looked over to where Amanda was waiting for their drinks.

"And mountains," he added under his breath. "The composer. Russian. He has to be Russian."

He sat back and listened to the piped music being played in the reception and bar areas of The Westbury. Was it the same song?

Less than an hour earlier, he and Amanda had left the offices of her brother's publishing business, City Fiction, situated in the Royal Exchange, opposite the Bank of England, and had taken the Central Line from Bank, in the heart of the City of London, and travelled west to Oxford Street. From there, they had strolled down Regent Street, before turning right into Conduit Street. Ten minutes in the late afternoon pedestrian traffic. The Americans were back in town, many having stayed on after the royal wedding and the presidential visit, and there were lots of Chinese and other East Asian visitors, too. A bustling, cosmopolitan crowd.

He'd first heard this composition one month earlier, when driving in Holborn near to Lincoln's Inn Fields. It was stirring and nationalistic. He'd turned up the volume so that he could make a note of the composer and the title of the piece. He usually tuned in to Classic FM but on this occasion had pressed the wrong button and found a foreign station.

As the music had stopped, a taxi driver and a cyclist – who was riding one of the London Mayor's Barclays-sponsored hire scheme bikes – decided to dispute the right-of-way. The driver had resorted to his cab horn and the rider, who had paid her £3.00 registration fee and £1.00 for using the bike for twenty-four hours, delivered a fearful lashing of obscenities. Unsurprisingly, her attention had wavered and she'd crashed into a fresh fruit stall. Boxes of oranges, apples, peaches, grapes and plums had cascaded into the road. As the market trader had gone to help her, his foot slipped on the spilt fruit, and down he went.

Oliver had tried, with difficulty, to manoeuvre his car around the debris, while watching the girl, whose skirt had risen high up around her waist, and, at the same time, to hear the answer to the question he was asking of the DJ from the long wave radio station.

He had caught "ascent..." – but had he also heard the word "mountain"? Something registered "mountain" but it wasn't the actual word "mountain". The composer. Who was the composer?

The cyclist had struggled up and was straightening her clothing, only to find that she'd torn her blouse. She'd cursed again.

"Russian," Oliver had cried under his breath. "It sounded Russian."

A police motor cyclist had then arrived on the scene only to watch the taxi driver accelerate away. Oliver had put his car back into gear and left the officer taking notes from the girl, who had been rather angry.

He glanced around the Polo Bar and his eyes settled on Amanda, who was still waiting for their drinks at the counter.

Three movements, he thought. One theme repeated twice, or was it just once? He'd looked at his watch as he drove away from the cycle accident and estimated a playing time of around eight minutes. It comprised piano and orchestra. A mini-concerto, he'd decided. He wanted to hear it again and play it in the tranquillity of his flat. He was determined to identify the composer and its title.

"Why don't you just pour it over your cornflakes?"

Lucy Harriman almost spat out the words as she watched her husband's hand hover with a bottle of vodka over an empty glass.

Charles Harriman looked at Scarlett, aged nine, Lily, who was almost seven, and Tabitha, now four years old. All three daughters continued eating their breakfast, although Scarlett was edging closer to her mother.

Their father was chief executive at White, Harriman and Boyle. Mr White had retired several years earlier, as the increasing regulatory pressures being applied by the Financial Services Authority (universally known as the FSA) persuaded him that corporate finance work was best left to younger men.

Charles had assumed control only to find that Bryan White had been his mentor and protector. After more than two years in office he'd begun to react to the business pressures with an ever increasing dependency on alcohol. He'd always controlled the glasses of wine at lunchtime and was popular with his clients, who enjoyed his hospitality. But before too long there were drinks after work, which he justified as staff liaison duties. A pint of strong lager before catching the tube train west to Ealing – where he was usually met by Lucy and his daughters – became two pints and perhaps a whisky to complete the day's work. He'd begun to rely on a glass of spirits in the evening about a year earlier. Lucy, however, hadn't seen him with a vodka bottle at the breakfast table until that morning.

They had already recognised that he had an alcoholic dependency and had agreed to fight the problem together.

She'd arranged for Charles to see a consultant at the Priory Grange clinic in Hemel Hempstead. She wanted the visit to be away from West London to ensure there was no possible leak in their gossipy community. Lucy didn't know whether the two-hour session had been constructive.

"He was efficient," Charles had told her when they'd discussed his appointment the previous evening. "He was keen to tell me about the people he'd helped. But he had difficulty understanding my work. I thought I'd explained things pretty well, but he seemed unable to comprehend that my difficulty is how our deals are structured."

Lucy said that she'd experienced the same problem in trying to understand his daily work. She asked her husband to take her through the issues again, although she was really motivated by her wish to keep him talking. Of course the difficulty wasn't with his work, but with his reliance on alcohol. But it was late into the evening and she was becoming increasingly concerned by his slurred speech and nervous mannerisms.

"It's the system, Lucy," Charles had explained after drinking some more wine. The flood gates opened. He'd detailed the process, which usually involved one of White, Harriman and Boyle's City contacts (often a law firm or an accounting practice) introducing a potential client. "They always want to raise money now or later." He'd slammed his hand on the table. "It's always about raising money."

He'd paused before going on. "We're part of the capital markets. Which are so called because they're a mechanism by which the directors of companies can offer shares – which we call capital or equity – in their company to outside investors. These might be financial institutions or private individuals."

"Name me a financial institution," she'd asked as she sipped her cup of coffee.

"A pension fund," he'd responded. "They invest their savers' contributions to try and increase the value of their clients' savings with them."

He'd stopped and opened another bottle of wine. He'd poured them both glasses of chardonnay, not noticing that Lucy's first glass was now under her chair. He'd continued as though he had forgotten the answer he had given to Lucy's question.

"There are many funds which are seeking a return on the money entrusted to them by their clients or private individuals. There are many funds," he'd repeated, "and a variety of legal structures. Private investors can range from retired army officers to speculators looking for above average returns."

Lucy was lost again, but had wanted him to continue without further interruption.

"Once the corporate finance house has decided it can and will act for a client, and terms are agreed, there will be a four to six month period during which a share promotion document is prepared. At this point the fund-raising can begin. It is exhausting, Lucy, and can be an emotional exercise for the directors of the client company. Sometimes it involves fifty or sixty presentations to individual fund managers."

"What's so emotional about it?" Lucy had thought to herself, but although now tiring, she'd still wanted him to continue talking.

"If, and when, the money is raised, and this, Lucy, is quite a complicated process, finally the company receives bank transferred funds net of the costs. On a fund-raising of ten million pounds, the costs could be as much as one point two million pounds."

"How much, Charles?!" she'd exclaimed, but he hadn't answered. He'd carried on as though he hadn't heard her.

"We can earn around three to four hundred thousand pounds if the deal is completed. But Lucy, if the transaction fails to raise the funds and collapses before the completion of the objectives agreed with the client, the advisers will receive abort fees. These are much reduced non-completion amounts, or no fees at all." He'd paused. "Imagine that, Lucy. No fees after all that fucking work!"

She'd realised that her husband had every intention of talking into the hours past midnight.

While waiting for the drinks at the Polo Bar, Amanda found her mind wandering back to the events of the previous weekend.

She and Zach had driven to Stratford-upon-Avon to watch the RSC's production of Hamlet. She had loved every moment of the production and was remembering some of the speech in which Polonius tells Laertes some home truths.

'This above all: to thine own self be true,
And it must follow, as the night the day,
Thou canst not then be false to any man.'

Zach was a successful independent film maker, specialising in social documentaries, several of which had been shown on prime-time television. He was, in many ways, ahead of his time and his analysis of the broken society would be re-shown following the August street riots and the temporary collapse of law and order in many cities across the country.

Amanda enjoyed his conversation. He was serious but fun. He was passionate and loving. And he was also married with two young children. He claimed his wife was having an affair with the headmaster at the school where she taught and he was preparing to leave her. He was putting no pressure on Amanda. He'd told her the situation as it was and said that he wasn't fighting for custody as his wife was seemingly being reasonable about access. He said that it wasn't ideal, but he loved Amanda and wanted to spend much more time in her company. He had bought her a ring and become a little emotional when he placed it on her finger.

They'd returned to London on Sunday afternoon and spent the evening reading the papers and listening to music. That night, in bed, their love-making had had an added intensity.

The following morning she'd left Zach sleeping and sat at the kitchen table. She'd taken some time to compose a letter to him. "Why, oh why, must he be married?" she'd mused to herself.

She knew that she was attractive to men. During her long sessions at the gym she often found herself in conversation with various athletic suitors. Over the previous three years she'd been with several decent partners. But somehow the relationships never lasted. There weren't arguments, nor rows – nor, in fact, much passion. Whenever she'd tried to dig deeper she'd found a void.

She had met Zach at the launch of one of City Fiction's new titles. He was a friend of a friend and had been persuaded to attend the evening event. He'd met Amanda after being accidentally pushed in the back and spilling his glass of champagne down her blouse. It proved an effective way of breaking the ice and within a week they were involved. Immediately, she'd found him interesting and witty. He spoke passionately about his work and cared about the social issues which his documentaries exposed.

So why was she proposing to end their relationship? She wasn't completely sure herself. There was just a nagging doubt. To break up a marriage... And she couldn't understand why Zach wasn't fighting harder to keep his family together. There were two boys aged five and three to consider. She just didn't understand – or much like – how he could seemingly walk out on his responsibilities.

She'd placed the letter on the table and walked out of the house. She knew what her brother Alistair would say; he was convinced she was unable to consummate longer term relationships. She knew that he cared for her and wanted her to find some stability. She'd groaned inwardly as she started to plan how to tell him.

She shook her head to clear her mind of these reflections. She paid for their drinks and turned round to carry the glasses over to Oliver.

Charles was now on a roll. He was drinking even more quickly as he explained his business to his wife.

"Bryan White built up the business by never taking up-front fees," he'd continued. "The reason was that his experience had taught him that the relationship between the client and the adviser was stronger if both parties needed a success before the corporate finance house was paid. I always agreed with him on that principle."

"That's like saying a doctor should only be paid if he cures the patient," Lucy had said.

9

"Good point. The difference is that the doctor is paid a salary. In our case we earn commission based on a successful transaction. They're big fees. Our clients are happier if they only pay us for achieving results."

They'd discussed her husband's work on many occasions but never before had he spoken with such intensity and energy.

He'd told her that while this strategy had underpinned the growth of White, Harriman and Boyle, he found that he was becoming increasingly exposed as various deals reached their end game. In the space of seven weeks he'd lost three transactions. The first, a speculative new ecology printing process, failed to interest investors and ended with the three directors threatening Charles with litigation and grievous bodily harm.

The second business, a leasing company involved with helicopters, raised the money they wanted but not at the valuation they were willing to accept. Charles had spent nearly a day and a half in meetings and phone calls to the fund managers who were willing to invest. The directors assessed their business at a valuation of one hundred and twenty million pounds and the fund managers were only willing to invest at a valuation of seventy million pounds. He'd experienced a frustration the like of which he'd never known before. At seven o'clock in the morning he'd found a pub in Smithfield market where he'd downed nearly a third of a bottle of scotch.

Lucy had wondered whether she should make a phone call in the morning. The Priory Grange clinic had said, in a private telephone call with her alone, that she could take Charles in at any time. She'd let him continue talking.

He'd described how the third transaction collapsed when the chief executive of a Sunderland-based oil-surveying company fell in love with his finance director. They had always been professionally close and she and her husband, a professional musician, played bridge with the chief executive and his wife. However, several evenings in a London hotel during a series of twenty-three institutional presentations had led to illicit night games. At first they had both fought against temptation and breaching the sanctity of their marriages. The finance director had thought of returning home to the north. However, following one rather tense session with a fund manager who had spent two hours arguing over her financial forecasting model, they had found themselves in Bloomsbury. They'd gone to a champagne bar and ended up in bed. The next day they decided to return to Sunderland and set up home together.

When he had finally stopped talking, Lucy had looked helplessly at her husband. It was rather easier in the surgery. There was a set procedure for dealing with this type of patient, albeit within a ten minute time scale. It was proving rather more challenging with her own partner. She decided that she must check on the girls. Luckily, Charles had abruptly announced that he was going to bed.

The following morning he asked his wife if it was too early for a drink.

She immediately regretted her response, although the moment she suggested he pour vodka over his breakfast cereal proved to be the turning point.

He put down the bottle and looked in turn at Lucy, Scarlett, Lily and Tabitha. He put his hands up to his face.

"Lucy," he said. "I'll never go back to that clinic."

The drinks menu provided for guests at the Polo Bar suggested *"it is a haven for lovers sharing a moment for a romantic cocktail"*.

Amanda placed the glasses on their table, sat down and radiated a smile in Oliver's direction.

She was at that moment hardly a lover. She was a client. She was the foreign rights editor at City Fiction, a rapidly expanding publishing company founded by her brother, Alistair, five years ago. Oliver was a corporate financier who was hoping to raise two million pounds for their business.

"Did you hear the music being played?" he asked.

"No, Oliver, I was trying to buy you a drink."

"I heard the same piece on my car radio a few weeks ago. I'm trying to discover what it's called." He explained about the bicycle incident and the few clues he'd heard.

"Ascent, mountain, Russian. Good luck with that," she said.

He would return to The Westbury the following morning to ask the manager if he could trace the CD which had been playing the previous evening. After a few minutes it transpired that it was a track from a disc brought in by a temporary member of the bar staff, who had left the employment of the hotel that evening.

The corporate financier was now concentrating his attention on Amanda. He was enjoying the glass of white wine she'd bought for him.

"That was a good meeting, Oliver. Thank you. Alistair was clearly pleased."

"So where's he gone tonight?"

"He travels all the time to meet authors. He's flying up to Scotland to dine with a retired stockbroker who wants to tell his story."

"And will that sell?"

"No, probably not," replied Amanda. "Alistair will want him to pay for the cost of production. We then publish the title and, if it sells, so much the better."

"Don't they call that 'vanity publishing?'"

"It's an old-fashioned word with a stigma attached to it. We refer to 'marketing and promotional costs' but that's exactly what it is. Alistair spotted the gap in the market. The stockbroker will be filthy rich and will want to tell his stories. Many of them have the same ambition. We produce a lovely book, they pay for it, and occasionally they sell quite well."

She excused herself and went out of the bar in search of the ladies' cloakroom. He watched her go. She was blonde and her hair almost touched the collar of her two-piece dark blue suit. She was wearing a white blouse and Oliver could see the sleeves extending beyond the cuffs. She was about five foot eight, not allowing for the high kitten heels on her blue tinted shoes. Her skirt fell just above her knees and her tanned skin shone with health. The calves of her legs were gently muscular and her ankles were toned and narrow. As he lifted his eyes he focused on her buttocks, which were pressing rather alluringly against the tightness of her skirt.

She turned around and smiled at him before disappearing from view.

12

The subdued lighting in the bar had briefly caught her face in its glow. Her hair was swept across her forehead and her eye-brows were natural. Although Oliver couldn't see from his seat he remembered that her eyes were blue.

As he waited the waitress appeared and he ordered a second round of drinks. The music playing in the Polo Bar was now the more usual jazz-based themes. He pondered his search further. He was certain the composer was Russian. He hadn't caught the name but it had sounded full of piano and orchestra and patriotism.

Amanda returned as the drinks were served. She smiled – she liked being taken out of the City into the West End.

"It's good to meet you," she said. She explained that she'd been in Europe for the last week and had missed the introduction made by Alistair's solicitor to Oliver.

They went on to discuss the work of a corporate financier and why this one was interested in trying to raise funds for City Fiction.

"Great name by the way," he said.

"Alistair at his best," said Amanda. "He's really inspirational. He took his idea around the City and raised half a million pounds to get the business going."

She raised her glass to her lips.

"Alistair and I are close, Oliver. I'll be so grateful if you're able to help us. Alistair can see how to expand the company. He just needs the money to do so… and I'm going to help him all I can."

"I do like the business, but you must understand that conditions are pretty tough at the moment. It won't be easy to raise the funds you need, please understand that."

She put her hand over his.

"But, Oliver," she said. "My instinct is that if anybody can, it's you, and I'm rarely wrong about men."

The top two buttons of her white blouse were undone. Her jacket was open and a black belt fitted snugly around her waist, accentuating her figure. She had applied virtually no make-up apart from a little mascara around her eyes and no jewellery apart from a gold crucifix around her neck.

She smiled at Oliver and then became a little more serious.

"Alistair is everything I have," she continued. She picked up her glass and took a small sip. "He's the hardest working human being I've ever known."

He reached for his glass of wine and gulped a mouthful.

"He's building a great business, Amanda, but publishing is..."

"Publishing is about finding winners, Oliver. Alistair just needs to find his J K Rowling."

"Well, City Fiction is certainly a good company," he acknowledged. "And you've done well to expand beyond just vanity books. Alistair is a gifted publisher. In five years, and almost from nothing, he's created a serious publishing business with over ninety books on his list. It's an impressive record. That's why we're so interested in trying to work with you."

"So, you're going to raise the money he wants?" Amanda flashed Oliver her most winning smile.

Sara Flemming was seriously fed-up.

She could accept his arrogance. She tolerated the occasional wandering hand and the suggestive language. He was rich, so what. He was on his way upwards, a Cameron favourite. He'd convinced her that the Tories would win the next general election in 2015 and that he would become a minister. He had told her that a PPS wasn't too far away. She'd had to ask a friend what PPS meant – not that she understood what a Permanent Private Secretary did anyway. But she liked Portcullis House, overlooking the Thames towards the South Bank and she enjoyed the parties. She'd now slept with three Members of Parliament. To this day she could never understand why one of them insisted on putting a photograph of his wife beside the hotel bed. Still, it was a particularly vigorous experience. So far, she'd notched up a Conservative, a Lib-Dem and a Scottish Nationalist. Not bad going.

But now she was upset because of Charlie Stanford's hypocrisy. He adapted his policies as required by the situation. At first he was totally for the proposed reform of the National Health Service. Sara sent letter after letter to his constituents praising

Andrew Lansley's budgetary changes. "I love the thought of patient choice and GPs holding the purse strings," he would write. "Dear Mrs Roseacre. It is a disgrace that you have waited six months for your replacement knee joint. I send you my sincere best wishes and know that under Andrew Lansley's proposals the financial power being given to your doctor will change things for the better."

Charlie was street-wise, charming and ambitious. He was also intellectually limited. While at a university in the north, a classmate had once famously said to him, in front of thirty others, "Charlie, if you had a second brain, it would be rather lonely."

Thus Charlie was slower than many to realise that, by May, David Cameron had already decided that Andrew Lansley was the fall guy when, as was expected, Lib-Dem pressure meant the proposed NHS reforms were to be drastically revised.

Once he finally grasped the drift, there was a marked change in his letter writing.

"Dear Mr Hickman. I am so sorry that you are facing a two month wait to see a consultant about your hip. We in the coalition government are finding it difficult to repair the damage caused to this country by Gordon Brown. I am sending your letter to the authorities with a request that they expedite your case."

"Charlie," interrupted Sara. "I thought we were telling your constituents that the NHS reforms are going to..."

"Oh, shut your mouth, Sara. I dictate, you type, got it?"

"Charlie, all I said was that I thought you were excited by the health reforms. You said you chose me because, to use your word, I was 'interested'."

"Sara. You have two functions in life: to serve me because of the life I can offer you here, including a bloody good wage..."

"And?"

"To screw around all you want. From what I hear that's not going too badly. Now, you are never again to utter Andrew Lansley's name in this office. Right?"

Sara smiled innocently. "Did you enjoy your drink with the Prime Minister last night, Charlie?"

On leaving, she decided to walk past several tube stations before catching her ride to Aldgate and the ten minute walk to her flat from which she could see the Tower of London. She mulled over recent events and decided it was time she grow up a bit. She was twenty-four years old. She decided to respond to Alex's text suggestion and meet in their favourite wine bar. She needed to talk about her decision.

"Lisbeth Salander was twenty-four," said Alex.

"Why do you say that?" asked Sara, as she sipped her glass of Chardonnay.

"Come on, Sara. You can't fool me. All this drama about walking out on an MP. You're trying to be the English version of *The Girl with the Dragon Tattoo* aren't you?"

"Piss off, Alex. Never entered my head." She laughed. "Anyway I haven't got any tattoos."

"So how many did Lisbeth have?" laughed her companion.

"Three... er... four... er... well the dragon was on her left shoulder blade."

"That's one – what were the others?"

"There was a WASP tattoo on her neck."

"Two. Go on."

"Give up. Who cares?"

"You do, Miss Wannabe Salander. Four. She had loops around the bicep of her left arm and her left ankle."

"Oh, whatever!" Sara laughed. "I'm a redhead anyway. Nothing like her."

"Wrong again. Lisbeth was a redhead but she dyed her hair raven black."

"What's all this about, Alex? It's you who's obsessed with this sodding woman."

"Ever since you read the book you've imagined you were her." A hand rested on her knee. "When you read that she had imagination..."

"No. That was Dragan Armansky, her boss at Milton Security. He thought that she had..."

"Got it, Sara? You know that book word for..."

"Piss off, Alex. She was anorexic."

"No she wasn't. She was just thin."

"And flat chested."

Alex laughed. "Thank God there's one difference between you." A hand disappeared inside Sara's shirt, and she groaned softly in anticipation of the pleasures which would come later.

The next morning, when Charlie Stanford arrived for work at Portcullis House, he found a brief letter from Sara on his desk.

Oliver had parked his car in the basement and switched off his radio after listening to Jane Jones on Classic FM presenting uninterrupted classical performances. He nodded to the care-taker as he caught the lift to the fourth floor of his Clerkenwell flat. He was tired after his evening workout in the gym. He threw his jacket onto the table, poured himself a drink and put on the CD he had bought earlier in the day at the HMV shop in Moorgate. He was determined to track down the piece of music he had heard on his car radio four weeks ago and then again in The Westbury the previous evening. He was able to repeat the theme and decided his best option was to try to identify the composer. He'd telephoned his brother-in-law, who was in his chambers at Gray's Inn in Holborn.

"Edward," he asked. "Who's the most famous Russian com-poser of piano music?"

"Rachmaninov," he'd replied.

He now had a choice of four piano concertos. For no par-ticular reason, he selected No.3 in D minor, op.30. Sergei Rachmaninov had written this masterpiece during a stay at Ivanovka, his family's estate near Moscow, in October 1909. He then crossed the Atlantic and premiered the concerto on 28 November at the New Theatre, New York. Initially its great length, over forty-five minutes' playing time, caused some critical reservations, but eventually the brilliant first movement ('allegro ma non tanto'), with its colour and emotion and its climax in the cadenza, paved the way for its eventual acclaim.

Oliver closed his eyes as the pianist began to play. It wasn't the style of music for which he was searching, but slowly he became immersed in its lyrical and flowing melodies. He raised his feet and laid them on the arm of his sofa.

Vladimir Ashkenazy and the London Symphony Orchestra, conducted by André Previn, led Oliver into the second movement ('intermezzo adagio') and finally to the 'Finale (alla breve)'. However, by this time, Oliver's mind was wandering to a different place.

He was recalling her physical shape. He hadn't seen the flesh of her thighs but his imagination was vivid. He retraced her calf muscles and the tanned skin of her lower body... the silky smooth legs. He was becoming aroused.

Amanda was sipping wine in her flat on Elm Tree Road on the north side, overlooking Lord's cricket ground. She was twenty-eight years old and reflecting on her decision to reject the chance of a longer term relationship with Zach. During her time at Oxford she'd had a few relatively serious boyfriends as a result of her production work for a theatre group. However, Zach was the closest she'd come to a life partner. She was reading a letter he'd sent her – it was composed with Zach's typical tact and sensitivity.

He analysed her decision with some empathy and discussed why she'd questioned their relationship. He suggested that life wasn't always perfect and all choices had some form of defect ingrained in them. He wrote that there was no ideal relationship but he felt they were capable of building a good one.

She knew he was right. But she concentrated on what he had not written about. There was no comment on his marriage and, unbelievably, no reference to his two sons.

She chose not to reply. She'd made up her mind.

On Thursday morning, at the offices of Agnew Capital, situated in Queen Street, south of Mansion House tube station, Oliver met with Andrew Agnew and his other colleagues.

Andrew had founded his business in the early 1990s. Agnew Capital specialised in raising finance for entrepreneurial businesses. He'd been joined by Jody Boyle in 2002 and she was both finance director and responsible for regulatory matters. Oliver had known Andrew for a number of years before joining the firm in 2004. There were now eleven staff overall.

"As you know from my briefing paper," said Oliver, "City Fiction has been introduced to us by Nick Billings, their solicitor."

Oliver then described the formation of the company by Alistair Wavering and how he was joined by his sister Amanda two years later. Alistair had begun his career in regional newspapers and came to London when Tony Blair became Prime Minister. He'd worked for several specialist financial publications until he spotted a gap in the market: he'd realised that there were a number of people in the City who wanted to tell their stories. Some were coming to the end of their careers and were keen to write their autobiographies, others thought they could explain aspects of City finance, and a surprising number thought they had a novel in them.

Alistair had realised that he must be based in the City and so he'd rented offices in the Royal Exchange. He housed his key staff here but also ran a production and sales team from cheaper premises in Camden Town.

He was lucky to the extent that he'd begun trading in the boom years of the Blair/Brown era. Even though the recession was beginning to show, he'd had no difficulty in finding titles and people willing to pay for their publication. He'd quickly extended into fiction publishing and begun to build his reputation as an innovative operator. He'd made one acquisition which added twenty-seven titles to his list and brought in three talented young people. They were ahead in their understanding of the power of eBooks and the impact of the Kindle.

"The company," continued Oliver, "needs an injection of new capital to finance its growth. Jody has their financial projections. My advice is that they raise perhaps two million pounds now and then, in a year or two, join one of the smaller stock markets to develop their appeal to shareholders."

"Thanks, Oliver," interrupted Andrew. "This is a good report. Jody, your thoughts please."

Jody smiled across the table.

"Andrew," she said. "I think this has potential. But, Oliver, please just summarise for me and for Andrew again, in no more than three minutes, why we should accept it."

Oliver smiled back at the finance director.

"City Fiction," said Oliver, "has now published over ninety books. They have two award-winning authors and they're ahead in their understanding of electronic publishing. They were under-capitalised from the beginning. The initial half million pounds that was raised was insufficient to finance their rapid expansion. They had an eighty thousand pound government guaranteed bank loan which they have nearly repaid. They've issued some more shares under the Enterprise Investment Scheme, which raised an additional one hundred thousand pounds, and they have thirty-six shareholders."

Abbi Highfield, the marketing manager, nodded before speaking.

"It really does help the story when the shares attract EIS relief," she said. "The twenty percent upfront tax relief and the fact that dividends and gains will be tax free are both attractive." She paused and then continued. "Andrew, I do like this story. Our investors will be able to relate to the company. They can go online and order the books if they wish."

Oliver looked gratefully at Abbi. She usually supported his proposals.

"But the balance sheet, Oliver," she went on, "it shows net assets of only five hundred and fifty thousand pounds. My assessment is that their cash position is tight and they are struggling to pay their bills on time. They're borrowing from other sources by factoring their debtors. Just explain that for me please."

Jody clarified that it was possible for companies to use their debtors – customers' bills which remained unpaid – as security for lenders who might advance as much as eighty percent of the face value, an operation known as factoring.

"City Fiction has repaid its bank loan, Jody," continued Oliver, "and now the bank is refusing to extend a fresh overdraft facility. That's why they want us to raise them two million pounds. The larger sum will address the issues you've identified, Jody, and allow them to invest in more titles."

"So, they want to raise two million pounds for thirty percent of the company. I think we can get that from the investment funds and our clients here in London," Oliver went on, looking at Jody.

"I did like Alistair," said Abbi. "And was that his sister in the suit?"

"Yes," said Oliver. "She deals with foreign rights and spends much of her time in Europe. She told me that she's planning a visit to Hong Kong and the Far East."

"Jody," asked Andrew, "have you met with their finance team?"

"Well, Andrew, it's hardly a team. It's often the case with these smaller companies. Their financial support lags behind their growth. They have a part-time finance director, David Singleton, whom I liked. He produces management accounts by the tenth of the month. There is a finance manager and she's really good. So overall, it's competent. But I must say that a fund-raising process will test them. It'll put a lot of pressure on the two individuals."

"This is pre-public markets, Jody," said Oliver, "for that very reason. My strategy for them is that they'll be ready for a flotation, hopefully on the London Stock Exchange junior market, in about two years. So we'll raise the money using an EIS document."

"Yes," said Abbi. "Our clients will like the EIS tax benefits."

"Abbi," said Andrew, "I understand your enthusiasm for the tax relief for investors that the EIS means, but remember that the investment story must stand up in its own right. Tax relief does not make a bad investment into a good proposition."

Abbi nodded and smiled at Oliver.

"You know, Andrew," said Jody, "I do like this deal. But I think the problem is that Oliver hasn't had the chance to really research the publishing industry. We all know things are changing. On the tube these days more and more people seem to be reading books on their Kindles."

"Jody is saying what I was thinking," continued Andrew. "Oliver, I know you're stretched at the moment but most of the information in your proposal is just what the company has told you. I thought the same about the retail marketing venture we looked at last week. I think we need to recruit a research analyst who can provide reports of greater depth."

"Good luck with that," said Oliver, under his breath.

The forty-eight hours which had passed since Charles Harriman had started the process of coming to terms with his alcoholism had catapulted him into the supporting arms of his wife. For two days they had been locked together.

Lucy took her left hand and, using her handkerchief, wiped the perspiration away from her husband's face. With her other hand she held Charles's arm and squeezed hard. The children had been taken to school by their neighbour and they were now sitting alone in their kitchen.

"There's nothing in this world, Charles," she said, "that Scarlett, Lily, Tabitha and I wouldn't do for you. You are a wonderful man. You're needed by your children. We'll sell the house. I've arranged with the surgery that I can return to work for three days a week starting next Tuesday."

Lucy produced a sheet of paper from her case. She was the type of woman to be very organised in a crisis. "Here's a summary of the finances. The bank is bridging the sale. The credit cards will be cleared. That's eighty thousand pounds we owe. The mortgage is four hundred and fifteen thousand pounds. After costs we will have around two hundred thousand pounds. We'll rent for a year while we stabilise our position. With the recession there are a number of properties for rental in this area. We'll start looking almost immediately."

Lucy put her hand on Charles's arm. "We need to know if your business can pull through, Charles. That's where you are going to put all your effort. I'll deal with everything else." She stopped for a moment and then continued. "Charles, all I need to know from you is, are you truly serious about staying off the drink? It's a huge challenge for you, I know. I don't underestimate it."

The telephone rang but they let it continue until the answerphone clicked in.

"They were kind to me at the clinic, Lucy, but suddenly I realised that I was being treated as a patient. They said I was ill. It was humiliating. I've been drinking too much because of work pressures. I'm not ill. Of course I can stop."

Lucy stood up. "We have a lot to do, Charles," she said abruptly.

"You said that the children need me – but what about you, Lucy?"

She smiled tightly but didn't speak. There was a long silence.

"What if I can't resist it, Lucy?" Charles said quietly. "What if I have another drink?"

Lucy reached inside her case and took out what seemed to be a piece of card. She handed it to her husband and he turned it over. It was a photograph of his three children taken in late February during a winter's walk in the forest. Scarlett was dressed all in red and was wearing a white, fluffy hat. Lily was clinging on to Scarlett's back and waving and laughing. Tabitha had fallen over in the snow but was still managing to look at the camera held by her mother.

"Keep this with you at all times, Charles. You must understand one thing. You're not giving up drink. You are making a choice. You're deciding what life you want to lead."

On Friday afternoon Oliver met with Alistair and Amanda at a coffee house in Old Broad Street. Alistair spent an hour telling him about developments at City Fiction and Amanda spoke persuasively to him on the potential of their foreign rights. She was wearing a green jacket and skirt. Her hair was full of bounce and Oliver noticed again her impossibly radiant skin – and her skirt rising halfway up her thighs. She insisted on smiling at him. It was a modest gesture. It completely took him apart.

"So what do you think, Oliver?" asked Alistair.

"Yes," confirmed Oliver. "Andrew is there to be persuaded and Jody generally backs me."

"So it's a 'yes'. You'll raise the money for us?"

"It's *almost* a 'yes', Alistair. Andrew wants a more detailed report on the publishing industry. He's seen that Waterstones have been in trouble recently. He is, of course, right to the extent that we're relying on you for all our information. A separate analysis does make sense. It shouldn't hold matters up. I'll prepare the client engagement letter for you and we need to complete client take-on procedures and money laundering checks. I want to spend a day with you next week. I'll start the preparation of the share promotion document. I think you understand our process?"

"Out of ten, Oliver," asked Alistair abruptly, "what are the chances of you raising the money for us?"

"Well, I really like your business and we've all been watching Bloomsbury Publishing and the Harry Potter magic. Jody likes your financial controls, although there is some work to be done there. We really do think that you're a publisher with a great future."

"Yes, but out of ten?"

"The economy is weak, Alistair. Cameron seems to want to save the world while Middle England collapses. Consumer spending is really struggling. Investors are cautious."

"Alistair is a committed Tory," interrupted Amanda. "I understand that your father was a vice-chairman of the party at one time?"

"My father was part of the inner circle during the Thatcher years," responded Oliver. "He and my mother emigrated to Australia about ten years ago. Dad hated Blair and the doctors suggested that the heat of Queensland could help my mother's arthritis."

"Out of ten, Oliver?" Alistair repeated.

"I'll give it everything I can, Alistair. If it's possible, I'll get it."

"You still haven't answered my question."

"Seven, on a good day."

"And on a bad day?"

"Seven. Every day in corporate finance is a bad day."

Amanda leaned forward, put her hand on Oliver's thigh and squeezed.

"With you on our side, Oliver," she said, "I reckon it's a nine."

"Thanks for coming in," said Andrew.

Sara Flemming smiled. "I only posted the letter on Thursday, Mr Agnew. I'm impressed that you work on a Saturday." She sat down on the chair that was offered to her.

"You did business studies at Manchester. You then worked in Paris for two years researching impressionist art and, most recently, you worked for a Conservative Member of Parliament?"

"That's about it, Mr Agnew."

"How did you get our details?"

"I was reading a research paper about publishing companies and the difficulties they have in raising money. The article mentioned a number of finance houses which specialise in the sector. I wrote to ten of those companies."

"Is the publishing world something that interests you, Sara?" asked Andrew. "Sorry, would you like a coffee?"

"I called at Starbucks on my way here, thank you, Mr Agnew. I like researching and understanding about things. I'm an English Lisbeth Salander." She paused, feeling rather pleased with that line.

"The girl with the dragon tattoo!" he exclaimed.

"Yes," she laughed, "without the tattoos, the hang-ups, the drugs and the occasional violence. But, like Lisbeth, I have good IT skills and I love to ferret. I like gaining knowledge." She smiled. "I also have imagination."

"Well, it is indeed a coincidence that you came across us in the way that you did, as I actually need a report on the publishing industry," said Andrew.

"Why?"

"I have to make a decision on whether to commit my corporate finance team to raising two million pounds for a publishing house."

"Which one?"

"I can't tell you that, Sara, I'm afraid. Client confidentiality."

"Which publishing house, Mr Agnew?"

He looked at her and smiled.

"Well...since you've pressed me – City Fiction... they're a..."

"Wow. They published *Twenty Four Hours to Meltdown*. Did you enjoy it?"

"Well... I haven't quite reached that..."

"Ronan Murphy. Former City journalist. He won a big literary award in 2010. I looked up their website. They have some great titles."

"It's hard work making money in publishing, Sara. I have to be certain before I can ask our investors to consider it."

"The world is changing, Mr Agnew. Everybody is talking about eBooks, but that's just scratching the surface. You want to know if City Fiction fully understand what is happening in their industry."

"Can you do a report in two weeks, Sara?"

"Would Lisbeth have agreed a deadline?" she asked with a smile.

As she left the chief executive's office, Andrew remembered they hadn't discussed fees. He called her back and raised the question.

"Whatever I charge, Mr Agnew, I'll be worth it," said Sara.

Saturday was a typical May bank holiday. Sun, showers, hot, clouds, cold.

Gemma sighed in frustration and disappointment. She'd reached a decision to end her relationship with Oliver. They had met in the gym a few months earlier when he had fallen over a trailing rope and she had kissed his bruised knee better. They'd begun a passionate affair which she'd thought was beginning to mature into something more meaningful. She was now having doubts.

They had been walking and talking together for over an hour as they followed the trails of Regent's Park. She could feel him becoming more and more remote and his mind seemed to be somewhere completely different. She told him that she objected to being taken for granted. He remained silent. He said nothing as she told him that it was over.

The last thing he did was to buy her an ice-cream. As her lips closed around the chocolate flake he experienced a slight pang of regret. They had been pretty good together.

"Goodbye, Oliver," said Gemma, as she tried to control her frustration. She knew there was someone else.

On Sunday evening, with a bank holiday Monday ahead, Oliver stayed up late into the evening and decided to listen to Rachmaninov's piano concerto No. 2 in C Minor, op.18, which starts with one of the greatest moderatos in piano music. Listeners of Classic FM regularly picked it at the top of their various charts.

Rachmaninov died in 1943, two years before David Lean directed *Brief Encounter* and used the music, performed by Eileen Joyce, as the background to one of the most famous love affairs in film.

Vladimir Ashkenazy had moved on to the adagio sostenuto so, for over twelve minutes, Oliver allowed his mind to be hypnotised by André Previn and the London Symphony Orchestra.

He was slowly arriving at two conclusions. There was indeed somebody else; and Sergei Rachmaninov wasn't the composer of the music he had heard on the radio.

That had begun with an introduction of piano and violins. Da-de-da, da-de-da. The violins dominated and went up the octaves, then some trumpets and drums, followed by dum, dum, dum, dum and then the pianist came in again followed by the orchestra and...

Oliver fell asleep on the sofa in the early hours of the bank holiday. As he slipped into dreams, he thought about a skirt rising up some sun-tanned thighs.

Chapter Two

Lucy Harriman began her first surgery of the new contract at the Whiteoaks Practice, about three miles west of Ealing, on the Tuesday morning. Although there were two doctors ready to see patients from 7.30am onwards, the senior partner, who was pleased to have a female doctor in his team, agreed that for her three days each week, she could start at 9.00am and finish at 4.00pm. There had been some logistical organisation to accommodate school runs. Charles was able to cope with the mornings and a neighbour had agreed, temporarily, to collect Scarlett and Lily from their school and wait for Lucy to come and get them at around 4.45pm. Tabitha would remain at her nursery school in the care of the duty teacher until Lucy arrived.

She paused briefly before calling in her first patient. Charles had been particularly disturbed during the previous evening and had insisted on telling her about a visit he had been forced to make to meet with the regulatory authorities.

"It was so intimidating," he'd said. "Catching the Docklands Light Railway from Bank Tube down to Canary Wharf. It's like entering a futuristic world, Lucy. The offices are huge. There's glass everywhere. There are shopping malls full of coffee houses." He had paused to take a drink of fresh orange juice. "You go into the FSA building. It's massive. It takes ages to reach reception. It's like a seven star hotel. You get signed in and the guard takes you to the lift. The corridors are wide and the meeting room we were in was six times the size of this lounge." He'd drunk some more of his juice and seemed genuinely distressed at the memory.

She'd studied her husband's face and knew that he had yet to understand the devastating effects of alcohol. She was certain that he had not fully grasped that drinking merely disguised intense and scary feelings that he would, one day, need to face. He needed to talk about his real fears. But she'd found herself having to listen to his description of the regulatory interview.

"There were four of them sitting in a row opposite me and my solicitor. They had sheets of paper. The main officer started by saying that they had twenty-two questions on which they wanted answers." He'd slapped his open hand on the table. "We were there on a routine matter. We wanted to discuss adding to our permissions. In your language, Lucy, what we were allowed to do."

She'd noticed the sweat on his forehead.

"Routine, my ar... sorry, Lucy. Routine. It made the KGB look like Punch and Judy. Two lawyers and one barrister. We were there for two hours and, afterwards, my solicitor made me write a four page letter which, he said, was to correct all the errors I had made. We won't get their decision for six weeks."

He had retired to bed and she had followed her increasingly frequent habit of sleeping in the spare room.

Now, the following morning, she knew she had to focus on her medical duties.

Her first three patients were men. Philip was a sports fanatic whose daily workouts at the gym had given him piles. A thorough examination and a prescription for suppositories and cream completed the appointment.

The second was a marketing manager for a toy manufacturer who had arrived back from China the previous day convinced he had skin cancer. At Lucy's request he lowered his trousers and showed her his infected thigh. There was a vivid red and brown blistered patch from the top of the leg almost to his knee. Across it were lines where the victim had been scratching.

"Your skin is rather dry, Mr Henderson."

"Is it...?"

"It's discoid eczema, Mr Henderson. It's often caused by stress. It's quite common with long distance fliers. How long is the flight from Beijing? Twelve, perhaps, thirteen hours? But we can help with the skin dryness. I can refer you to a dermatologist if you wish, but it's eczema. It's not an unusual condition."

"It's not...?"

"Occasionally it can be what we call tinea corporis, which is better known as ringworm infection. But you have eczema. It should clear up over time. I want you to take regular showers using a body wash I'm going to prescribe for you. Please dry the area carefully and then apply the hydrocortisone cream I'm giving you twice a day for the next week."

"You are sure? Well, thank you, doctor."

Lucy smiled inwardly. "Mr Henderson. I don't want you to worry if it doesn't improve immediately. It should clear up after a few days. Please come and see me in ten days' time. Tell the receptionist that I want to see you myself."

"I made my appointment myself on your computer system. I'll book in on my laptop. Thanks, doctor."

Computer booking system? Lucy was behind the times.

Her third patient came to hear the results of his cholesterol test.

Lucy looked at the screen and studied the series of readings under 'Blood fats'. Cholesterol 4.8, Triglycerides 1.14, HDL Cholesterol 1.20, LDL (Calculation) 5.40, HDL/Cholesterol Ratio .36 and Cholesterol/HDL Ratio 6.31.

"Mr Surrinder, I'd like to weigh you please," she said.

The Ealing businessman removed his jacket and stood on the scales. They showed a reading of 98.2 kilos.

He dressed, sat down and smiled at the doctor.

"You're a little heavier than I would wish, Mr Surrinder, but your main cholesterol reading is good. You registered 4.8 against 5.3 last time. Your LDL reading is a bit on the high side but we will watch that."

"Thank you, doctor," the patient said, as he rose from the chair.

"Mr Surrinder, please sit down." As he did as she asked, Lucy studied the screen on her computer. "You saw Doctor Phillips last time. Doctor Phillips asked for a full blood test. There are some results here under 'liver and enzyme tests'. The readings are concerning me. Total protein is 96 and your gamma GT is 79. Mr Surrinder, you have lost eight kilos in the last year telling me you're being careful with your diet, although you do have more to lose."

Awal Surrinder smiled. He liked praise.

"Mr Surrinder, do you drink alcohol?"

"I came here about my cholesterol. I am well. Thank you."

"Mr Surrinder. I can smell the alcohol on your breath. Please, have you had a drink this morning?"

"I was nervous."

"The evidence I have, Mr Surrinder, shows that you are damaging your liver. We can do something about that. The liver recovers well but I must understand the underlying cause."

"I want to see a male doctor. You women don't know what you're talking about!" he shouted.

"Of course, Mr Surrinder. I'll arrange for you to see one of my colleagues. But I would like to know why you are drinking alcohol so early in the day."

The businessman stood up and tugged at his jacket. He paused and sat down again. He looked deflated.

"Panatha. My wife. She abuses me," he said quietly.

"How does she abuse you, Mr Surrinder?"

"We have four children, two boys and two girls. She wraps them around her. I work long hours and my business has been under pressure from the bank. When I get home all she wants to do is tell me about the children. Then she makes nasty comments about me to them."

"Have you tried to talk to her?"

"Panatha is an intelligent person. I feel I have lost her respect."

"Do you have, shall we say, relations, Mr Surrinder?"

"We have four children, doctor. We have had some good times. But in the last two years, she turns her back."

Time was pressing and Lucy asked Mr Surrinder to return to the surgery in two months' time for a further blood test.

As he left her room, Mr Surrinder turned back and looked at the doctor.

He spoke softly.

"I have lost the respect of my wife, doctor. That is why I drink."

Lucy watched as he left the surgery. A few minutes later the phone rang. She had forgotten to press the 'next patient' button.

Sara and Alex had exchanged some sharp words. Secretly she liked the comparison with Lisbeth Salander but she rejected the suggestion of having a ring through her lip and she most certainly was not going to pierce her nose. While she accepted that she had her wilder side she did not see herself as a social misfit. She most certainly was not going to wear Doc Marten boots.

No, it was the professional qualities that Sara wanted to emulate. She re-read the passages about how Lisbeth prepared her reports for Milton Security. Her use of footnotes, quotations and source references. Her IT research skills and her ability to ferret. That is what she wanted to apply to the task at hand.

The one thing that she was certain about was that the chief executive of Agnew Capital didn't want a report specifically on the publishing industry. She would produce one anyway, but she suspected that her task required some lateral thinking.

She felt boosted by the change in her circumstances. From being a parliamentary researcher she had managed to set up on her own. The meeting with Andrew Agnew and the awarding of a commission impressed and pleased Sara and she was not easily impressed by anything.

She pulled the bed covers over her naked body. She'd remained in bed all day Tuesday after arriving back at Paddington Station late on Monday evening. She had spent the bank holiday weekend visiting her mother, who was in a Bristol care home. She had cleaned the room, removed fresh linen from the stores, persuaded the cook to prepare some soft foods for her mother, cut her nails, cleaned and dressed a bed sore, phoned the doctor and made her drink some fluids. By the time she left, her mother's kidneys were working again. She could not challenge the staff because she knew her mother would suffer. She thought about contacting her sister in Exeter, but she was busy changing husbands and didn't really care. She so missed her father. He had educated her, loved her, made her laugh and visited her many times at Manchester. When he had his stroke no one knew that his finances were in such a mess, least of all her mother.

She reached once more for the email attachment which Andrew had sent her on the Saturday, before she'd left for the West Country. She'd read the project specification several times. Her verdict was that it was crap. He could obtain any amount of material on publishing that he wanted. She'd started by reading the annual report of Bloomsbury Publishing, where JK Rowling had ignited revenues. The chairman Nigel Newton's statement to shareholders was a valuable commentary on the publishing industry. He was enthused by technology and electronic publishing, though she noticed he was cautious about future sales revenues.

"Perhaps Harry Potter should establish the Hogwarts school of mystic publishing: principal Lord Voldemort!" she'd laughed.

She had used the journey to Bristol and back to read *A Long Winter* on her Kindle. It was an intense love story involving two City professionals, their desires and their destruction. It was typical of the newer publications from City Fiction. It was written by a lawyer who was using his own libidinous activities as his source material.

The notes about the author said that he'd been a corporate solicitor for nearly twenty years before he met Alistair Wavering and asked him to read his draft document. He was now on his third title, which had already been sold to a television drama production company.

Now back at home she reached over to the bedside table and poured herself a glass of wine. She sat up and let the covers fall away.

"You have doubts, Mr Agnew," she said to herself.

Sara went through a mental checklist: the company, the finances, the chief executive, the senior team, the books, the sales operation. Perhaps his concerns were integral to his company. She realised that if the money wasn't raised Agnew Capital would have invested its cash and resources for little or even no return.

She made her checklist. She would initially meet Alistair Wavering and Oliver Chatham.

From her university studies she'd become aware of the difficulties many authors had finding a publisher. John Masters – and she had read nearly all his books – was turned away many times before finding success. And even JK Rowling said she had received many rejections before securing a backer.

She needed to turn the question around. What are the special qualities of a publisher which allow him or her to discover a bestseller? Is it a numbers game? The more you publish the better the odds? Sara's brain was now buzzing and she found that sleep evaded her.

She realised that niche publishers are a different proposition. It is so much easier to define the target market. *Luxury Holidays in the Far East* is simply a marketing exercise.

City Fiction had now changed into a generalist publisher looking for the bestseller. The book that would change its fortunes. She was aware that publishers receive hundreds of manuscripts every year, which is why securing an agent is the optimum route for the unpublished writer to take.

Agents themselves are always looking for their own winners, a Jack Higgins, a Gerald Seymour or a Frederick Forsythe... City Fiction had already published over ninety books and had a number of successes. But it was obvious they were searching for their one big winner.

"Can they find it? Is that the question Andrew is asking of me?" she mused.

Amanda wrapped her fingers around the stem of the wine glass.

Oliver had booked the table for two at one of his favourite restaurants, One Lombard, opposite Bank tube station, and was enjoying seeing the foreign rights editor again.

"Alistair is so sorry, Oliver," she said. "He's delayed in Amsterdam. He was due back this morning but another opportunity came up." She put the glass down and smiled. "Will I do?"

June had started with some Mediterranean sunshine and was becoming warmer by the day. Amanda was wearing a thin white dress. Several diners had turned to look at her when she walked in.

They decided to share a starter of cold meats and olives. Amanda selected the salmon and Oliver, having been shown the cuts of meats, went for a fillet steak. He ordered sparkling water and a French cabernet sauvignon.

"Business first and then let's talk about you, Oliver," Amanda said. "Alistair was hoping to receive your contract by today."

"It's on its way. I think we are agreed. But the boss wants one more document."

"Anything we can help with?"

"He's having a report on the publishing industry prepared."

"But there's nothing that Alistair doesn't know about publishing. How strange."

"Regulations, Amanda. The rules are that our files must demonstrate that we have undertaken stringent checks before we can offer the shares to investors. We have to do it. I sometimes think that what the regulatory authorities want is a risk market without risk for the investors."

"Do we represent risk?"

"All investments are risky. The greater the potential reward the higher the risk."

"I don't really understand that, but we trust you. Alistair is convinced you'll get us the money." She raised her glass and smiled. She then waited while their plates were cleared.

He coughed politely. "So do you live on... with... er... do you share?"

"I live on my own. I have a flat in St. John's Wood. I can see the corner of the cricket ground from my living room window."

"You have a partner?"

"A cat called Jingles," she said. "He actually belongs to the people in the flat above me but he's adopted my balcony as his second home." She paused, looking at Oliver with a smile playing about her lips. "Why, would it make any difference if I did have somebody?"

"Er, no, nothing to do with me," he stuttered. "I was just wondering if... er… well..."

"You were so confident in our first meeting," she said. "Why are you dithering now?"

"I'm not... er… oh... dithering as you put it," he retorted. "Dithering," he repeated. "I've never been accused of that before."

"But perhaps you've never been with somebody like me before?"

The waiter cleared their plates and served the main courses. He then refilled their glasses with some sparkling water.

"I've actually just finished with my boyfriend, Zach," said Amanda. She paused because she was surprised she had revealed this detail. She glanced at Oliver. She couldn't help noticing that he was very handsome.

"Zach?"

"Ten months together."

"So what did Zach do wrong?"

"Hey, he might have ditched me."

"Highly unlikely." Oliver immediately regretted his words. She raised her eyebrows and her glass of wine.

"He was a lovely man and I'm missing him dreadfully."

Oliver cut up more of his steak and indicated to the waiter that he would like their wine glasses refilled.

"Zach was the closest thing I've found to the man I might choose to spend my life with," she continued. "But there was something I couldn't rationalise… I don't know."

He dared not speak. What had Zach, the idiot, done to lose this woman? Was he fucking mad?

Suddenly she brightened and smiled.

"What really frustrates me, Oliver, is that being together was so good."

At that moment his mobile phone rang.

"Sorry," he mouthed as he listened to the voice of his chief executive.

"Oliver. Get back to the office now. The FSA are here. Fast as you can."

Lucy's first day free of medical duties was on Friday.

She started cleaning the house at five in the morning, prepared breakfast with a smile on her face and took the girls to school. Charles was pre-occupied with reading business papers and left early. Lucy collected the girls in the afternoon and Scarlett noticed a difference when they arrived home. She sniffed the air in the house and asked her younger sister what smell she could detect. "Peaches," said Lily.

Lucy sent text messages to Charles on three occasions and received one reply.

He arrived home at six thirty in the evening. When he entered their bedroom he found that some casual clothing was laid out on the bed. There was also a wrapped present. The label read: "Darling Daddy / Charles. We love you lots. Scarlett, Lily, Tabitha and Lucy xxx."

He opened it and found a book inside. *For Those in Peril* by Wilbur Smith. His favourite author. He would never forget reading *When the Lions Feed*, his first masterpiece. Thirty books later they kept coming. It was signed inside. "Fondest love. Lucy. 3 June 2011."

Charles went downstairs and initially could not find anybody. As he reached the patio doors he smelt the barbecue. Scarlett was cooking the meats, Lily stood behind the salad bowl with some plastic forks and spoons and Tabitha was holding a jug of fresh cordial.

It wasn't long before the four of them were seated at the wooden table, each with a plate of food. Charles realised the music being played was Leonard Bernstein's 'West Side Story', a modern day Romeo and Juliet musical set in New York.

"Mrs Allen was horrible today," said Lily.

"Later," ordered Lucy. "Charles, I think you had a board meeting today? We want to know what happened."

He looked at the girls and drank some cordial.

"Well, I sacked a broker," said Charles.

"Can you do that?" she asked.

Before he could answer her question his eldest daughter chipped in with one of her own.

"What did he do, Daddy?"

"He was rude to a client. It has been going on for some time. I can't abide that."

"Is that a sacking offence?" asked Lucy.

"No. But his expenses are. It's the oldest trick in the book. I went in early this morning to go through his returns for the last six months. He has a girlfriend. He took her to Paris. He shouted and screamed and then I showed him the hotel and restaurant invoices. He walked out."

"And is that the end of the matter?"

"He'll go to a lawyer and we'll end up paying him two hundred thousand pounds and then he will secure another position. That's the way the City works."

"So why sack him, Daddy?" asked Scarlett.

"I want to live my life with people I can trust, my darling," replied her father.

"Like me," said Tabitha.

"Like you, Tabitha," he laughed as he sipped his drink.

Sara had spent the morning at her computer compiling an initial report on the publishing industry. It was a fairly straightforward task. She had been trained in this activity and knew many of the tricks of the trade. One was sheer volume. It never ceased to amaze her that there was an immediate payoff between size and quality. Time and again in her government work she saw volumes of meaningless research papers which would hardly be read. She understood that the work lying behind these tomes provided the basis for the recommendations which might, at a later stage, be considered. It was the system and Westminster worked on the system.

She wanted her report for Agnew Capital to offer originality. She therefore spent the afternoon in Charing Cross Road visiting a number of bookshops. She spoke to some of the staff and asked what books people were reading. She asked what they themselves were reading too. It proved difficult to identify patterns. She studied the bestseller lists; fiction and non-fiction, hardback and paperback. She used Google to analyse the latest information on eBooks.

At 5.30pm she had reached Leicester Square. She found a wine bar and treated herself to a glass of Chardonnay. She raised her glass and said a silent "cheers" to herself. She had decided that she knew what Andrew Agnew wanted.

She felt her mood beginning to lighten with the wine. She didn't touch drugs anymore after several unhappy experiences at university, but drank liqueurs with Alex – Schnapps, Kahlua, Crème de Menthe, the sweeter the better. She remembered the many happy evenings… Yet she never lost her perplexity at the unpredictability of their relationship. Sara understood her life in clear straight lines. In her professional work she was adept at thinking laterally. But it was in her personal dealings that she experienced the vagaries of the human spirit. Why, on some occasions, was their sex warm and loving and then, for no good reason that Sara could identify, did their physicality lack any passion? She hated the situation, especially as they seemed unable to talk about it. The rows were long gone. She had become used to accepting it. The lure was that when the spark was there it was really, really good.

Charles Harriman looked around the breakfast area of The Landmark London. It was located beneath a soaring eight-storey glass roof atrium. He noted several familiar faces. A former Labour cabinet minister was reading the *Financial Times* and a retired England test captain was in animated conversation with a companion.

He'd left his car in Dorset Square near to Marylebone Station and had met his guest in the reception area of the hotel, where the Presidential Two Bedroom Lifestyle Suites are available at £4,400 per night. They were shown to a vacant table and offered menus.

"I'll start with the fresh fruit from the buffet bar and then order an English breakfast," Charles said to the waiter.

Andrew Agnew nodded in agreement and told the waiter to bring him some Earl Grey tea. Charles ordered coffee and then the two businessmen walked over to the buffet area. Andrew selected mixed fruits, including prunes and figs, and Charles served himself some freshly prepared melon and citrus fruits.

"It's good of you to meet like this," said Andrew.

"Just tell it as it is, Andrew," Charles replied.

"Always to the point," laughed his friend. "We had a visit on Wednesday from the FSA. As the judge said, 'you will be given a fair trial, then hung'. They had already decided on their conclusions. They pretended to look at some files but they were in no mood to listen. They'd received several complaints about two of our deals. They said our due diligence work was inadequate."

"That's not good."

"There was a director of one of our client companies who had concealed a previous disciplinary action and we failed to pick it up. Actually it was the lawyers who didn't check properly because he was a Hong Kong resident, but the FSA don't have time for excuses. I was given a lecture about our 'know your client' procedures."

"So what did they say?"

"They said that they would be impressed by the introduction of new management." He paused and drank some tea. "Initially I was offended and called our solicitors in to consider our position. They read the riot act and said we had a massive fight on our hands to retain our regulatory permissions." He stopped again and wiped his forehead with his napkin.

"It was Oliver who really took charge. He sent a four-page letter to the FSA that evening detailing the immediate action we were taking to address their concerns. Jody was calm too and helped the whole situation. The FSA inspectors had interviewed her for over an hour but she seemed to be able to handle the stress." He drank some water. "Stress is the right word I can tell you. These regulators make you feel guilty whatever the situation."

Charles understood the issue of personal pressure all too well. He signalled to the waiter that he required a refill of his coffee cup. Their plates were cleared and quickly followed up with two cooked breakfasts: poached eggs, bacon, sausage, tomatoes, black pudding and a hash brown. A rack of toasted granary bread was delivered by a waitress.

"You want me to help you," said the corporate financier, "in what way?"

"I'm hoping that we might merge our firms," replied Andrew. "We have eleven staff and you are seven according to your website."

It was only later in the day that Andrew realised how quickly Charles had eased into the concept of merging their firms.

They spent the next hour in detailed discussion on how the two businesses might unite. White, Harriman and Boyle was regaining some momentum but had experienced a difficult time in the recession; Agnew Capital was also ticking over. They quickly agreed on some key matters: chairman, Charles Harriman, chief executive, Andrew Agnew, finance director, Jody Boyle (whose father had been a founder of their merger partner), head of corporate finance, Oliver Chatham, head of brokerage, Gavin Swain, and head of compliance, Melanie Reid. It was agreed to move to the offices of Agnew Capital in Queen Street by Mansion House tube station. The new name would be Harriman Agnew Capital LLP.

They paid their bill and moved into the lounge area for morning coffee, where they began to discuss their various pending transactions.

"We have a two million fund-raising for a publisher, City Fiction," said Andrew. "I'm just waiting for a report on the industry but I'm keen to sign them up."

With the business discussion at an end Andrew and Charles stood up and shook hands.

When Charles got home Lucy wanted to know all about his breakfast meeting. She seemed genuinely interested and wanted to know every detail. He told her gladly.

Amanda scanned around the lower part of Regent's Park, shielding her eyes with her hand, and spotted Oliver hurrying towards her. They met and decided to walk over to the tented coffee shop, where Amanda ordered a large skinny latte and Oliver had English tea. They both selected a pain au chocolat before sitting down at a table.

"It's been a hectic two days," he said.

He knew that he should be exercising caution but he chose to tell her about his discussions yesterday afternoon with Andrew. They both agreed that the FSA were sending a clear message. Initially Oliver had proposed the recruitment of several additional staff members. However, after hearing Andrew's suggestion that they offer Charles Harriman a merger, he was warming to that strategy.

They left the café together. Amanda was making the most of the tanning potential by exposing a lot of skin to the late morning sunshine. It was growing very warm, so they strolled over to the lake and walked round its perimeter before finally finding a small, and rather secluded, grass-covered knoll. As they settled down, Oliver took a bottle of champagne and two glasses from his bag. He extracted the cork expertly and poured them each a drink. Amanda looked around before slipping off her dress to reveal her yellow bikini. She produced a tube of suntan cream and invited Oliver to rub the liquid on to her back. She then straightened the towel which she'd laid on the ground and settled back down onto it with a sigh.

"I enjoyed our lunch together," she said, "before you rushed off leaving me with the bill!"

"Oh, sorry," he said. "I'll settle that up for you."

"Don't worry," she laughed. "You had other matters on your mind."

"And you were missing Zach," he said.

"Zach's history." She pushed herself up and adjusted her bikini top.

Oliver retrieved the bottle of champagne and filled their glasses. He paused, slightly uncomfortably, before looking down at the sun-bathing goddess. The skin of her stomach was tanning well and without a blemish.

"Oliver," she said. "Please come and sit down." She patted the grass by her side and smiled as he joined her. She put her right hand across his shoulders. "Tell me about your girlfriends."

"Why?"

"I told you about Zach."

"But you chose to. You just started talking about him."

She squeezed his shoulder tightly. "I still want to know about them."

He laughed. "Not much to tell. I work hard and I play a lot of sport. I go to the gym every day, just like you. I play squash and rugby in the winter and tennis in the summer. I go skiing when I can."

"No girlfriends?"

He pulled away from her.

"Look, Amanda. I'm sorry. You're a client. This is getting too personal. But... if you must know, the truth is that girls are not a problem for me. If I want company it's usually available at the squash club, in the gym or somewhere. I never mix up my personal life and the office. I prefer it that way. I always find a partner for my winter trips. That's the way the girls want it and it suits me fine."

"If I wasn't a client do you think I might be a candidate? Do you think I might be one of your girls?"

The danger signals rang. He took a deep breath.

"I can't believe the effect you're having on me," he said. "I promised myself I wouldn't talk in this way. It's so tricky... Andrew would be furious if he overheard this conversation..."

She reached up and pulled him towards her.

"But he's not here is he, Oliver? You're here and I'm here. We're adults." She kissed him gently on the lips. "But I also have a problem..."

"Problem?"

"Well, we know we're going to sleep together, don't we?"

"We do?" Oliver could barely contain his enthusiasm.

"But there's a condition."

"Before we sleep together?"

"Yes."

"One condition?"

"Just one."

"When am I going to find out about this condition?"

A languorous smile spread seductively across her lips.

"It's not really a condition. It's a situation. I want for Alistair more than I can explain. The fund-raising is everything. It'll allow him to expand the business beyond his wildest dreams. And you're going to secure the investment of two million pounds."

She paused.

"I simply can't prioritise a personal act. It would be selfish. You know that we'll go to bed together eventually… but help me out, Oliver. Raise the money first."

"That's the condition, Amanda? I've got to raise two million pounds before you'll go to bed with me."

"Oliver. If that's the way you want things. I'll lie on the bed and you do what you want. I'll think of England."

He looked at her in amazement. She was so hard to read. "There are plenty of girls at the gym who'll do that."

She smiled. "You want what I want, don't you?"

"I'm moving in that direction."

He stood up and looked around for his jacket.

"Where are you going?"

"Where do you think? To raise two million pounds, Amanda. I think you've just redefined a 'banker's bonus'!"

Sara sighed with contentment. Her anger at receiving a phone call from a Member of Parliament suggesting they should get together for dinner was fading. She recalled meeting him but couldn't remember much more. She decided to check him out on www.sexymp.co.uk, the website that ranks MPs according to their (alleged) sexiness. To her horror she discovered that her prospective dinner partner came in at around number four hundred and fifty. She sent a curt text message to the disappointed parliamentarian.

She ran her hands over Alex's body and, underneath the bed clothes, allowed her fingers to creep ever lower. She knew already that tonight would be one of those evenings when their relationship failed to meet the heights of passion she craved.

Was it her fault? She was becoming obsessed with her report on City Fiction. She was sleeping fitfully and spending many early morning hours reading her research papers. She was walking daily around the grounds of the Tower of London, thinking through the conundrum of publishing.

Oliver received the text message early on Sunday afternoon. He'd spent most of the morning in the gym and lunchtime with pals in his local pub in Clerkenwell. When he returned to his flat he checked his mobile for messages. There were three: one from Abbi Highfield, another from Andrew, and a third which he hesitated over before opening.

He had wanted to spend the afternoon reflecting on his visit to Andrew's home late on Saturday. He needed to think about the merger, although the decision had already been made.

Now he had a text message to ponder. He already knew the number well. He so wanted it to be positive. Finally he opened it.

"Oliver. I want so much to be with you today. When we are together my world comes alive. You must, however, raise the money for Alistair. Deal? Love. Amanda x."

He replied immediately.

"Deal. Oliver x."

He lay back and listened to the orchestral music playing on Classic FM. His mind drifted back to Regent's Park. It seemed pretty crude. He was basically being offered sex with Amanda provided he raise two million pounds for her brother's publishing business. He recalled the film starring the stunning Demi Moore – Robert Redford offered her husband one million dollars if he could go to bed with her. Had Amanda, too, made an indecent proposal?

Why had she worn such a brief bikini? If it was strategic, bloody hell, it had worked! She had an exquisite body, which he was sure was the result of personal discipline and hours spent in the gym. Although they had been hidden from public view on the grassy knoll Oliver couldn't recall having seen any other woman wearing a bikini in Regent's Park that day. Though he had certainly observed couples in the heat of a summer's afternoon, after the lunchtime wine, clearly aroused and passionate.

The music played on with a loud burst from the trumpeters. Oliver realised that he was becoming hypnotised by his desire to have sex with Amanda. At first he had tried to empathise with her love for her brother. He knew that he had played it right by going along with her condition that was not a condition. But the issue for him was that somehow her foibles – were they such? – her personality traits – whatever they were – simply added up to one hell of a woman. He couldn't fully explain it. He knew she tantalised him but he felt something more too… Could he be falling in love? He had to go to bed with her. That much he knew. The answer was to seduce her as soon as possible.

But he knew that was not going to happen. She meant every word. He must raise two million pounds for City Fiction if he was to experience the fulfilment he knew was awaiting him.

He should have been... something. Disgusted, appalled, humiliated – perhaps, angry.

No, he loved it. He would raise the money in any case. And at the end of the transaction he would call in the deal. He would experience the summit of his desires. He would win Amanda.

The music had finished. He re-read a long email from his father in Australia. After his mother's hip replacement operation, the drought and his father's dissection of East Asian politics ("Watch North Korea, son"), he considered again his father's opinion on what the piece of music might be.

"You say Russian. That's a start. You have eliminated Rachmaninov. You think you heard the word 'ascent' and possibly 'mountain'. You estimate the playing time at about eight minutes but that could be misleading if it is part of a longer piece. It has to be Shostakovich. I suggest you listen to the 'Leningrad' and by the end you will know whether Shostakovich wrote the piece you are trying to find. Take care of yourself, son. Your loving father."

Oliver had spent part of the evening reading up on Dimitri Shostakovich. He'd been born in Leningrad in 1906 and died in Moscow in 1975. He'd lived in Russia all his life and, at times, found his composing affected by the wishes of his communist leaders.

When he realised the depth of Shostakovich's musical output, he began to understand why his father had suggested he listen to the 'Leningrad'. Shostakovich's compositions included fifteen symphonies, two piano concertos, two violin concertos, two cello concertos, twenty-four preludes and fugues for the piano, the Age of Gold ballet and lots of film scores.

He had visited a music shop and bought a CD of Symphony No. 7 in C Major known as 'Leningrad'. He had read the cover notes carefully. It was thought that its underlying purpose was a protest against the suffering caused by the communist state. For some it was simply a battle symphony.

He decided to listen again to the whole performance, which lasted well over an hour through four movements: Allegretto, Moderato (Poco allegretto), Adagio and Allegro non troppo.

He became absorbed by the large orchestra's rendition of the Shostakovich masterpiece.

At the conclusion of the performance he replayed the final section, the allegro.

He then knew that the piece of music he was searching for had not been composed by Dimitri Shostakovich. The style was different.

Twelve people packed into the board room at what was already being called Harriman Agnew Capital. Introductions were made and Charles explained the basis of the merger of the two firms. Andrew took over as chief executive and dealt with the bad news immediately.

"Three colleagues have already left this morning," he said. "We have, of course, paid them their full entitlements and in two cases we have added some additional salary."

"Who decided who should go?" asked Duncan Hocken.

"They've gone. Let's move on as well," replied Andrew.

He explained individual roles and there was little comment. The two companies merged together so neatly that nearly everybody involved could see the logic.

"Can you tell us more about the FSA visit please, Andrew?" asked Abbi. "What happens now?"

"Thanks, Abbi. I'll ask Melanie to answer your question because she has been liaising with the inspector."

"Well," said the compliance officer, "my understanding is that it was a low grade inspection in the first place. We know that other firms in our sector are also being contacted. I spoke to our contact at the FSA this morning and told him about the merger. There will be lots of form filling but he seemed reasonably happy with the detail I gave him."

"Why is Oliver head of corporate finance?" asked Gavin.

"Because you are head of brokerage," replied Andrew.

"I have more experience. I should have been considered."

"You were, Gavin. But we think you're too valuable in brokerage. You're the best fund-raiser we have."

"Yeah, Oliver, hear that. Try bossing me around, mate, and..."

"Gavin. Cool it," said Andrew. "We need each other. These are difficult times. Oliver will bring in some good deals for us."

"Like City Fiction you mean, Andrew? I read the summary. It's crap. I'm not selling that to the clients."

"It's an interesting case," said Abbi.

"Who the fuck are you to tell me what's a good deal?" snapped Gavin.

"Gavin," said Oliver. "I'm more than happy to go through the papers with you afterwards. It has real merit."

"I'm busy," said Gavin.

Gavin was in grave danger of attracting a fight. He wouldn't have taken a backwards step if one had started. It was only the calming influence of his friend Duncan that prevented his mood escalating out of control in the dark interior of the Embankment bar.

"Dunc," he slurred, "see that fucking river... what's it called? The Thames. The fucking river Thames. Well, Dunc, that's where fucking Oliver fucking, Lord Muck – what's his sodding name, Dunc? – that's where he should be..."

Duncan noticed that the bar manager was becoming agitated by Gavin's foul language.

"Gavin," he said, taking his companion by the arm, "let's go and decide where you're going to dump him."

"Fucking good idea, Dunc. You're my best friend aren't you, Dunc? Lead on. I'll select the deepest fucking part for Lord..."

They exited the bar and Gavin staggered towards the riverside railings.

"See, Dunc," he cried, pointing towards the incoming tidal waters. "That's where Lord Oliver Crumpet is fucking going to end up."

"Oliver Chatham," said Duncan. "He's not a Lord, but he's certainly landed gentry and public school."

"Fucking Eton, Dunc. I went to state school and done good." He grabbed his friend by the arm. "I've done ok haven't I, Dunc? Bloody good I am. I never fail to raise the money, Dunc. I'm the best of the best, me..."

"Gavin, you're the top man as far as I'm concerned."

"Then why am I not the head of corporate finance? Tell me that, Dunc. What did Charlie say? It's fifty fifty. It's a merger. It's fucking not. I'm the best. I should be head honcho, Dunc. If Oliver fucking… er… Crumpet tells me what to do he'll go in that fucking river."

"We need to give it a chance, Gav. I must say the combined operation looks much better. Charles has been off the boil for some time."

"I've no fuckin' choice, Dunc. The wife is preggers again."

"God, how many is that, Gav?"

"Martine says we've got four. I've lost count." He roared with laughter.

Lucy Harriman packed Lily off to bed and settled down in the lounge. Scarlett had gone upstairs earlier and Lucy found her and Tabitha together in the back bedroom.

The 'For Sale' sign was now outside their house and she had found it difficult to explain to the girls why they were selling their home, though when they knew they were staying at the same school things improved. Scarlett, being a bit older, understood better than the other two.

Charles was watching a film on the TV. Lucy edged up beside him. He turned the volume down.

"Thanks," he said. "Thanks for organising everything. I've had a look at the properties you want to see at the weekend. The one on the edge of the Common looks alright. £1,450 a month. Can we afford that?"

"I was surprised how optimistic the estate agent was about selling ours," she replied. "We seem in the right price range for selling houses at the moment. He said it's the cheaper properties that they can't move."

Lucy ran her hand across his forehead. "How is Harriman Agnew Capital getting on?"

"Early days. It's like two boxers eying each other. Gavin is upset but he always is." Charles picked up his cold cup of coffee. "Are you enjoying the surgery?" he asked.

"Oh, I don't know. I can't seem to cure a simple case of eczema," replied Lucy.

"Then it's not simple."

"You might have a point. The patient is intelligent but he won't accept a referral to a consultant. He says I will do."

"He's trying to tell you something."

Lucy looked at her husband. "What do you mean exactly?"

"This is the businessman you mentioned to me last week? You told me eczema is stress related. This chap travels and you say the schedule he is following, and the flights to China, are the cause."

"Yes. Probably. So what are you saying?"

"Lots of people work hard and take long distance flights, Lucy. They don't all get skin complaints. The stress is coming from somewhere else."

"From where though? He never stops talking. He's told me his life story."

"No he hasn't. He's told you the bits he wants you to hear. My guess is that he's beating around the bush. What's the most likely event in his life that might be resulting in the stress – money, career or women?"

"The bloody obvious!" she cried. "An affair... you should never stop looking for the obvious."

She looked up and their eyes met.

"You haven't asked me," he said.

"I suppose I'm a bit scared to." She was surprised by the sudden switching of the conversation.

"Nearly two weeks, Lucy," said Charles. "Not a drop."

She wrapped herself around her husband. She was proud of him, but she wondered whether he was truly facing up to the reality of his situation. He was not just giving up drinking alcohol; he was selecting a new way of life. The challenges would come later and then he would be tested to an extent which, at that moment in time, he could not imagine.

Amanda was lying on her bed thinking about Zach. She was not doubting her decision to end their relationship, especially now she had met Oliver. They were so different – possibly because Zach had been married and was a father, while Oliver retained the enthusiasm of youth. He went about his professional duties

51

with an energy and commitment which was infectious. Zach was more of a thinker. He spent many hours on the script of a documentary long before a camera rolled. He studied people and selected his interviewees with great care.

She realised that she acted differently with the two of them. When she was with Zach she was more serious and took a real interest in his work. There were many nights when Zach had either gone home or slept in her spare room. They never discussed the issue: it just happened.

With Oliver she was much more flirtatious. She already loved teasing him and watching him struggling to match her humour. She was more provocative too, partly because she enjoyed using her sexuality and partly because he turned her on so much. He was so good looking and had an athleticism and virility which made her desire him intensely.

She did not, however, have any concerns over the terms of their deal. She was delighted at the spirit with which Oliver had accepted its imposition. He had not argued or even sulked: he was, after all, a man! She knew that he would raise the money and she was already anticipating their first night together. She would wear a two-piece outfit made of silk. She would arouse him slowly and take her time removing her lingerie. He would discover that she was still hiding her modesty with tight white knickers.

She closed her eyes and allowed her dreams to overtake her.

Chapter Three

Sara Flemming was late. She had misjudged the walk from Bloomsbury towards Clerkenwell and then struggled to find Bleeding Heart Yard off Greville Street, near Smithfield Market.

She pounded over the cobbled courtyard and paused at the top of the stairs, where she adjusted her jacket collar and ruffled her hair, before going in to the wooden entrance hall and asking for Alistair Wavering. She was directed down the steps and towards a dark corner where a man sat alone. Nearly all the other tables were occupied by the Hatton Garden business community.

She shook hands with her host and sat down. He was six feet tall, slim with fair hair. She knew instantly that Alistair was not a flirt.

The publisher poured a glass of white wine and passed it to her. He then filled another glass with sparkling water and repeated the process. The waiter arrived and handed them menus before placing a basket of bread, a small dish of olive oil and a bowl of olives between the two diners.

"Are you comfortable?" asked Alistair.

"Very," she replied. She was congratulating herself on her choice of a dark green two-piece outfit. She had decided not to wear a blouse and now she felt comfortable. It was mid-week in early June and the weather was getting warmer each day.

"Oliver says I must impress you," he said.

She lifted her glass of wine.

"To you and City Fiction," she toasted. "I've never been here before. I must say, Bleeding Heart is an unusual name for a restaurant."

"It's called 'The Bleeding Heart' because, in 1626, Lady Hatton was bludgeoned to death by her lover." Alistair paused and sipped some wine. "He left her dismembered body in the courtyard. They say that the locals were transfixed by her heart continuing to pump blood over the cobbles."

He handed her a menu.

"Wow. I generally eat vegetarian food," said Sara.

The waiter returned. Sara selected the trinity of baby beetroot with goat's cheese mousseline and a walnut and cider dressing as a starter, followed by a pappardelle of roast wild mushrooms with chervil. The waiter said "merci" and turned to Alistair, who waved his hand in the air. The waiter wrote something down and nodded.

"You're a regular here?" she said.

"They know I'll always choose the sea bass if they have it and I like a Caesar salad as a starter."

"Is food important to you, Alistair?"

"I can't resist food and decent company," he replied. "Often I'm with authors or agents, sometimes both. But then I have to work."

"What will you be trying to achieve?" she continued, as she sipped the water and then drank some more wine.

"The job has changed from when we first started," he said. "Initially we specialised in finance books, many of which were, essentially, vanity publishing."

"That's where the author pays to have his book published?"

"Yes. In the world of publishing it's the cheap end. A professional publisher would only commission a book if he thought it saleable and worthy of his list." He sipped some water. "I thought there was a market there and I was right. I found that lots of people in the City thought that they could write and I gave them an opportunity. Production costs, and especially printing overheads, have been falling in recent years so it's not as expensive as in the past."

"So what has changed?"

"As we became profitable and acquired more titles I started to want to enter the world of general publishing. I was being offered new books all the time. We tried a few and realised that a small niche publisher had a future."

"I'm never certain what the word 'niche' means." Sara said, as she smiled at her host and sipped some wine. She was not only listening to his responses, but also studying his face. He was treating each of her points with genuine gravity and trying

54

hard to provide full answers. She found herself beginning to relax and enjoy the lunch. She was being taken seriously.

"In my world I think it reflects a choice," he said. "City Fiction concentrates on thrillers and political stories reflecting the world of finance in modern times. Forgive the lack of modesty, but I give the business an edge by being in the City and by knowing people. I find that the books come to us now either from agents or from City people themselves."

"And so you spend more time with authors?" Again she smiled, but then hid her expression behind her glass of water.

"Our authors are our assets," he replied. "The newer ones can be nervous, perhaps uncertain. They can be lonely. Writing is a solitary occupation. As they become more experienced, and especially if their book, or books, are selling, the issues of advances and royalties will surface. It's easier to transact deals with their agents. I do enjoy my time with the authors though. They can be very interesting in their own right, of course."

The waiter arrived to serve the starters and to replenish the wine glasses. He raised the bottle slightly and Alistair nodded.

"We haven't finished the first one," she laughed.

"We will," he responded. "It's only a matter of time."

"So, is publishing basically a numbers game?"

"In general fiction – which is what we now publish – yes. The objective is to try to create a backlist of titles so that what we call annuity income, by which we mean repeat annual sales, aggregates to fifty percent of the company's turnover. Put another way, on the first of January each year, we hope to have banked guaranteed sales of our existing titles to pay the overheads in the year ahead."

Sara sipped some wine.

"You have over ninety titles now. What are your... er... annuity earnings now?"

"Annuity income is the usual term, Sara. You might as well get it right in your report."

"I'll decide what goes in the report, Alistair. What's the answer to the question?"

"Our year end is June so I'll have our final results fairly soon. We think it will be around thirty-two percent this time."

"You should have these statistics at your finger tips, Alistair. 'Around thirty-two percent' isn't good enough."

"Hey, I'm a publisher, remember."

"What's that got to do with it?"

"Everything," he replied. "Amanda and I have flogged ourselves to death getting the company to where it is today. It needs a managing director to run it. I want to be a publisher free of cash-flow worries, independent of the bank and the Inland Revenue, not having to deal with staff matters. I want to work with my authors."

"What's stopping you?"

"Two million pounds."

Their plates were cleared and almost immediately the pappardelle of wild mushrooms and Alistair's sea bass arrived with steaming vegetables. A second waiter opened the new bottle of wine and invited Alistair to sample it. Their glasses were swiftly refilled.

"I think publishing is gambling," said Sara. "You produce, say, ten books and hope that three will sell."

"That's more the American approach, Sara. If Sarah Palin runs off with a new boyfriend, the Yanks will have *Alaskan Lovers* piled high in the book shops within days."

She laughed and looked more closely at Alistair. She was liking him more and more.

"What you need, Alistair, is some winners."

"One winner will do," he laughed.

He reached beneath the table and produced a book which he handed to her.

"As I said, mostly we're publishing financial and political fiction books. There really are some decent authors around. This is *Sub-prime* which was written by a chap in one of the broking houses. He's used his knowledge of finance and the tricks that are played to good effect. It's now sold thirty thousand copies."

Sara looked at the book and read the cover notes.

Alistair put his knife and fork down and drank some water. He was unhurried and gave the impression of having plenty of time. Sara realised she was feeling very at ease in his company.

"What do you read, Sara?"

"Hey, I'm asking the questions." She smiled playfully.

"Do you want to know about the team back at the office?"

"No," she said. "I want to know why JK Rowling was turned down by so many publishers."

"The conundrum of publishing, Sara. We ask ourselves the same question on a daily basis. At City Fiction we receive on average about ten books a week. We live in fear we might miss the big one. Sometimes the agent approaches us which helps. We know the good ones from the time wasters." He drank some wine. "You should also look at those authors who only publish one title. It's as hard to get past the first book as it is to be published in the first place. Now, shall we talk about eBooks and Kindles?"

"No," she said. "These ten books you receive each week. What do you do with them?"

"It's a poor answer but I rely on instinct. We have a 'submissions policy' statement on our website and if the author has followed that they are more likely to be read."

The waiter cleared their plates and tidied the glasses.

"Coffee?" asked Alistair.

"Green tea, please."

The waiter poured the last of the wine and left to organise the hot drinks.

"I'm due to meet Amanda tonight," said Sara.

"She'll tell you about foreign rights," he said. "She travels the world selling our books. She really is beginning to build up our European sales. She's talking about going to Hong Kong and China."

"Tell me about her."

"Find out for yourself."

"I will," she said. "But I would have thought that you could discuss her value to the business with me."

"I know she's my sister," Alistair said, "but I can honestly say that she's one of the loveliest people I've ever known. Our parents divorced when we were in our teens so we only had each other. My father went off to the Far East and we lost contact. My mother lives in Hastings and Amanda sees her regularly. She never recovered from the separation and lives alone, though her health is good."

"And Amanda lives in St. John's Wood?"

"Yes. She's a fitness fanatic and works out every morning. She's dedicated to City Fiction. She reads many of the proofs we receive and, as I say, she travels."

"Sounds like Miss Perfect."

"You might learn something then!" teased Alistair. "Though definitely not about men."

"What do you mean by that?" Sara was surprised at Alistair's indiscretion.

"She gets herself in a mess with men – but I never said that."

Alistair handed the waiter his credit card. Their lunch was coming to an end.

"You want two million pounds?"

"Two million pounds."

"To gamble away on new titles which you hope will sell?"

"To build our business up to a trade sale for many millions of pounds so that, in five years' time, I can become financially free and travel the world."

"Well, thanks for lunch, Alistair."

They stood up and shook hands, before leaving the restaurant with Sara in front. She stumbled over the first of the wooden steps but quickly regained her poise. Later she sent a text message.

"Alistair. Thanks. Please email me 500 words on the impact of eBooks on your business. Sara."

Dr. Lucy Harriman had found the day's surgery rather wearing. Perhaps it was, in part, a reaction to the previous day's drama. Lucy had been in the main office looking for a file when she heard a receptionist taking an incoming call. She indicated that she would talk to the caller. She had already heard enough to have concerns. She listened to the worried mother explaining that she was on her own and her daughter was unusually listless and had been unwell for over a day. In answer to Lucy's question she said there were no signs of a rash.

Lucy had decided, on pure instinct, to visit and asked that her patients be advised that there would be a delay in their appointments that morning. She'd reached the house in less than ten minutes and found the mother in the driveway.

"There's a rash!" she'd shouted as Lucy reached her. She'd run into the house and asked the mother for a glass. Her fears were confirmed when she placed it over the rash and the marks remained visible. She'd wrapped the child in a blanket and picked her up.

"We need to get her to hospital now. It'll be quicker if I take her myself."

She'd carried her to the car and put her on the back seat, fastening a seat belt around her.

"Close up the house and come to the hospital as soon as you can," Lucy had said.

She'd reached Ealing General Hospital in eight minutes. She'd parked in the A & E entrance, picked the child up out of the car and rushed in to the desk. She'd said to the receptionist that she was a doctor from Whiteoaks Practice and she thought the child had meningitis. After she was satisfied that the child was being cared for, she'd returned to the surgery and resumed her duties.

Later that afternoon she'd received a call from a doctor at the hospital who confirmed that they had started antibiotics immediately and the child was now out of danger.

"Rather impressive, Dr. Harriman, if we may say so. It's so difficult to diagnose in young children."

That day, the man with the eczema had returned and Lucy managed the situation badly. The skin condition was worse and she'd suggested that she should refer him to a consultant. However, she'd added, "unless there is anything else you think I should know about?"

The patient asked what she might have in mind.

"Perhaps there are other matters troubling you?" she had suggested.

"Like what?" he'd asked. He'd then added that this was his third visit and if the doctor hadn't got all the information she needed to make a correct diagnosis it might be better if he did see a consultant.

It was, however, the mid-morning couple that had really tested her. In many ways she regretted reading Kate McCann's book. The story of the disappearance of Madeleine McCann from Praia da Luz in Southern Portugal on Thursday 3rd May 2007 had become a world event. Kate was a GP, like her, but the McCanns had used IVF treatment to have children. It was impossible for Lucy, reading page after page, detailing both the search for Madeleine and the personal agony suffered by Kate, not to relate the situation the McCanns faced to Scarlett, Lily and Tabitha.

There was one passage when Kate McCann explained why she felt she could never return to her medical work. She wrote that in their surgeries doctors have to deal with many medically trivial complaints. She was worried, after what she'd been through, that she would struggle to offer the degree of understanding and attention that her training required of her.

The husband and wife sitting in front of Lucy weren't succeeding in their wish to have children. They had gone through test after test, which the husband had hated. They were fit, active, healthy and, apparently, fertile. Now they were beginning to start questioning whether to pay for private help.

Lucy just wanted to say to them, "Go away, get absolutely blotto, fuck each other to kingdom come and wait for the Boot's kit to test positive."

But she'd smiled in her best caring manner. "We can recommend three clinics, each with their own good features."

She was finding the three days a week at Whiteoaks Practice was working well. Her pay was excellent and she enjoyed the mental stimulus of diagnostic medicine. Her patients were so much better informed these days and she was used to being given an internet printout of what the individual thought might be wrong with them.

She was conscious of the dangers of routine. She faced a number of trivial illnesses but tried to take each seriously. The "come back in seven days if you do not feel better" approach cured many cases. There was much more administration, government returns and internal processes but, nevertheless, she enjoyed most days. Yesterday had been a surgery she would remember for a long time. Perhaps she had saved a young life.

Today was an exception and she knew in part that her thoughts were with her husband. They were talking continuously and she acknowledged that he was fighting to stay off alcohol. But she also realised that one relapse, just one, would put them back to where they started.

She'd always thought that her status as a doctor had impressed Charles from the beginning. They'd met at a party organised by the senior partner of her previous practice. She remembered thinking at the time that he was partial to alcohol, but she found herself attracted by his vivid stories of life in the City. She began to think less as a doctor and more as a potential wife. Alcohol made him happy and then silly. They began to spend more and more time together. When, to her complete amazement, she found that she was pregnant (having forgotten to take one of her birth control pills) they drifted into marriage, both agreeing that there was no possibility of termination. And she did love his stories of life in the financial centre.

There were five people sitting around the table at the City Fiction management meeting. As always, cash-flow seemed to dominate the agenda, but Alistair wanted to discuss publishing matters.

"Alistair, I can control things, but you must understand the HMV problem," pleaded the long suffering David Singleton. "HMV own Waterstones and are under pressure from their shareholders. They are fighting massive debt problems. They've tried to improve Waterstones' balance sheet by returning thousands of books to the trade. As a consequence, our expected payment at the end of June is thirty thousand pounds down."

"But Waterstones have been bought by that Russian bloke, haven't they?" said Glenn Davis, the PR and marketing manager.

"Right," said David. "Alexander Mamut, that Russian bloke, is paying fifty-three million pounds for it, subject to shareholders' approval, but we can guess how that works."

"In fact," contributed Amanda, "it's good news. Waterstones is vital to the book publishing industry. I understand that the trade is convinced this Russian guy will expand the business."

"I've spoken to their finance people and they're expecting that the books will be wanted back and so we should probably get our money in September," advised David. "The fact remains. We need a capital injection."

Amanda banged her fist on the table.

"Are you saying that the owners of Waterstones, HMV or whatever they're called, have improved their balance sheet – sorry, the figures of Waterstones – by returning all our books so that they can debit our account, but you aren't worried because they'll ask for them back again? And in the meantime they've left us short of money?"

"In a word 'yes'."

"So what do we do?" she asked.

"My cue, I think. We push on with our fund-raising," said Alistair. "Our corporate advisers are now called Harriman Agnew Capital and remain in Queen Street. The merged business looks stronger. Oliver Chatham is head of corporate finance."

"So do we have our contract letter?" asked David.

Alistair and Amanda looked at each other.

"They've employed an analyst called Sara Flemming. I met her for lunch today. She's preparing a research note on us."

"Did you know that she came into the office yesterday afternoon? We all went for rather a lot of wine with her in Leadenhall Market," said Glenn. "Quite a girl."

"You should have told me," said Alistair. "I was on my mobile."

"Why?" asked Glenn.

"Well, what did she want to know about?" snapped Alistair.

"What were our opinions of you," he responded. "One or two of us told her what we thought."

"Is it asking too much to enquire what you said to her?"

"Ask away. We're not telling you. But she seemed pretty pleased that we were so open with her."

After the meeting was over and the other three had left, Alistair and Amanda shut the door.

"You're meeting her tonight?" Alistair asked.

"We're having a drink in St. John's Wood," Amanda replied. "How do you think your lunch went?"

"She's not easy to sum up. She seems quite sure of herself and she undoubtedly knows how to research a subject. I just wonder what Oliver expects to get out of her report."

"Whatever it is, I get the impression it's quite important to them," his sister replied.

Oliver had decided to complete a second session at the gym and didn't arrive back at his flat in Clerkenwell until after nine o'clock. He listened to Jane Jones on Classic FM on his way back and recalled his lunchtime chat with Edward, his barrister brother-in-law, who was himself well versed in modern classical music. He'd come up with a surprise suggestion.

Oliver had again explained to Edward the only clues he had on the piece of music he was trying to identify.

"I definitely heard the first word, which I thought was 'ascent' or something similar," he had told him. "Then I gained an impression of a mountain. Can't think why. The name of the composer was definitely Russian or sounded very similar."

"And you say it was about eight minutes long?"

"Yes. I noticed the clock on the dashboard of the car."

"You're sure it was not the first part of a concerto?"

"Not certain, no, but my sense was that it was complete in itself."

"So it must be a mini-concerto because you say it started with piano and then the orchestra came in."

"Definitely. There were three movements each starting with the piano. Da-de-da."

"We've ruled out Rachmaninov. Fair enough. Are you sure you've given Shostakovich enough consideration? He wrote an awful lot of music. Have you thought of listening to some of his film scores? Try 'The Fall of Berlin', which I think he composed in 1949." Edward had paused. "Though, to be fair, you don't normally get a mini-piano concerto in the middle of a film

63

theme." He'd sipped his glass of water. "I've had one thought," he'd said.

Oliver had never heard of Nikolai Karlovich Medtner. When he googled his name he was amazed at what he read: "Born in January 1880 Medtner became a Russian master in the composition of piano music. This included fourteen piano sonatas, three violin sonatas, three piano concertos and thirty-eight piano pieces to which he gave a title of 'Fairy Tales'."

Oliver played the CD which he had bought from the Barbican music shop. He listened to the First Piano Sonata in F Minor which Medtner composed in 1903. It is said he was influenced by Rachmaninov. This was followed by the second, third and fourth piano sonatas (which were published as the 'Sonata-Triad'). It was the fifth sonata which Oliver enjoyed the most. This had been written in 1910 (in G Minor, Op 25) and its sixteen minutes are said by some critics to contain several of Medtner's best harmonies.

But the drums and the powerful strings were missing. Oliver knew that Medtner wasn't the composer of the piece of music he was searching for.

He wondered what Amanda was doing. Should he send a text? Perhaps not tonight, he decided. He was finding it difficult to force the pace of their relationship. She was not going to revise the terms of their deal and yet, when they were together, she was so warm and affectionate. It drove him mad.

Amanda was back at her flat in Elm Tree Road reflecting on her meeting with Sara in a local wine bar. It had started badly. They argued about who should buy the drinks and then they could not agree where to sit, which was influenced by Amanda's wish to be private. She had given some thought to the questions which Sara might ask but nothing prepared her for the opening barrage.

"Alistair says that you get yourself in a mess with men," said Sara.

Amanda was apoplectic.

"I'm here to talk about City Fiction, young lady, nothing more!" she snapped.

"Young lady?" repeated Sara. "I can teach you better put-downs than that if you wish."

"What I want is to finish this conversation as soon as possible. Now what do you want to know about Alistair and City Fiction?"

"Nothing."

"Good. I suggest we drink up and then we can go."

"I want to know about you, Amanda. So stop being so uptight and relax. You are Alistair's sister. He adores you. You are obviously his prop. You back him totally. I want to understand how stable you are."

"So I'm unstable now, am I?" she said. "Who are you to judge me?"

"What's the name of your present boyfriend?" asked Sara.

"Er... well... he works in the City. What's this got to do with publishing exactly?"

"How long have you been together?"

"You don't give up do you? Well, he's a total Adonis, if you must know. Six foot tall, handsome and great company. Ok?"

"How long have you been together?"

"It's a newish relationship. Can we please talk about City Fiction now?"

"Who was your last boyfriend?" asked Sara.

Amanda groaned. She really didn't want to talk about Zach. But the strange thing was that she did. She was falling into the trap of relieving her frustrations by telling somebody about them. She started to tell Sara the whole story. Even more surprising was Sara's reaction.

"So, let's understand this better. Zach was everything you wanted. You accepted he was married. He puts a ring on your finger. You had this great weekend in Stratford – and you get up the next day and end the relationship because he is not seemingly considering his wife and his children."

Despite her sudden openness, Amanda still felt slightly uncomfortable talking so personally to Sara. But she knew her report was very important and, anyway, she had already given away enough to make further revelations pretty harmless.

"That's about it. We really were good together... but I just couldn't understand how he was just absolving himself of his responsibilities."

"Perhaps he was protecting you."

Amanda pondered Sara's point for several moments.

"Why? We were always open with each other."

"Do you think that perhaps he was concerned that he might lose you if he talked about his family too much?"

Amanda considered this statement. "It's ironic but I suppose if that's the case he's managed to get it completely wrong!"

"Hmm, maybe so," said Sara, taking a sip from her drink.

"Now, shall we talk about foreign rights?" Amanda prompted.

Sara agreed immediately. She had, believe it or not, been nervous about meeting Amanda and had decided that a direct approach was her only chance of understanding the woman who seemed to have such an influence on the chief executive of the publishing company.

Detective Chief Inspector Sarah Rudd left Ealing police station at nine o'clock in the evening. She would use the twenty minutes of her journey home to Nick and the children, who would pretend to be asleep, to plan the long weekend ahead. She had taken three days holiday and booked a cottage for them in North Devon. They would be leaving early the following morning and expected to be travelling along the M4 by eight o'clock.

During the last four weeks she had led a team of detectives in closing down an illegal operation masterminded by a gang from Eastern Europe. They had devised a way of tampering with cash machines and succeeded in grossing around three hundred thousand pounds.

After she had arrived home and parked her car she let herself into the house to find her husband asleep in front of the television. She woke him up with a cup of tea and told him about her recent success at work. Nick was always interested in what she did, although he worried about her safety.

"They were pretty nasty, Nick," she confided. "We were well prepared but the armed guys had to step in."

She then told her husband how well her posting from Paddington Green police station was working out.

"It's never easy to settle in and some of the officers have been there for a number of years," she said, pausing to drink some tea. "So far it's going ok. I just don't want a problem case. You know what I mean. A rapist on the loose."

"Or worse," said Nick.

"Or worse," she agreed. "So, let's go to North Devon."

"Let's go to bed," suggested Nick.

At the end of the week, at eleven in the morning, Sara Flemming was shown into the board room of Harriman Agnew Capital.

She looked quizzically at Andrew. She did not like surprises.

"Sara," he said, "this is Charles Harriman. Since we met we've merged our firms. Charles is our chairman."

Sara ignored the chairman. Despite an invitation to take a seat, she remained standing and handed Andrew four envelopes.

Andrew opened the first envelope.

"That is my report," said Sara. "There are ten printed copies in your outer office."

He flicked through it and handed it to the chairman, who started to turn the pages. It was later agreed by the members of the corporate finance team that Sara's report on the publishing industry was one of the best and most informative on any sector that they had ever received.

Andrew picked up the second package. "What's this?" he asked.

"My invoice," she said.

The chief executive opened the envelope and looked at the single piece of paper. He nodded.

"The funds will be in your bank account on Monday morning," he said. "Thank you, Sara."

"There are two more envelopes," observed Charles.

Sara did not take her eyes off Andrew.

"You'll not read my report," she said. "People like you never do. You're like MPs. Half page summaries are your limit."

Charles and Andrew looked at each other in amazement.

"The third envelope is what you really want."

Andrew sliced the packet open and took out a single piece of paper. He read it aloud.

"Strictly Confidential

To: Andrew Agnew
From: Sara Flemming
Date: 9 June 2011
Subject: Should you accept City Fiction (CF) as a client and raise them two million pounds.

1. *CF is a gamble.*
2. *CF is building up its annuity income very well indeed. They will have one hundred and ten titles in 2012. They are currently generating 34% of their revenues from this source. It will exceed 40% next year.*
3. *That pays the overheads. It leaves nothing for shareholders.*
4. *CF has a great staff. Young, enthusiastic, committed. They worship Alistair Wavering (see below).*
5. *Amanda Wavering is important. She holds Alistair together and is calculating, clever and charming.*
6. *CF will do well. BUT it is a gamble because it is desperately difficult to find the bestsellers. CF has some excellent authors but try as he might Alistair Wavering has yet to find the bestseller that will turn his fortunes.*
7. *Alistair told me something I did not know. Bestsellers come from word of mouth. Existing authors, as an example Wilbur Smith, find success and simply keep writing books which have guaranteed sales. But to succeed, the CFs of this world must find their bestseller. Somebody needs to read a book and recommend it to others and tweet about it. Book clubs need to pick it up. Reviews help.*
8. *Therefore to justify your investors' money you must be certain that CF will, someday, find its bestseller(s).*

Recommendation

Alistair Wavering is as good as they come.
I have an instinct that one day he will find his Holy Grail and repay
investors many, many times over.
Go for it, Andrew.

Sara Flemming
London."

The two executives remained silent. They exchanged glances.

"There's a fourth envelope," said Andrew.

"You don't necessarily need to open that one," suggested Sara.

"Why?" asked Charles.

Sara continued to look at Andrew.

"If you decide to appoint me as head of your research department, those are my terms."

Sara turned and walked out of the offices of Harriman Agnew Capital.

Charles groaned inwardly. He knew he should have discussed the latest Simon Cowell controversy or their newest computer game. But he'd chosen to tell Lucy, Scarlett, Lily and Tabitha about the events, earlier in the day, at Harriman Agnew Capital.

It was a glorious June day and the late afternoon barbecue was in full swing. Lucy had taken ever greater care washing the salad items because of the E.coli scare sweeping across Europe from Germany. She had washed every item several times and although, as a doctor, she knew it was simple scaremongering, she had discarded the cucumber. She encouraged her family to stay off the red meats and had selected chicken, tuna steak and vegetarian burgers.

Lucy's senior partner at the surgery bounded up, breaking through her reverie. He seemed in an ebullient mood.

"Lucy," he had said the previous day, "these Lansley reforms are fantastic. We had a meeting yesterday of the local practitioners and our early calculations are that GP salaries will go up by a basic thirty thousand pounds a year."

"For doing what?" Lucy had asked.

"We'll have budget responsibilities."

"Which we'll exercise in surgery time…"

"Yes, of course, we all work too hard as it is. But think, Lucy, of the stress of trying to balance the allocation of hospital services."

"John, I read that the health minister said that the rationalisation of the structure your committee are working on will cost one billion and save five billion."

"Well," Dr. Templeman had responded, "he's certainly got one of the figures right. I was looking at the costs of dismantling the local PCTs alone. There are one hundred and fifty of them. It will be at least one billion nationally, we think, and some of us suspect it will be near two billion."

"And the savings?"

"We think Mr Lansley is rather visionary."

Lucy was brought back to reality as her daughter continued with her questions.

"So, Daddy," demanded Scarlett. "Her name is Sara. How tall is she?"

Her father had described the events which had taken place earlier in the day at Harriman Agnew Capital. All four female members of the Harriman tribe had latched on to the Sara character. Tabitha was spilling coleslaw down her front but nobody noticed.

"How tall? Five foot five. Just a little shorter than your mother."

"Her hair," said Lily. "How was she wearing it?"

"Er... well it was fair, on top of her head."

"It normally is, Charles," said Lucy. "It does sound quite a performance. Did you like her?"

"Did I like her?" pondered Charles. "Did I like her?" He drank some fresh orange juice. "I agreed with Andrew that we should employ her. The report she did was remarkable. Several of the team have partly read her full document. Ninety pages. But her summary to Andrew hit every nail on the head. Brilliant."

"What was she wearing?" asked Scarlett.

70

"Jeans and a blazer," said Charles. "Most unusual for business, but somehow it worked. She's not what I might call good looking. She has a vitality though. Her face is her personality."

"Is she thin?" asked Scarlett.

"Trim," replied her father.

"How old is she?" asked Lucy.

"Twenty-four."

Sara read the text message again.

"Terms agreed. Start Monday. Andrew."

She rolled over and on top of the warm body beside her in the bed.

"I'm horny," she whispered into Alex's ear.

"Lisbeth Salander triumphs again," Alex replied.

"Actually, it's Sara Flemming who has a new job. Anyway Lisbeth rarely talked about herself. You know everything about me."

"Everything?"

Sara giggled in anticipation as Alex ducked beneath the bed covers.

Oliver and Amanda met on Saturday morning and went together to her gym. They then left London and drove west along the Thames Valley and found a river bank. She had prepared a picnic which she spread out between them. He was dazzled by the fare. His eyes focused on a trio of melon pieces, goat's cheese and red pepper tartlets, a Caesar salad with barbecued chicken, prawns in a sweet chilli sauce and some crusty French bread. He opened the wine and vowed to keep to two glasses.

He began to tell Amanda again about the piece of music he could not identify. She was watching the river traffic and a couple arguing in a motor boat.

"Russian," repeated Amanda. "You're sure?"

"I went through all this with my brother-in-law. I heard the name. It sounded Russian. If it had been Chopin..."

"But not Rachmaninov, nor Shostakovich nor Medtner?"

"There were drums and violins and trumpets."

"Oliver, there are drums, violins and trumpets in lots of compositions!"

"Let me tell you about it. It started with the piano, da-de-da with the emphasis on the first da. Got it? Da-de-da and again, da-de-da, and then the violins raced away up the scales. This produced trumpets and drums. It was stirring music. Then it started again."

"Why Russian definitely?"

He explained the accident involving the taxi and the cyclist. "I was trying to listen at the end. I caught the 'ascent' and I thought I heard something about a mountain. The DJ said the composer's name but I was being distracted by her... er... the police arriving."

She looked a little quizzical. "So you missed the name completely?"

"Definitely Russian."

"Long or short?" she asked. She leant across him and picked up the bottle of wine. She filled their glasses and raised her own to her lips.

"Long or short?" she repeated.

"Long or short what?" he asked.

"The name of the composer. Was it a long name?"

"Er. Longish. Quite long. Hell, Amanda, I can only remember the sound. I was dealing with a road accident."

"Involving, no doubt, a pretty girl," she laughed.

"Well... er." He stopped at that moment as he decided that admitting he had been watching the rider with her skirt riding up might not create quite the right impression.

Oliver knew that his thoughts were drifting. Amanda was wearing a simple pink blouse and skirt and not much else. She had tanned to perfection in the early summer sun and her daily regime in the gym had toned her muscles perfectly. Her hair was natural. Her face was relaxed and her smile was gentle. She put her hand on his lower thigh.

"Thank you, Oliver, for your work so far," she said as her thoughts returned to City Fiction. She kissed him on his cheek.

The contract was going to be signed on Monday and Oliver knew what was awaiting him when the two million pounds were raised. He lay back on the grass and felt Amanda by his side. She undid the buttons of his shirt and began to run her fingers across his stomach.

"There's not much doubt that you'll raise the money now is there?"

"None at all," he spluttered, as he felt her fingers probing down towards his groin. He brushed his hand against her midriff. It was sensational. She made no move as his fingers reached her left breast. He squeezed her gently through the silk material.

"Mmm," she moaned softly.

"A down payment," laughed Oliver.

"Yes, of course. Our deal," said Amanda. "I never, ever, change my mind. You must understand that, Oliver."

He had now moved his fingers inside the edge of her panties and discovered that she'd had a Brazilian wax. He wondered if he dare go further.

Amanda turned towards him, wrapped herself around him, reached his lips, thrust her tongue inside his mouth and left his hand exactly where it was. He moved his hand a little further down. She froze and pulled away. Oliver was utterly perplexed. And worse was to follow. Amanda went quiet and refused to answer his gently whispered questions. Within thirty minutes they were driving back to London in silence.

Andrew Agnew met his partner, Rachel, outside the Prince Edward Theatre. They were going to see Jersey Boys. Within five minutes they were joined by Charles and Lucy Harriman. They were too late for a pre-theatre drink and were shown to their box almost immediately.

Towards the end of the first half of the show, the four players broke into hit songs from the past, and they clapped along with the rest of the audience. It was truly electric.

During the interval, Rachel and Lucy chatted happily. Rachel was full of enthusiasm for the flourishing corporate finance business.

"Andrew is coming home a different man," she said to Lucy. "What about Charles?"

Lucy hesitated before replying. "He is, what can I say, happier... than I can remember for some time. He's really pleased with the way people have merged together."

"I see he's not drinking tonight," said Rachel.

Lucy hesitated. She surely must know. "He's driving," she said.

The five minutes bell rang.

"I'm so pleased the men suggested we should meet, Lucy. I just feel, well, excited about what's happening."

"Yes," said Lucy, "the signs are propitious. But – actually, you may not know – I'm a doctor and we're taught to be cautious. It goes with the job, I suppose."

"But still, I want you to have a good time tonight," said Rachel.

"Yes, of course, and I am," said Lucy, smiling. "We'll worry about tomorrow, tomorrow," and they both laughed as they headed back to their box.

During the second half the hits just kept coming: 'Beggin', 'Bye Bye Baby, Baby Goodbye', 'Can't take My Eyes Off You' and 'Rag Doll'. They all left the theatre in an exhilarated mood.

But, in the coming week, Lucy would have cause to remember her ominous words – for her daughter, Tabitha, was to vanish off the face of the earth.

Oliver did his best to impose himself on the meeting between City Fiction and Harriman Agnew Capital. He also tried to avoid eye contact with Amanda. He was still puzzled by the turn of events on Saturday afternoon. Her sudden request that they return back to London. Her rather dismissive attitude as he left her outside her flat. Oliver had watched his mobile for the rest of the weekend but there was no text from her.

She was wearing a business suit and white blouse. She smiled at everybody and when Alistair signed the contract on behalf of City Fiction she clapped her hands together. She seemed her usual, radiant self.

Melanie Reid then painfully instructed everybody on the regulatory processes that would follow. There was much more interest in the draft timetable which Gavin and his team, together with Martin Daboute, who was to play an increasingly significant role in the deal, and Abbi, had prepared.

Oliver focused on one item. "Completion: funds to company: w/b 25 July 2011."

He had six weeks to wait. He completed the formalities, said some pleasant words about the client and then walked out of the room with Amanda. The smile never left her lips – until they entered the lift together. Oliver pressed the ground floor button. Once they had both left the building he asked Amanda to stop. She turned and faced him.

"I'd rather you didn't say anything please, Oliver."

"But, Amanda. On Saturday we were..."

"That seems a long time ago. Today is business. It's an important day for Alistair. I'm so grateful to be working with you. I know you'll bring us the success we need."

"So, what happens over the next six weeks?"

"You'll raise the money. What else?"

They had to move to one side as a street cleaning machine clambered past them.

He put his hands on her shoulders.

"You know what I'm talking about. What happened on Saturday... I didn't plan that."

"Things happen, Oliver."

"You're going to make me wait for six weeks, aren't you?"

She turned and started to walk towards Holborn, striding out and using the wide pavements so she could move faster. As she passed Gray's Inn Road the tears of frustration she had been holding back began to trickle down her face.

Chapter Four

"What are the bloody terms?"

Gavin's words hung in the air, his question, as yet, unanswered.

Oliver had decided that the late morning meeting at Harriman Agnew gave him an opportunity to assert his authority.

"And why did I have to read this crap?" Gavin continued. He threw Sara's report into the centre of the conference room table.

"Why's she here anyway?" he continued. "Andrew announces that we have a new head of research and this skinny teenager turns up. It's a joke." He snatched the jug of water and poured a glass for himself. "What do you say, Dunc? Is it a bloody farce or what??"

Oliver groaned inwardly. He had spent an hour with Gavin and Duncan over breakfast, discussing business in general and conditions in their market sector. They had agreed that the coalition government was struggling to stimulate the British economy. Gavin had summarised the problems faced by the Eurozone, as Germany and France tried to sort out the difficulties being faced by Greece, which were now spreading to Spain and Italy. Duncan was more interested in the United States, where President Obama was continuing to face difficulties in getting the Tea Party-dominated Republicans to agree a debt reduction programme with the Democrats. They discussed what a borrowing requirement of eight trillion dollars really meant.

"A lot of fucking green-backs," laughed Gavin.

Oliver told them about an email he'd received from his father overnight. He was worried about China. Gavin surprised the other two by displaying considerable knowledge about China's investment policies and their recent support for Spanish bonds.

"I know you think I'm an East End London boy," he said, "but I have to know what our clients want to talk about. Their average profile is male, aged over fifty, retired or on their way, wealthy and reading *The Daily Telegraph* every morning." He drank his coffee and munched a bacon sandwich. "That's what they read about and they expect us to tell them what's going on. It's not easy for the lads. Duncan and I have to lead. Ian is a good head of sales but you have little idea how hard we work. Before the recession we could sell shares totalling one hundred thousand pounds in a day. Now it's very tough. Dunc, what was our best last week?"

"Monday. Ten thousand."

"Do you understand, Oliver? Bring in all the fucking deals you want. It's us who have to sell the shares."

Oliver had left the breakfast gathering feeling that he had made some progress in building team morale. However, as soon as Gavin found himself in an open conference he reverted to type.

"Hey, skinny. Why should my salesmen read your fucking report?"

"My name is Sara and as far as I'm concerned you can..."

"Gavin," interrupted Abbi, "Sara just did what Andrew asked her to do..."

She was stopped in mid-sentence.

"I'll answer for myself, Abbi," Sara snapped, turning to face Gavin, "but not to you, you bald-headed lout!"

Oliver tried to bring some order to the proceedings but the damage was done.

Tabitha Harriman was snatched on Tuesday 14 June at around four o'clock.

The 999 call was made about this time and was answered in the central operations room. It reached Ealing police station a few minutes later. Detective Chief Inspector Sarah Rudd was already aware of a major incident taking place at the western end of Ealing Broadway, where it becomes the Uxbridge Road.

At 4.50pm she was told that a frantic mother was demanding to see her. She was being continually briefed on the situation.

An hour earlier at 3.50pm, on a normal Tuesday afternoon, the nearside tyre of a tanker carrying inflammable chemicals had burst. The vehicle had slewed sideways into a car which was attempting to exit a car-park into the Broadway. A second driver had lost control and ploughed into the back of the lorry. In the car-park another driver was using her mobile phone and had reacted three seconds too late. Her state-of-the-art Range Rover had crashed into the back of the first car, which was crushed further into the lorry. At this point a member of the public, standing on the opposite side of the street, had spotted that liquid was leaking onto the Uxbridge Road.

The calls from the public flooded into the operations room and the police quickly launched their well-practised disaster procedures. Five fire engines arrived at the site of the accident. The second policeman on the scene was experienced in the Hazchem Emergency Response Service (HERS).

He searched for the identification decal. The information disc provided the HERS telephone number. Within minutes he was speaking to the trained chemists at the National Chemical Emergency Centre. In line with the Emergency Response Protocol it was agreed that this was a level 2 situation. With the agreement of the owners of the truck, specialists were on their way to advise on the clean-up procedures.

The officers were told that the chemicals were highly toxic and that the area must be evacuated. The ambulance services were dealing with a seriously injured tanker driver who hadn't been wearing his safety harness in his cab. The driver of the first car was already dead. The fire brigade team, using breathing apparatus, were struggling to extract the driver of the vehicle that had crashed into the back of the tanker. A local doctor had already given a pain-killing injection. The woman in the Range Rover was again on her mobile and arguing with her husband. She noticed the policeman approaching her vehicle and rang off. The medical services had already sent five people with breathing difficulties two miles west towards Southall to Ealing Hospital.

Heathrow Airport was put on an alert warning. The District tube line service was suspended at Acton Town and Ealing Common station was closed. The railway police decided to halt all trains on the Paddington to Bristol/Cardiff lines for a precautionary period. The M4 and M40 motorways were quickly affected as the side roads became gridlocked and the motorway junctions were blocked. The Uxbridge Road was closed for many hours. By four-thirty the driver of the tanker was on his way to hospital and his vehicle was being covered with foam. At Ealing police station, Superintendent Daniel Obuma was in charge of operations. He had notified his boss, Chief Superintendent Avril Gardner, who was being driven back to Ealing by the Metropolitan traffic police from a conference in Westminster.

At the beginning of all this, a call was received by the police from a local shopkeeper, from a phone located on the opposite side of Ealing Broadway. He reported that he had seen a young child being forced into a car.

Amanda sat on the balcony of her flat and looked out over St. John's Wood. The bright afternoon sunshine was reflecting on the buildings. She was thinking about Oliver, re-living the Saturday picnic and their passion on the river bank.

She so enjoyed his company. He was quiet, yet entertaining – and so slim and fit. She had watched how he approached his sessions in the gym. She was competitive, but he attacked the challenges posed by the various pieces of equipment with a demonstrable will to win.

Looks and personality. It was an irresistible combination. She wanted him now more than ever. She remembered his hand inside her clothes and wanted again to feel his fingers on her. She remembered the taste of his mouth.

She wanted to tell him why she had had no choice on the Saturday afternoon but to stop his hand going any further. She had realised that if he had carried on, she would not have been able to control herself. At that moment, and more than at any time with any man she had ever been with, she had wanted – and believed in – her personal completeness. She was with the person she was beginning to believe might be her life partner. The moment had been perfect: her body was screaming out for him.

"Damn the deal," she said to herself. She knew he would raise the money. Why wait six weeks? She bitterly regretted her initial approach. At the time she understood her own motivation in wanting the fund-raising to come before any romantic relationship. She was still thinking about Zach and it had never occurred to her that she would feel such a strong attraction for another man so soon. But she had and it was happening all too quickly.

She wondered if she would be letting Alistair down if she released Oliver from her terms. Perhaps it might send the wrong message. Was this the selfish streak – which previous boyfriends had delighted in pointing out to her – rearing its head? Could it, perhaps, affect the raising of the two million pounds?

This was the Amanda no other person ever knew. The confident, determined businesswoman – who somehow never managed to completely get her life together, in the way she wanted, when it came to her personal relationships. She had thought she might be on her way with Zach.

She also knew she had to accept her other demon. Why had she not removed Oliver's hand, kissed him and whispered in his ear, "Oliver. I'm falling for you and want to be with you. But we've agreed a way forward and you know we have to keep to it."

And he might have accepted that, despite his arousal. But, somehow, Amanda simply could not speak those words. She had written to Zach rather than talk to him. She had run away before and now she was running away again. What made matters worse was that she did not even know why she was running or where she was going.

She'd decided to allow things to settle down but, even so, she felt a need to make contact with him. She thought through several options and then remembered their conversation about a silly piece of music where he was searching for the composer and the title. She spent the next hour at her computer googling "Russian composers". Surprised at how many there were, she decided to find a name which she recognised. Finally she sent a text message:

"Oliver. It could be Tchaikovsky. His piano concerto no.1 is often played on the radio. Love. Amanda. x"

The tensions between Oliver and Gavin boiled over early in the afternoon, after the latter had spent nearly two hours in the pub. He was beginning to earn the sobriquet "a legend in his own lunchtime", often used in the City by drinkers about other drinkers.

Oliver decided to reconvene the morning meeting, against the advice of his colleagues, Abbi and Martin. Once he had everybody together he attempted to review the process they would be following over the next few days.

Gavin wasn't interested and kept snapping. His first target was inevitably Sara, to whom he had taken an intense dislike. She was rude back to him and seemed not to care.

"What the fuck are we paying you to do?" Gavin barked.

Sara ignored him, which added to his tension.

"Gavin," said Abbi, "Sara is giving us a vital resource. We've agreed in the past that our research facilities are limited. If you think about it, Sara will help your salesmen sell shares."

Martin nodded in approval and looked at Oliver, who was also quietly impressed.

"You're just a pathetic little girl," said Gavin, staring at Sara evilly.

"What's that got to do with anything at all?" said Abbi. "You have to stop with these personal and sexist comments, Gavin."

"You don't understand the pressures we're working under," said Duncan. "The salesmen depend on commission for their living. We're not finding the right deals. Gavin and I have real concerns about City Fiction. It's not going to be easy to sell their shares to our clients."

"Why?" asked Oliver. "It's a good story. You've read Sara's report. Whatever Gavin might think, the advent of electronic publishing gives the salesmen something to talk about. And Abbi is capturing that in her script."

"That's an important point Oliver is making," added Abbi. "I will try to emphasise the excitement of the digital era in the salesmen's selling story. Amazon is thought to be matching

Waterstones in terms of total sales. Sales of Kindles are soaring and the readers are getting used to downloading their books at cheaper prices."

"Which is where my report is relevant," said Sara.

Gavin looked at her with his mouth wide open.

"The day you're relevant..."

"I get that," interrupted Duncan. "Perhaps it might help if you spent some time with us and heard some of the discussions we have with the investors. They want shares that have an added excitement. Can't you find us a gold mine in Africa or an oil exploration company in Asia?"

"Then you'd need me, Gavin," said Sara. "You'd never get that sort of deal away without the right research."

"The day I need you, skinny, is the day I retire."

Lucy was beginning to panic. Her neighbour couldn't collect Tabitha that day and so she had to be at the school at four o'clock. She had been delayed at the surgery, stitching a cut on the back of the hand of a housewife who had been over-enthusiastic with her kitchen knife. She could have sent her to the local hospital but she knew that it only needed two stitches. But despite her best efforts the cut would not stop bleeding.

She phoned the school and was reassured that Tabitha was safe and looking forward to seeing her. A massive row between three of the teaching staff would ensue later about who was actually responsible for looking after the child. What was in no doubt was that she had somehow slipped out of the playground, through the locked school gates and onto the Broadway to await the arrival of her mother.

Gerald Masters and his wife Alice ran a confectionary shop on Ealing Broadway. They made a steady, if modest, living and were well used to having the school children in their shop. On that afternoon, once the shop was clear of the school kids, Gerald had slipped out onto the main road to light up a cigarette. He had tried and failed to give up.

He told the police in rather vivid detail that as he was watching the activities of the emergency services about two hundred yards down the Broadway on the opposite side of the street, suddenly, on his side of the road, about thirty, perhaps forty, yards away, a dark green car pulled up. A woman got out and went over to a small child on the pavement. He noticed that the young girl seemed to be trying to pull away, but at that moment two fire engines, with their sirens bellowing out, thundered past and diverted his attention. He was to tell the police how he went back into the shop and told his wife about the small girl. Alice insisted he phoned the emergency services.

Lucy couldn't reach the school because of the traffic chaos. She abandoned her car and ran the last half mile. She could not find Tabitha. She tracked down the head teacher, who was himself desperately searching the school for any remaining pupils because a policeman had rushed up and warned him about the possibility of an explosion.

Lucy finally found one of the three teachers who would later be accused of negligence. The woman said that Tabitha was there in reception when she heard that her mother was delayed. She could not remember seeing her again.

At this point a policewoman ran into the school and asked if they had any children on the premises. She was met by the caretaker, Nigel Brewer, who immediately took charge of the situation. He took her to the head teacher who explained that the children had, in most cases, left for home before the incident on the Broadway had taken place. A number of teachers were still on the premises as they were unable to exit their cars into Uxbridge Road. Nigel, a former army officer who had served with distinction in the Falklands War, offered to organise for the police officer to look around the school premises. The policewoman, however, was using her radio.

It was not until 5.15pm that Detective Chief Inspector Sarah Rudd managed to begin to piece everything together. There was a major incident in the Broadway. On the opposite side of the street about two hundred yards away, a shopkeeper had reported that he had seen a small girl being pushed into a green car. DCI Rudd was now with Lucy on the pavement where Tabitha was thought to have been taken. Lucy was demanding to speak to the shopkeeper. DCI Rudd explained that this was not possible. Lucy phoned her husband again, whose mobile phone was now turned on. He had arrived home and was perplexed by the police officers outside their home.

DCI Rudd contacted the chief superintendent by phone.

"Ma'am. We have a missing child."

Abbi was reviewing her file on City Fiction. As marketing manager at Harriman Agnew Capital, her function was to work with Martin Daboute on the documentation and to produce the promotional material. This would be used by the brokers when talking to their clients, who were potential investors in the shares they were selling.

She looked up and stopped writing as she saw that Sara had sat down opposite her.

"Hi," said Abbi.

"So. Marketing manager. What's that exactly?" asked Sara.

"I'm more than happy to tell you," replied Abbi, "but why don't you drop the aggro bit?"

Sara remained silent.

"Ever since you walked in here you've had an attitude. Forget your start with Andrew. You need to earn your place with the rest of us. You missed a real opportunity this morning to start building bridges with Gavin."

"He's an idiot."

"Gavin runs a successful department. It's not easy selling shares in these market conditions. You heard what Duncan was saying at the meeting. They really are a good team. If we don't raise funds for our clients we have no future."

"He's a prick and I don't trust him. What's a marketing manager?"

"Ok. I'll tell you," said Abbi. "Within the business we have corporate finance and brokerage."

"Oliver is corporate finance and Gavin and Duncan are brokerage," said Sara.

"Right. You have been listening," said Abbi. "You sit there with such a vacant expression on your face I never know what you're thinking. Corporate finance, which is Oliver and his team, find and approve the deals. You are part of that process. Eventually a decision is made by the bosses to take on the client. When the transaction is ready Gavin and his team, which we call brokerage, will try to sell the shares to our private and professional clients."

Abbi poured some water for them both and asked Sara if she was feeling better after her bout with Gavin.

"It takes time to settle in here," she said.

"I'm fine. I can take care of myself," responded Sara.

"Do you understand what Melanie does?"

"No."

"You need to know, Sara. She is God – or thinks she is at any rate. She is our compliance officer. Regulation is everything these days. Melanie walks the corridors dispensing fear."

Sara laughed. "Nonsense."

"It's not far from the truth, I promise you."

"What's it all in aid of?"

"It's about ensuring that we understand our clients and treat them fairly. This is why the directors' backgrounds are checked so carefully. Melanie is paranoid about that. All must pass money laundering checks. We have lawyers and accountants who verify all the information we produce."

"So what is brokerage?" asked Sara.

Abbi poured some more water and produced two chocolate bars. Sara shook her head. Abbi patted her stomach.

"Jonathan says I need to lose a few pounds," she said, as she unwrapped her snack.

"Jonathan?" asked Sara.

"Brokerage," she said, ignoring the question. "When we have the deal ready, my job is to prepare an investor story. This is a script that will be used by Gavin and his team when they talk to potential investors. It's simply the process of selling shares to our clients. That's what brokerage is all about."

"Why is the door to their office locked?"

"Chinese Walls," replied Abbi. "Melanie makes sure that the corporate finance team can't talk to the brokers. She wants to make sure that they can't influence the sales process."

"So what happens when they're all in the pub together?"

"They talk to each other. Crazy, isn't it?"

"This script you produce –"

86

"It will come under your responsibilities once you've settled in," said Abbi. "It's a research function. I will then work with you to ensure the wording is something the salesmen can use." She drank some water.

"It has to be approved by Melanie first," she continued. "She then allows Gavin and the salesmen to use it. They phone our clients and try to sell them the shares in the company being featured."

Abbi stood up and indicated to Sara that she should follow. They arrived at the door leading to the sales team, most of whom could be seen through the glass and were on the telephone.

"This is the Dealing Room," she said. She punched in a number and pushed open the door. She indicated to Sara that she should look across the desks.

"Can you see that girl with the headphones on?" Abbi asked. Sara nodded.

"She works for Melanie. She can, at any time, listen in to any of the sales team's calls. Her job is to check that they are sticking to the agreed script about the investment they are selling. All calls are taped. If there's any concern the call will be replayed and if the salesman has exceeded the brief, the client will be offered their money back. It's a serious matter and we've lost two salesmen in recent months."

"They live on commission," said Sara.

"You catch on quickly."

"No. I just listen to them talking in the pub and it's what Duncan was saying. They're all short of money."

"It's not easy at the moment," said Abbi. "Anyway, we're about done here, I think. Buy you a glass of wine?"

"Thanks," responded Sara. She paused. "What about mobile phones?"

"What about them?"

"Are they recorded?"

"No. That's smart. Oliver was telling me that the regulators are thinking about imposing new rules and they want them caught by the tapes."

"How will that work?"

"No idea. Come on. Drinks time."

At 7.00pm, Gerald Masters was interviewed by a team of police officers led by DCI Rudd.

He was later to sign a statement which, from the police's point of view, was frustratingly short of detail. Gerald was clear about his timings. He said it was a green car. A dark green car. He looked blank when asked if he had noted the registration number. The police now had a picture of Tabitha which they showed to their witness. He hadn't seen her face. He said his instinct was that she was about four years old and it might be her. She was young: this he had confirmed. Her hair was blonde and she wasn't wearing anything on her head. Tabitha had fair hair and hadn't been wearing a hat that day. Their witness was to state that he couldn't remember seeing this girl in their shop at any time. Mrs Masters, after studying the photograph, also later confirmed this statement.

DCI Rudd wanted to spend more time with her witness, but he was impatient about collecting his van from the garage, where he said the mechanic was waiting for him, and reaching the Cash and Carry before eight o'clock. She had no choice but to let him go.

At this point DCI Rudd was told that the school caretaker had arrived at the police station and was asking to speak to the officer in charge. He was waiting in an interview room.

"It's Mr Brewer, isn't it?" she said. "We met briefly earlier. Thank you for the help you gave my officers."

"I'm a military man, madam. I'll come straight to the point. I saw her. I can't believe that I didn't react. I'm making excuses, but there were police and fire engines and ambulances. The teachers were panicking. It was mayhem."

"Where and when did you see her?"

"Very briefly. The pavement was full of people. She'd wandered away from the school."

"And you didn't do anything, Mr Brewer?"

"I took a shell at Port Stanley. Bloody Argies. It was about the only one they managed to land. I get dizzy spells and all the commotion must have triggered one off."

Surprisingly late in the day, the police realised that the green car was facing west and thus on the wrong side of the street. The road further down was blocked by the emergency services. Had Gerald Masters seen the car turn right into one of the side roads? The shopkeeper couldn't answer this question because he had hurried back into the shop to tell his wife what he'd seen.

DCI Rudd sat with Alice Masters for over thirty minutes and shared a cup of tea with her. They talked about the shop, the school children and how hard she and Gerald worked. They didn't have any children of their own. She told DCI Rudd that they had decided to apply for adoption, but their problem was that they couldn't afford to employ additional staff in the shop and she had to continue working.

"Alice, I appreciate that this is a difficult matter but may I ask how you and your husband are getting on with the adoption application?"

"What's that to do with you, if you don't mind?" asked Alice. "I must phone Gerald. He wouldn't like this."

"Well, I for one always admire people who take that course of action. Adoption, I mean."

"It's been difficult. Gerald wanted his own children and it took me a long time to persuade him to go for the tests." She paused. "When we found out it was him he became quite depressed."

"So how's the adoption process going?"

"We've got some brochures. But Gerald says he's too busy in the shop to attend the meetings. I'm hoping to get him there soon."

"But your husband is committed to adopting a baby?"

"Oh yes," smiled Alice. "It's what we both want."

At 8.30pm in the evening, and with the agreement of Alice, who telephoned her husband to check, a team of police officers, together with a sniffer dog, searched the shop and living accommodation of the confectionary shop where they lived. Nothing was found.

Alice seemed troubled and continually went outside to see if her husband had returned from the Cash and Carry. She explained that he always stocked up mid-week with ice creams for the weekend trade.

"Our sales pick up on Friday, and Saturday is always our best day," she said.

Nobody was interested when she informed them that a new flavour, peach melba, was currently their bestseller. "The children. They tell each other," she added.

Abbi and Sara had secured a spare table in the wine bar. They shared the cost of a bottle of wine and Sara had found a bowl of olives from somewhere. They had been chatting for a few minutes when Oliver appeared.

"Abbi," he said. "I was told that you might be here."

He sat down and Abbi got another glass and poured him some wine.

"Thanks. Can you join me and Gavin tomorrow morning at eight o'clock? We're going to start the process of preparing the selling story for City Fiction."

"That's fine," responded Abbi.

"But not me?" said Sara.

"No," he said. "Right, I must go. I want to get to the gym. Sara, it was a great report but you need to move on. Please try to make your peace with Gavin. Get to know Duncan better. As you've seen, he's more level headed."

"I seem to be getting plenty of advice," Sara said.

"Perhaps you need it," said Abbi.

As Oliver left, Sara picked up her glass of wine. She looked at Abbi and smiled.

"Abbi. Short for Abigail. From the Hebrew meaning 'father's joy'."

Abbi laughed. "Spot on."

"Abigail was the wife of King David and was said to be intelligent and beautiful. She was one of the great female prophetesses in the bible."

"You know your stuff, don't you?"

"Not really. I just looked it up on Wikipedia the other day."

"Why?"

"Because I hoped there might be an opportunity to impress you." She took a sip of wine. "See, Abbi. I'm actually trying."

Lucy arrived home and found her husband in a dreadful state.

"What do we do?" pleaded Charles.

She said they would deal with the police first. She found the officer in charge, who told her that DCI Rudd would be coming later in the evening. She said that they'd completed their searches of the house, garden and surrounding areas.

"How would Tabitha have got here from the school?" asked Lucy, an edge of hysteria in her voice.

"We are simply part of a process, Mrs Harriman. I'll be leaving two family liaison officers overnight. It's your choice. I'd prefer you allowed them in the house but they'll decamp to their vehicles if you want."

"Don't you trust us with our own children?" asked Lucy.

"Mrs Harriman. I don't trust anyone. I want to find Tabitha."

Lucy agreed to the police staying in the house but asked them to settle in the kitchen. She assembled the family in the lounge and went through their movements from four to six o'clock one by one. Then they each prepared a list of Tabitha's best friends and compared the names, before phoning each one and slowly ticking them off. Lucy prepared some tea, although only Lily seemed hungry. She spoke privately to Scarlett, who confirmed that Tabitha had seemed fine in the morning.

The two girls went to bed. They realised something was very wrong but they were tired and, anyway, Mummy always sorted out the problems. Charles and Lucy settled in the lounge to await the arrival of DCI Rudd. The phone rang on several occasions, but in each case it was a parent returning their earlier call.

Charles and Lucy could not look at each other. On several occasions each began to say something, only to stop.

Superintendent Daniel Obuma had grown fond of Sarah Rudd. When she'd first arrived from Paddington Green station he'd wondered if she'd been over-promoted. But she'd slowly gained his confidence.

91

The tanker had now been removed from the Broadway and the roads and rail transport systems re-opened. The two senior police officers were discussing the missing child.

"Sarah. We have to rule out the Masters. Childless couple. Nobody else saw anything. She's been abducted. It's all too obvious."

"But if it's the Masters, then where is Tabitha?" asked Sarah. "She's not on the shop premises. The dog would have found her."

"Search again," ordered the superintendent.

"On what grounds?"

"No idea. Send the team in."

"We're both tired."

"I hate missing kids. More than anything else. When we get the bastards, the judge will tell them how naughty they are, read them their human rights and leave us to watch the lives that have been destroyed."

"We usually find them within twenty-four hours, sir."

"Well, will you find Tabitha, Sarah?"

"This feels wrong. It feels very wrong to me."

She thought through the many hours of training which she had received for the event of a missing child. She had been taught to focus on the obvious. She remembered the words of the college officer. "You're not fucking David Jason or Colombo. You're a police officer. The fucking child is in the most obvious place. Stop worrying about detective work. The child is nearly always found and it will be where you should have looked for it in the beginning. Fucking got it?"

She had got it and she was going over and over the obvious. It was just that they could not find her.

"How many officers have we got out there?"

"We've had over thirty officers out with photographs, sir, on the high street. We've completed house to house, or rather shop to shop. We're searching the whole area. We've brought in three dog teams from other divisions."

"The school?"

"Well, that was quickly eliminated. Because of the risk of an explosion from the traffic accident we visited the premises almost immediately." She paused. "The caretaker, Nigel Brewer, has been particularly helpful. He approached two of our officers and suggested that the school children occasionally try to hide behind the parade of shops. He offered to help look for Tabitha. He came in earlier this evening. Funny really. He wanted to talk and then admitted that he was a war veteran and gets dizzy spells. He says he saw Tabitha briefly on the pavement."

"Search the school again," ordered the senior policeman. "And I assume you've checked out this Nigel Brewer?"

"We're checking, sir, but we're thin on resources. The petrol tanker incident has literally drained us. I did put a dog team in. We have Tabitha's DNA. She's not on the school premises."

"Have you checked Mr Brewer's car?"

"We've asked him. It's in the garage for repairs."

"Check it asap. The family?"

"We have a child protection team at the house. The mother is a doctor. The father works in the City. There are two other daughters."

"Have you seen them?"

"I met the mother in the high street. I'm going over to see them later."

"The car. Dark green."

"That's all we have. Absolutely nothing else. We've checked stolen vehicles. We have some CCTV lower down the high street but we can't begin checking that until the morning."

"Why?"

"Lack of staff," Sarah sighed. "I must have some fresh officers in the morning. We've asked the local authority if they have people available."

"Are you sure you're paying enough attention to the car?"

"What car? Nobody else has seen a dark green car. The roads were gridlocked and closed. It's the most unlikely kidnapping I've ever known. If it had been abandoned we would have it by now. We've had officers on the Broadway for the last eight hours. Nobody else saw a dark green car. We'll return tomorrow but I suspect it'll be the same result."

"So Gerald Masters is lying and he kidnapped Tabitha."

"That's too easy. We would have found her by now. They don't have her."

"But he's lying about the car."

"There was so much happening. He might have seen something. God knows."

"So what happens now?"

"I'm seeing the chief superintendent in ten minutes, sir, and then I'm off to meet with the parents."

"And what, Sarah, do you plan to say to them exactly?"

Oliver didn't really need to read up about Pyotr Ilyich Tchaikovsky. He knew his music quite well. He did, however, listen to the Piano Concerto No 1 in B-flat minor, opus 23, and immediately recognised the piece. It was finished in 1875.

Oliver decided to text Amanda.

"Thanks. Not Tchaikovsky. Wrong piano style. O x"

He was surprised to receive a message back within minutes.

"Call in, if you wish. I have a large CD collection. A x"

He read, and re-read, the text message. He was becoming increasingly puzzled by the mixed signals he was receiving. What was she trying to say?

Amanda was slumped on her settee, wearing a silk kaftan. It was a hot evening. She was watching her mobile, hoping for a response from Oliver, while feeling annoyed at herself for doing so. She'd be leaving for Paris tomorrow morning and would be away for a week.

As the minutes ticked by she wondered whether Oliver would indeed be coming to her flat that evening. She tidied away the papers and plumped up the cushions on her sofa. She wiped the table on her balcony and stroked Jingles for a few minutes, before the cat ran away. She placed two wine glasses in the centre of the glass top table. She breathed deeply and enjoyed the warm evening air. She went back and checked her mobile phone.

Charles and Lucy sat on the sofa in their lounge and pleaded with their eyes.

DCI Rudd had asked the two family liaison officers to remain in the kitchen. She held her cup of tea in her left hand and used her other to emphasise her points.

She was taking Charles and Lucy through the procedures being followed by the police. It was now nearing midnight. The phone rang several times and Lucy, on each occasion, jumped up, only to be disappointed.

Sarah asked to see Tabitha's bedroom. She picked up her toys and smelt them. She looked at the pictures the child had drawn. The lines were firm and the colours bright and happy. This was an intelligent girl.

She suggested to Charles and Lucy that they go to bed. One of the liaison officers would wake them up if there was any news.

"You must already have some idea where she is," said Lucy, desperately.

"To assume would be dangerous, Mrs Harriman. We're investigating every possibility. I've explained that we've not yet found the car our witness reported. We've got officers everywhere looking for it."

"Surely the CCTV cameras will have picked it up?" asked Charles.

"We received the tapes less than two hours ago. One of the cameras is out of action. The officers will be viewing them in the morning."

"Why not now?"

"Mr Harriman. I understand that you are upset, but please leave the process to me."

As Sarah indicated that she was leaving the house, Lucy asked her if she had children of her own.

"I will find Tabitha," was all the policewoman replied.

Lucy showed her out through the door without another word. When she returned to the lounge Charles was sitting there with an unopened bottle of scotch and a glass on the table in front of him.

"Do you think that will help to find our daughter?" she snapped.

"It would help if we hadn't lost her," replied Charles.

Lucy picked the bottle up, put it back in the cabinet and closed the door. She went upstairs and checked Scarlett and Lily. They were sleeping in the same bed with their arms around each other. She went back to the kitchen and wearily showed the two police officers where she kept the tea and coffee.

"If you hear anything, just knock on our bedroom door, please. It's facing you at the top of the stairs."

They promised that they would and settled down for the long night ahead. But they could not help hearing the vicious argument taking place in the bedroom above them.

"It's because I'm fighting alcohol," hissed Charles. "It's making you feel and act in a superior way."

"What!" exclaimed Lucy. "We're working things out together. I completely understand that you want a drink tonight. Think just what you have achieved by resisting the temptation!"

"Why have you not apologised to me for losing my daughter?" shouted Charles.

She turned and looked at him in total amazement. She shut herself in the bathroom, slamming the door behind her. When she came out ten minutes later she found him sitting on the bed looking forlorn.

"Sorry," he mouthed.

She wrapped herself around him and whispered in his ear.

"We'll have her back soon, Charles. Let's have her back together."

He was going through a checklist in his mind. She was safe and warm and liked her toy. She wanted her mummy but understood that she must wait until tomorrow. She had drunk her warm milk. She did not like the dark but fell asleep quickly enough, clutching her baby panda bear. He locked the door knowing that she was safe for the night. He had fooled everybody. He laughed as he locked the back door.

Amanda looked at the clock on the wall. She checked her mobile yet again. She propped it up against the wall so that she would hear the bell that signalled a new text message.

She had decided that if he did come she would talk to him. Properly talk to him.

She lay back. She realised she was becoming aroused. This was unusual for Amanda. She had taught herself to masturbate in her teens and had tried a dildo without ever really enjoying it. A brief experiment with Ben Wa balls improved the tone of her pelvic muscles but achieved little else. She went long periods of time, especially during the years of studying, when she did not think too much about sex.

But now she felt herself becoming uncomfortably wet.

Zach had given her real pleasure, but she'd never felt this kind of raw longing. They'd just sort of found a way of making love together.

She grabbed her phone and rushed to the window to check the street outside her flat. She then hurried into the bathroom and stripped off her kaftan and panties, before dousing herself under a hard stream of cold water. After getting out of the shower and putting on a lightweight track suit, Amanda went over to the balcony, took the bottle of wine out of its iced container and poured herself a drink.

She could think of nothing else, only of Oliver. It was now ten o'clock. She glanced down at her mobile, and wondered whether she should send another text. A noise she thought she heard in the hallway sent her rushing to her feet. But when she opened the door, the corridor was empty and the lights on the lift were unlit.

She wondered, if he did come, whether she should go to bed with him. How important was the deal? She knew he wouldn't force the issue.

Amanda imagined grabbing Oliver's hand and silently leading him into the bedroom. There would be time for talking afterwards. She refilled her glass and continued sipping the wine.

The mobile phone was within inches of her right hand. She could not take her eyes off it. It was now approaching ten thirty.

Chapter Five

Amanda had checked herself in at Heathrow Airport and was awaiting her flight to Paris. Her first meeting was at lunchtime with the charming Monsieur Claude Chasseur. He would kiss her hand, pour her a glass of wine, tell her how wonderful she was and they would spend the afternoon visiting his five bookshops, which were all within two kilometres of the Arc de Triomphe. He would then take her to dinner and suggest they spend the night together. Amanda had said "oui" once, a year ago, but had declined on her next visit since she and Zach had become an item.

She was feeling rather subdued as she settled into the departure lounge. Oliver hadn't come to her flat the previous evening and she blamed herself. It had been unlikely after she'd sent such a ludicrous text. "I have a large CD collection," she repeated to herself, groaning inwardly. She also recalled their conversation on the pavement on Queen Street. She had thrust it down his throat. She'd told him that she was keeping to their deal.

Perhaps being in Paris for a few days would allow things to settle down. She intended to reflect, yet again, on her feelings, and she would meet with him on her return. The City Fiction contract was signed. Harriman Agnew would be raising two million pounds for Alistair and she had complete confidence in its successful outcome. She bought a second cup of coffee and decided against a freshly baked pain au chocolat.

She slumped back into her seat. She just couldn't get him out of her mind. They were in the gym together… and then her thoughts meandered back to the riverbank. She felt again his fingers as they probed her body. She felt his lips on hers and tasted his mouth.

"No, Amanda, don't," she pleaded with herself.

But she did. She took out her mobile phone and texted him.

"You stupid girl," she agonised, at the same time as she pressed the 'send' button.

"Oliver. At Heathrow. Will be in Paris for lunch. Selling books to Claude Chasseur. Missing you. Love. A x."

"You silly, silly…" she said to herself. After five minutes had passed, while she was checking her ticket and departure time, she received a response.

"In gym. Have beaten treadmill mile record. Thanks for text. Damn the fucking deal and no apologies for language used. Would have preferred to listen to Tchaikovsky with you in my arms. O x."

Amanda melted inside. She felt an almost adolescent excitement in the pit of her stomach. Here was she, a twenty-eight year old business woman, acting like a schoolgirl because she had just received a text message from a boyfriend. This was the stuff of Mills and Boon. This was crazy. What was she lacking in her life? She needed time to recover from her decision to part with Zach. They had been soulmates. Nearly. But it was the right move and now Oliver had been on the scene for, what, days, perhaps a few weeks. They were physically attracted but there were literally dozens of men in her gym to whom she was physically attracted. And she noticed the stares and the looks – she was only too aware of what her body offered. They were there for the picking.

And here she was refusing the advances of this handsome, lovely man. She was making him wait because she knew that the successful fund-raising for City Fiction would transform her brother's life. But she also realised that the demand she was making of Oliver wasn't going to make the slightest difference to the professional approach he would be taking to his work. He would succeed in his task regardless.

So why had she thought up this silly condition? She was now the one who was suffering. She wanted him more than she'd wanted anything ever. She shuddered as, once more, she remembered the feel of his fingers on her body and the smell and taste of their embrace. She remembered the final time that she and Zach had been together. It had been passionate and they had been close – but he was nothing like this new man. She realised that just holding hands with Oliver was different. She had been a jigsaw piece in Zach's life; Oliver approached her as though he wanted full ownership. Even when he looked at her she felt her juices flow. He was not promiscuous. He was never crude. He didn't waste time with schoolboy suggestions. He was just... something else. He was also stupidly sexy. The way his buttocks filled his trousers... she allowed her imagination to run riot.

She'd often mused over her sexual experience. She knew how to pleasure the man – and about one in three men knew how to pleasure her. One guy she'd been with from her gym had been entirely clueless at the outset but, three sessions later, he knew enough to show Amanda a pretty good evening. From the changing room gossip, she later heard that he'd put her tuition to good use.

Amanda never understood why men were often so selfish in bed. She understood the male libido and knew how to keep the pace; it was their lack of consideration that baffled her. Why not please her and allow her to approach satisfaction in an adult way. Did they not realise her response would be so much more dynamic? Several years earlier she had kept a log over a twelve month period. She'd had four boyfriends, all athletes. Their average time in completing matters was eleven and-a-half minutes. What a waste. The one who'd finished in less than eight minutes and then tuned straight in to 'Match of the Day' disappeared out through the front door, followed by his clothes.

She was broken from her reverie when her flight was called and she was instructed to proceed to her departure gate.

She picked up her mobile phone and surprised herself with the text she sent to Oliver.

"Willing to re-open negotiations on deal. Affectionately. A xx"

Her departure instructions were called for the final time. As she picked up her bag she saw the red flashing light on her mobile. She pressed the 'receive' button.

"Thank God. Travel safely. O x."

As the plane took off and climbed rapidly into the skies before turning starboard towards the French coast, she settled back into her seat. She felt the hand of the stewardess on her sleeve, opened her eyes and ordered a glass of wine, which she drank quickly. She thought guiltily that it was a little early in the day for alcohol but she needed to calm down. She had been disappointed when Oliver hadn't responded the evening before and the renewed contact had sent butterflies fluttering around her stomach. She pictured herself with him. They seemed to fit so well. She was three inches shorter than he was and when he put his arm around her it was a perfect match.

She had decided not to fight her desire any more. When she returned to London, she would allow Oliver whatever licence he wanted.

Lucy wasn't to know that at five o'clock in the morning Charles had ordered the police officers back to their car and was now sitting at the kitchen table with a bottle of scotch and an empty glass. He could not bring himself to look at the photograph Lucy had given him. Tabitha was missing. She might be tied up somewhere. She could be in pain. Was she being abused?

He began to wonder whether he should have a drink. It would help him cope with the stress. It might enable him to be more assertive. He needed to lead the hunt for Tabitha. She was his daughter and he would find her. He picked up the bottle and unscrewed the top. It hovered over the glass as his hand shook. He put the bottle back on the table with a clang. He then stood up and sluiced cold water over his face at the kitchen sink, before retreating back to the table. He stared at the alcoholic drink in front of him. He leant over and pushed it away from him. He sat still for the next few minutes.

He made a decision. He stood up and put the scotch bottle back in the cupboard and filled the glass with water. He told himself that he was not fighting drink. He was making a choice how he wanted his life to proceed. Lucy appeared in her dressing gown.

"No news," he said.

She made a pot of tea and took two mugs out to the policemen. They thanked her and resisted the temptation of saying something to make her feel better. They could see the despair on her face.

It was a wonderfully clear June morning and the birdsong was beautiful. Why did everything sound so normal when she was in so much pain? She shook her head and returned indoors.

"I'm going back to the school," said Charles. "They've lost our daughter. She's in Ealing. I'm certain of it."

"We have to stay here, Charles. That's what DCI Rudd said. We must work with the police. We'll start phoning at eight o'clock. There are several families I want to try to catch before they leave for school."

"Have you thought about our parents?" asked Charles. "Your father?"

"I'll phone later," said Lucy. "He'll probably call out the SAS."

"Oh my god. Where is she, Lucy?" asked Charles, his voice cracked and his forehead creased in agony.

"She's alive, Charles. She may be lost. Perhaps she's in a shed somewhere. She may be with someone else. The police have a good record with missing children. I liked Sarah Rudd. We have to put our faith in her."

Scarlett and Lily came into the kitchen wearing their pyjamas. They sat down with their mother. Lucy gathered them around her and asked Charles to sit closer. She talked the girls through what had happened. She told them about the police officers sitting in their car outside the house. She explained why more policemen would be coming to the house during the day.

"But what will Tabitha have for breakfast?" asked Lily.

Sara had woken early. Her eyes were still red from crying all night. Sara did not often shed tears. The last occasion that she could remember was during an Easter visit to Bristol to see her mother. She had discovered two bed sores on her mother's legs and could not interest the staff in her condition. She had allowed her emotions to spill over due to the utter hopelessness of the situation.

It was her and Alex's first row and it had started so suddenly. They had been arguing more frequently and so the dispute over the selection of the television programme was, in itself, not too worrying. The problems arose when several of the comments became rather too personal.

Sara had been reluctant to raise the issue of certain habits now taking place in the bathroom. Each was minor in its impact but together they were triggering a growing volatility between the two of them. Last night the underlying tensions had re-surfaced.

It had started with the rota for the washing-up. This was meticulously maintained by Sara, but she was finding that Alex was increasingly ignoring it. Initially she accepted the situation but on one evening, when she was particularly tired, her anger took over and she vented her frustrations, loudly. Matters were made worse when Alex totally ignored her anger.

Underlying everything was their deep affection for each other. They had been together for over a year after meeting at a social evening held in Portcullis House. They found that they had a similar sense of humour and they laughed together at the antics of the MPs. And a few months ago, almost without discussion, they had decided their occasional liaisons were developing into something more and that they should move in together. The lease for the flat was in Sara's name but they paid half the rent, rates and utility costs each.

Sara was not certain where these tensions had come from. She knew she had become more assertive since resigning from her job and becoming self-employed and she had felt empowered when she secured the job at Harriman Agnew. She had not changed in herself. Nor, she admitted to herself, had Alex.

She so wanted their relationship to continue.

Sarah Rudd and Daniel Obuma met with the chief superintendent at nine o'clock at Ealing police station.

"So, ma'am," concluded DCI Rudd. "That's all we have."

"Superintendent Obuma?" asked the senior officer.

"It doesn't feel like an abduction, but it must be. The obvious point is that we know that nearly every recorded child snatch has been carefully planned. Of course there is the occasional desperate woman who takes a child from a pram but that's usually a cry for help. We have over sixty-seven registered sex offenders within a five mile radius. We visited some of them last night and the team is out there now."

"It's kidnapping whether it's a childless woman or not," said the chief superintendent.

"Absolutely. I'm into motivation. There's no way that the driver of the green car could have predicted that Tabitha would have been on the street at that time. According to Mr Masters, the car pulled up quite sharply."

"So?"

"There are three clear possibilities. Masters is telling the truth and Tabitha has been abducted. Somehow this green car, despite our CCTV checks and searches, has been driven away with Tabitha inside. If so, we have a huge problem. Secondly, Masters is lying and he has her. Thirdly, Masters is a fantasist and she's lost somewhere else in Ealing. She might've been snatched off the street but we know that at four o'clock in the afternoon somebody would have seen her."

"I think it's far too early to arrive at any conclusion. DCI Rudd?"

"Children are capable of amazing things. Tabitha is bright. She might have wandered off... but it's hard to think where. The water authorities are helping us with the sewers and the local authority is checking its depots."

"The school?"

"We went in again at seven o'clock. The caretaker agreed to give us access and the head teacher met us there. They were both more than helpful. Brewer showed us Tabitha's classroom and one of the dogs picked out her desk. She's not there."

"Have we received the report on this Nigel Brewer?"

"He's clean. Good war record. He's been with the school for five years. Passed every check."

"Married?"

"His wife lives in Spain most of the time. They have a flat there."

"So what happened with the Masters this morning?"

"We had some trouble with Mrs Masters. We went in at eight o'clock. Her husband was already at the Cash and Carry. She told us he hadn't been able to get everything he wanted the previous evening. We then visited the Cash and Carry and they were able not only to identify him but also give us a copy of his till receipt."

"You've searched the premises again?"

"Top to bottom. We used fresh dogs. Tabitha is not there."

"What's at the back of the house?"

"There's a closed yard with just about enough space to park a van."

"You've checked every building?"

"We're working out there today along the parade."

The chief superintendent picked up her coffee cup and realised that her drink had gone cold. She picked up the telephone and ordered a fresh pot.

"Superintendent Obuma," she said, "please take me through your procedures."

"Of course. We'll have officers on the streets with a picture of Tabitha all day. We'll re-visit the school and the Masters' premises. We're working with the authorities checking empty buildings, drains and so on. We'll be visiting all local schools later this morning. We're in discussion with the individual head teachers, since we need their permission in every case. CID are out checking with their informers to see if there's news on the street." He paused and drank some water.

"However, our main focus is on the sex offenders. Of the sixty-seven we have on the register we saw five last night. We started again at six o'clock this morning and reports are coming in all the time. Nothing so far."

He then told the chief superintendent that DCI Rudd had visited the family.

"I went last night," Sarah said. "We've had officers there the whole time. We've searched the house and grounds. The family liaison team are there too. Lucy Harriman is dealing with things as well as can be expected. We're preparing them for TV and radio interviews and appeals so they'll be busy today. Her husband seems much less sure of himself. We're watching him."

The chief superintendent looked sharply at her two officers.

"We must find her in the next twenty-four hours."

As they were leaving her office, the chief superintendent called DCI Rudd back and told her to sit down.

"Tell me about the parents."

"Mrs Harriman, Lucy, is a doctor. She was in a bad way when I first met her in Ealing but later, back at the house, she had obviously taken control. She was conscious of the effect on the other two girls."

"And Mr Harriman?"

"Much more difficult to assess. He was edgy the whole time I was there. He seemed like he was searching for something."

"Have you ruled him out of any involvement?"

"Yes I have. It's not him."

Amanda read the text she had received from Oliver again.

"Must ask. Are you serious about renegotiating? O x."

She was in a buoyant mood. She'd had a successful afternoon with Claude – he'd increased his order from her previous visit and taken three of the five new titles she'd shown him. They'd enjoyed eating dinner together and Claude had realised there was to be no further contact that evening. He had kissed her with a certain fondness and left her at the hotel. She was now alone in her hotel room, feeling slightly light-headed. Was it the wine? Perhaps it was the atmosphere of Paris in June. She picked up her phone and prepared to send a text. She decided on a simple response. She pressed the button.

"No negotiation needed. A. x."

Back in London, Oliver read the message. What did she mean? Was it as obvious as it appeared to be? He was desperate not to illicit a wrong response. He quickly replied.

"You have too much time to change your mind. O. x."

On reading his message she smiled. She felt unbelievably turned on. She texted back.

"I have five days to anticipate your affection. A. x."

Oliver read the text and groaned. He typed his response and hesitated before pressing the 'send' button.

"No practising with handsome Frenchmen. x."

She read the message and laughed. She knew immediately what her response would be.

"No Frenchman can match you. Goodnight Oliver. xx."
He replied immediately.
"Take care. I wish I was with you. x."
She read his words and smiled.
"I have a vivid imagination. Bon soir, mon ami xx."

She took off her towelling robe and threw it on to the chair beside the bed. Naked, she slipped between the sheets and wrapped her arms around herself, embracing a distant man. She felt as though the final barriers between them were beginning to break down.

Just after midday, the Ealing police thought they might have the vital breakthrough in their search for Tabitha.

Superintendent Obuma called DCI Rudd from an address only half a mile from where the girl had disappeared. When Sarah arrived she saw two police cars outside a neglected terraced property. A police constable showed her inside the entrance and into the lounge. Daniel was sitting with a man of around sixty. He was untidy, unshaven and smirking. A cigarette dangled from his lips.

"Mr Watson," said the officer, "this is DCI Rudd. Mr Watson has agreed to invite us into his home."

"Oh yes, 'kindly agreed'. You'd have come in anyway!"

Sarah looked at Daniel. He turned back to the man.

"Mr Watson, please tell DCI Rudd where you were yesterday afternoon."

He looked at Sarah. "Six years ago I allowed myself to get a bit too friendly with a little girl on Ealing Common."

"You brought her here," said Daniel, "and held her for twenty-four hours against her will."

"The weather was bad and I was worried she might catch cold." Eugene Watson wiped his nose with the sleeve of his shirt. "I looked after her very well."

"You abused her, Mr Watson, and put your hands where you shouldn't. That's why you spent two years in prison."

A police officer came into the room. "It's here, sir," he said and handed Daniel the authorised search warrant. Four more officers went into the various rooms.

"We now have a warrant to search your house, Mr Watson."

"Go ahead. I would have agreed anyway."

"Where were you yesterday afternoon, Mr Watson?" asked DCI Rudd.

She watched as he signalled he was lying. His head kept dropping, although he knew enough to try to avoid this mannerism. He also kept looking to the left rather than meeting her eyes.

"I was on the Common all afternoon in the sunshine."

"Who did you meet?"

"No one. I keep myself to myself."

"How often do you visit the Common, Mr Watson?"

He was poking a finger inquisitively into one of his ears. He took it out and wiped it on his shirt before replying to the question.

"Most days, I suppose."

"Was it busy yesterday?"

"Oh yes."

"So people hadn't gone to watch the accident on the high street?"

"Oh that. Somebody said a car had crashed."

"You didn't hear anything then?"

"What was I supposed to have heard?"

"The sound of police cars and fire engines, perhaps?"

"What, for a car crash? I heard there was a bit of a commotion."

"You weren't on the Common yesterday, Mr Watson, were you?"

Two police officers came into the room and reported that they'd found nothing. Eugene Watson appeared to have neither a computer nor a mobile phone. They were asked to search again and to concentrate on the back garden as well as the rooms.

Sarah carried on with her questions.

"As I said, you were not in this area yesterday. If you were I find it hard to believe that you did not meet one of your friends and you were not aware of the major incident in the high street."

"You mean, did I meet another person on the register?"

"If that's the case, well, at least it proves you were there."
Sarah went into the kitchen and poured herself a glass of water.

"The little girl you're looking for. It's not me."

"I think it could be."

Eugene stood up and went over to the corner of the room. He found a piece of paper and wrote something down before handing it to Daniel Obuma. He'd written the address of a house less than a mile away.

"That's where I was," he said.

"What were you doing?" asked DCI Rudd.

"Watching movies with my friend. You'll find out when you get there. He's usually so drunk he won't care."

As DCI Rudd was leaving the house, he turned to her.

"I'll never lay my hand on another little girl," he said.

An hour later police officers arrested a fifty-six year old man for the possession of child pornography. A search of the house failed to find the missing child.

Oliver looked around the restaurant and noticed some familiar faces. The underground location of Gow's in Old Broad Street, adjacent to Liverpool Street Station, was where the City wealthy dined their clients. A combination of superb wines and the best fish dishes made this a popular venue for the investment community.

Andrew appeared and seemed a little tense. He settled down and drank some of the Riesling that Oliver had ordered and poured before he'd arrived.

"How was he?" Oliver asked.

"Not too good. There's no news on where Tabitha might be. There are police everywhere and they were filming the media appeal that's going out tomorrow."

He picked up the menu and gave it a cursory glance. He indicated to the waiter that he wanted to order a crab bake starter and the sea bass. Oliver chose the oysters and Dover sole off the bone.

"She disappeared yesterday afternoon?" he asked.

"Yes. Lucy was late arriving from the surgery and they think Tabitha must have wandered out of the school gates and into

110

the high street. A local shopkeeper spotted her being forced into a car. The whole series of events was complicated by the tanker accident and the chemical spillage. The police can't find any evidence of the car, though they still have hours of CCTV to watch."

"What is Charles proposing to do?"

"There's not a lot he can do. The police are insisting he and Lucy stay at home. They're phoning neighbours and the parents of Tabitha's friends and looking after their two girls. The phone never stopped while I was there."

"Well, I suppose life for the rest of us must go on, Andrew. You wanted to talk about Gavin?"

The waiter arrived with the starters and, at Oliver's request, produced a bottle of sparkling water.

"You're head of corporate finance, Oliver. The atmosphere in the office is not good and Gavin seems to be running wild." He sipped some water. "We can't afford to lose him. If the brokers can't, or don't, raise the money, we will simply lose our place in the pecking order. Deals are few and far between at the moment and the latest economic reports are worrying. We have to pull this around. Are you going to raise the funds for City Fiction?"

"It was you who imposed Sara on all of us, Andrew. You never discussed it with me. You and Charles made a unilateral decision. And now you expect me to clear it up."

"She's good though, isn't she?"

"She's different. She's unconventional. She understands corporate finance already. She doesn't care, either. She'll say anything to anybody."

"What did you think of her report on City Fiction?"

"The long report was remarkable given the time frame she had. She's an exceptional talent. The shorter version was inspirational. I accept that to some extent it stated the obvious. City Fiction needs to find winners. But she caught the imagination and the section on the evolvement of eBooks was brilliant. It's helped Abbi with her work a lot. No question, Andrew. She's good and we need her abilities."

"It's a matter of time. She'll settle in particularly well if she gets on with Jody and Abbi."

111

"Gavin is the problem, Andrew. He's aggressive by nature, but he's also drinking heavily and taking Duncan with him. We actually have a good sales team and they lead it well. It's the office side that's the issue."

"I'm afraid it's your problem, Oliver. Get it sorted."

As their starter plates were cleared away, their discussion turned to the current market conditions and the shortage of corporate finance opportunities. A number of the smaller brokerage businesses had either closed down or merged with their rivals.

"We must look east," said Andrew. "I'm thinking of going to Hong Kong and China." He raised his glass to his lips. "I've been looking at several of our competitors. They're picking up their opportunities across Asia. That's clearly the message for us."

"What about Africa? There's Chinese money going in there to back the mineral exploration companies."

"Yes. Possibly. But we must go to Asia."

"I'm dreaming of raising two million pounds for City Fiction," laughed Oliver.

"You won't do it without Gavin and Duncan."

They were well into their main courses when Andrew suddenly coughed.

"You seem nervous," said Oliver. "Why don't you tell me the real reason we're having this lunch?"

"There's talk in the office and Jody has spoken to me."

"About what?"

"You and Amanda Wavering. You were seen in Queen Street. You seemed to be arguing. Are you two involved?"

"That question is out of order, Andrew. Definitely not for discussion. I'm amazed you would listen to rumours."

"If you *are* involved with her I would consider it unfortunate."

"Are you questioning my professional integrity?"

Andrew pushed his plate away and gulped down some wine.

"Of course I'm not. But she's a client. You're on dangerous ground. And I note that you're not denying it."

"I'm not bloody well discussing it," Oliver snapped.

"Take it from me, Oliver. I probably know more than you realise. Tread carefully and think about what you're doing. Think very carefully."

It was unusual for Alistair Wavering and David Singleton to exchange words, but the tensions at City Fiction were mounting.

"You're acting as though we already have the two million," said David. "It's a long way off and, meanwhile, I'm the one who has to deal with the cash-flow pressures."

"Oliver will raise us the money. I simply want to expand the business."

"You want to commission this book, *The Legacy of Gordon Brown*? Crazy. There are books two a penny about bloody Gordon Brown."

"This one is what City Fiction was set up to do, David. The author is a very bright man at Goldman Sachs. He understands what happened and he thinks it was Brown's understanding of the crisis which saved the day. Don't forget Europe thought so at one point too."

"It was Brown who spent all the money, which is why we have a crisis now!"

"That's what Cameron peddles and there are some of us in the party who think he's taking it too far. A pal of mine says that if Labour had won the 2010 general election the bond market would have supported Alistair Darling's debt reduction programme and we wouldn't have the lack of growth we're seeing now."

"But what proof have you got, Alistair, that the book will sell?"

"The author is paying us ten thousand pounds in promotional costs."

David laughed. "Oh well, in that case, I take it all back – it sounds like an excellent book! Good work, Alistair!"

There seemed to be activity at the Harrimans' house all day long. The media process took over three hours and Charles in particular found the filming very difficult. At one point, he became extremely agitated and disappeared for over half an hour. When he returned he had taken a shower and changed his shirt.

They became confused about who represented the television company compiling the parents' appeal, who the plain clothes police officers, who the several civilians attached to the police, who the neighbours that seemed to come in from streets all around them and who the general media.

Around five o'clock it slowly became quieter and two hours later Lucy and Charles were together in the lounge, and Scarlett and Lily were upstairs watching a Harry Potter DVD.

Sarah Rudd arrived at the house at ten o'clock that evening. At her suggestion they went into the lounge and closed the door. Lucy's legs turned to jelly as she anticipated news she did not want to hear.

"We can't find her," she told the parents, before taking them through the whole of the police activities for the day. She took a long time over the detail because she knew they would want to know everything.

"Tomorrow we will use the media, which will be mainly TV, radio and newspapers. We are processing the pictures of Tabitha now," said Sarah. "Thank you for your co-operation. I've seen some of the footage and it looks good."

"How effective will that be?" asked Charles.

"It can be very helpful. Tabitha is a local child and will evoke enormous public sympathy. That's why we use media. They're great and will have the whole community looking for a lost child. We think Tabitha has been abducted. There is the risk that the publicity will scare her abductors, but we must take that chance."

"Take a chance with our daughter?" said Charles.

"We have considered it carefully," replied DCI Rudd. "The fact is that we can't find her as it is."

"Is Tabitha still alive, Sarah?" asked Lucy in a small voice.

"I have only my instinct to offer you, Lucy. But yes, I think that she's still alive. The police officers will be here again tonight. Please try to get some rest. Tomorrow is going to be a long one for you both."

After she left, Lucy checked the girls. They were both exhausted and nearly asleep.

She changed into her dressing gown and went downstairs. Charles was staring at the bottle of scotch which he had placed on the table in front of him, together with a glass.

"It's your choice, Charles," said Lucy. "Do as you want. I'm only thinking about Tabitha right now."

"There is no choice, Lucy. If I touch a drop, I'll be letting her down." He picked the bottle up and put it back in the cabinet.

They went to bed and, unusually, Lucy turned her back on her husband. She was lost in her dark, troubled thoughts.

Tabitha was scared. She cuddled the bear she had been given as a present. She also had milk in a cup and some biscuits. She'd been told that she must go to sleep and every so often she was aware that he was shining a torch on her. She'd enjoyed the fresh air and the picnic that they'd had together in the afternoon. But he'd got annoyed when she'd started crying. He would not say when she would see her mummy again. She put her thumb in her mouth and tried not to sob. She didn't want to be told off again. She cried out for Scarlett but there was no reply.

"Want to talk?"

"You need your sleep, Nick," replied his wife.

"You can't find her can you?"

"She's in Ealing and she's alive. I'll put my professional reputation on that."

"Why?"

"Why what?"

"You're so certain and yet you can't find her."

"I lost Lucy's trust tonight. She didn't believe me."

"Remember the Primrose Hill case. What was his name? David Rensburg. I remember walking through Broadway discussing it with you. The Welsh girl. Megan something..."

"That ended happily enough though, Nick. The murderer walked in and confessed!"

"And you were looking in the wrong direction. Think Sarah. I remember our chat so well. Please think, my darling. You were looking in the wrong direction."

"You've said that twice, Nick. Once is enough."

"So, are you going in the wrong direction with Tabitha too? Maybe there's some lateral thinking required?"

"Nick. We're a good team. Our procedures are text book. You can always do more but we've not had a single break on this one. Nothing, Nick. Every bloody witness might be unreliable. We've turned the sex offenders over like never before. The teams are exhausted."

"But you haven't found her."

"I know that, Nick. Please!"

"You were looking in the wrong place before."

"Believe me – she's in Ealing and she's alive."

Chapter Six

Sarah Rudd's bedside telephone rang at 2.37am in the early hours of Thursday morning. She answered it on the third ring, simultaneously trying to untangle her husband's arm from around her waist. She listened carefully to a brief message and replied that she would be at the station in less than an hour. She quietly got out of bed and took a quick shower. As she was putting on her uniform, Nick regained consciousness.

"Duty calls," she said. "The chief superintendent has called me in. I think I'll be looking at the body of a four year old child before long.

Nick leapt out of bed and gave his wife a quick hug.

"Would you like me to drive you? The kids can sleep in the back of the car."

"No," replied Sarah. "I'll be fine." She kissed him and went to leave the room, but turned back at the last moment. She put her arms around her husband and hugged him tightly. She turned and was gone.

As she entered Ealing police station she could sense the tension. She took the lift to the third floor and knocked on the door of Chief Superintendent Avril Gardner's office. She responded to the instruction to enter and found her boss reading a newspaper and pounding her fist on the desk.

"Look, Sarah," she exclaimed. "Look what they've done!"

Avril Gardner handed Sarah a copy of the local paper. She was shocked by the headline.

"Local doctor loses daughter in Madeleine McCann copycat case."

It was clever journalism. They had pulled all the facts together to make their impact: local female doctor... delayed leaving surgery and therefore late for her daughter... Tabitha left wandering the streets of Ealing... uncertainty as to who was responsible for her... reported abduction... possibly now out of the country.

117

But what was worse, far, far worse, were the two photographs side by side, one of Tabitha and the other of Madeleine McCann. The facial resemblances were remarkable. Both were fair-haired and very pretty.

Sarah Rudd slumped into a chair and covered her face with her hands.

"The circus is on its way," said Avril Gardner. "It's already been on Sky News."

"I'll go and see the parents," said Sarah. She stopped as she was leaving the office.

"Have you spoken to the editor?"

"He's not answering his phone. Be back here at seven please, Sarah. I've brought the morning meeting forward." Avril Gardner paused. "I suppose this gets us the publicity we need."

"Or an abductor who panics," Sarah replied, grimly.

Jody Boyle had woken early and was lying in bed, thinking about someone who meant a great deal to her. She was not the sort of person to obsess about the inequalities of life. Until that day in the autumn of 2007 when she was told the news, she had never heard of Lowe Syndrome. From that time onwards it was always to be referred to as LS.

She had accepted what she heard, although she later read up on the subject in great depth in the desperate hope that there was a cure. She knew it was a genetic condition which was caused by a single defective gene and resulted in an essential enzyme not being produced. She also learnt to her cost that it mainly affected boys.

She had spent the previous Sunday afternoon holding her son Ben's hand and talking to him. She'd repeated this activity on so many occasions that she could now anticipate his mood swings. She loved his gurgling laughter more than anything.

Her pregnancy had come as a complete shock. The weight she gained only showed quite late and she'd convinced the staff at Agnew Capital that she was fighting a battle with the weighing scales. There had been two possibilities as to who was the father. After Ben had been born she'd persuaded the most likely candidate to have a paternity test. When the result was known and she faced him with the letter from the clinic, he was kind-ness itself and vowed to do all he could to support them. He was in a relationship with a long-term partner and felt unable to marry her, but she accepted that their brief groping had led to a lot more than either expected, and respected his decision.

Time was against her and she'd negotiated six weeks extended leave from work so that she could visit her sister in New Zealand. The recession was already beginning to take effect in the United Kingdom and nobody at Agnew Capital thought her absence unusual. There was less work around and it seemed a good time to travel. Andrew had made public his approval of the idea, saying it was a reward for her outstanding service to the company and so it was accepted by everybody.

She had booked herself into a private clinic in London and given birth to a baby boy in July 2007. Within twenty-four hours she had been told that Benjamin William Boyle was suffering from LS. He was to spend three months at the health centre before being transferred to a specialist clinic in West London. He had several operations, including one for the removal of cataracts from both his eyes. He then developed glaucoma, kidney problems and, later, severe behavioural difficulties. She was told that his life expectancy was perhaps thirty years.

She determined from the beginning that she would raise him, as far as possible, as a normal boy. She talked to him for hours so that he would become comfortable with the sound of her voice. He slowly recognised her presence and when she fell into the routine of visiting him three times a week, he responded to her holding his hand and hearing her chatting with him. He was feeding well and putting on weight. After a time she no longer insisted on regular meetings with the doctors. She knew all there was to understand about LS and how Ben's life was to progress. All parties agreed that there would be a major re-evaluation when Ben reached five years of age. His father stayed in touch and visited Ben after he'd settled into the children's nursing home. The occasion so upset both father and son that she had decided that would be the last time she asked him to visit.

Ben grew to love Arsenal football club. Jody would read him the reports of their matches and he reserved a special gurgle for when they won a game. Jody convinced herself that he was improving and began to wonder what might lie ahead. When she left him she always told him how proud his father was of him.

He was in a room with three other beds. One boy stayed for a year but otherwise they came and went and Jody rarely had the opportunity to get to know the parents. She received a monthly financial report from the home. Payment was made by direct debit from her bank account but she found she continually had to ask about being charged the extra fees. The doctors could not change his drugs regime without her approval but there seemed to be a continual drip, drip, drip of additional costs. She spent many hours evaluating alternative health centres but always came to the conclusion that Ben was in the best place possible for him. The one thing she was certain about was that she would not let the NHS get hold of her son.

Jody wrapped up Ben's life in her own. Apart from the occasional discussion with his father she talked to nobody else. She was ferociously busy at Agnew Capital and had little free time of her own, apart from her Sunday night treat. She never missed a visit to see Ben and never gave up the hope that he might improve. She knew that he could face further health problems, but she would deal with these if and when they came. She had a number of photographs of the two of them together around her flat. When, on the odd occasion, she had a visitor, she packed them away.

Initially, in the autumn of 2007, as she began to understand the situation, Jody had thoughts of changing her way of life. She argued with Ben's father and then had to deal with the growing pressures of the declining business at Agnew Capital. She had to face one problem after another and began to dread the arrival of the post.

She never let Ben know any of this. She always dressed in bright colours and always made him laugh. Jody didn't indulge in self pity in any way, but as the months and years progressed she was to face challenges that would have defeated a weaker person.

But she had Ben to worry about. He was her son and she was all he had in life, however long that was to last.

Alistair Wavering, as he often did, was working at his home computer at five-thirty in the morning. He was completing a lengthy email to his sister in Paris. He was pleased with the orders she had generated from Monsieur Chasseur and the other two retailers she had already met in Paris. Amanda was usually cheerful and positive in her approach to customers, but Alistair sensed that she was on top form.

He'd been thinking about the future of City Fiction. He was certain that Oliver would raise the two million pounds and he'd found his lunch with Sara Flemming very thought provoking. Was she right in her assertion that publishing was a continuous gamble? Was it all about finding the right author writing the one bestselling book?

It was a little too simplistic for Alistair, but he recognised that one or more of his authors needed to deliver a big winner. He decided to tell Amanda about his plans. He set out his reasoning in some detail and then delivered his bombshell.

Amanda was sitting in the restaurant of her Paris hotel eating a bowl of fresh fruit and yoghurt in preparation for another busy day. She was reading the paper attached to Alistair's email. She covered her mouth with her hand as she read his proposals.

The red light on her mobile flashed to indicate an incoming message.

"Bonjour Amanda. Off to the gym. Missing you. x"

She returned to the paper she had just read. Alistair was convinced that he should become the full-time publisher and that the day-to-day operations should be run by a new chief operating officer – her! But he left the best till last. City Fiction was going places and, with two million pounds in the bank, would soon be ready to join a public market. For that, the board of directors would need a chairman and, since the team at City Fiction was young, he had decided that what was needed was a youthful City executive who was experienced in public companies... and he knew just that person – Oliver Chatham.

She texted Oliver back.

"Go for it tiger. xx"

She'd always liked compliments. The suggestion that she should be COO went down well – and she'd only recently been reading in the financial press about the City's obsession that there should be more women directors on the boards of public companies.

She read the passage on the proposed chairman again. Alistair had made the basis for his selection with complete logic. She agreed with her brother. Oliver, if he would accept the position, could be a dynamic chairman and help propel the business forward. She did not really understand 'the City', but she knew enough. It made sense to her to have a chairman familiar with public markets.

There was just one, small obstacle. As far as she was concerned the way was open for them to accelerate their relationship and she anticipated that, on her return to England, the deal would be re-negotiated and they would go to bed together.

"Oh Christ," she said.

DCI Rudd found both Lucy and Charles in a dreadful state. The media were already camped outside their house and several more police officers had arrived to try and ensure a certain amount of privacy for the family.

As she had walked up to the front door, her gaze had met that of the local reporter who had penned the article. She could not hold back her stare of disbelief.

She entered the house and went through to the kitchen. Charles was staring into space. He was unshaven and untidy. Lucy was sobbing into her hands. Her eyes were red with emotion and she shook as she faced DCI Rudd.

"I phoned the school," she pleaded. "I couldn't leave my patient. The school said she was fine. I didn't leave her in the street alone."

"This is your fault, you bitch!" shouted Charles. "I was against using newspapers from the beginning. You're risking my daughter's life! Get out of my house!"

Sarah moved towards Lucy and whispered something in her ear. She responded immediately as DCI Rudd told them both to join her in the lounge. She shut the door and faced them.

"I'm going back to the kitchen to make us all a cup of coffee," she said. "When I come back I hope we can talk in a civilised way." She stopped and turned to Charles. "You, Mr Harriman, can start by apologising to me for your rudeness. We will then work together to find Tabitha."

Five minutes later Sarah re-entered the lounge carrying a tray, from which she poured each of them a steaming mug of fresh coffee. As she handed a cup to Charles, he looked at her and muttered an apology.

Sarah started to pace slowly round the room, drawing the curtains and opening two of the front windows to let in some fresh air. She then turned and started speaking in a quiet voice.

"You have temporarily lost your daughter. The public tend to be hard in their judgements." She paused. "We must all focus on the day ahead of us."

"So were we wrong to involve the media?" asked Lucy.

"I understand how you feel. We can't, as yet, find Tabitha and one of the best weapons we have is the local people. Forget the hotheads. Most residents out there will want to help us find your daughter. They will ignore the newspapers."

"They'll all be accusing Lucy," Charles retorted.

"I doubt it. Most readers will realise it's the media with a clever headline."

"I really think this could have been avoided," said Charles.

"Stop thinking about yourself," Sarah snapped. "What's done is done. We now have maximum publicity. We're already taking calls at the station. Go upstairs and freshen yourself up. You are not to talk to the media unless I'm here. You do not go out of the house. The media will try every trick to get you to say something. You've already seen how they can turn words into sensational headlines. My officers will be with you all day. You must look after your other two children and prepare for Tabitha coming home."

Her eyes met Lucy's. "When will that be?" she asked.

"When I find her," Sarah replied.

As she walked out of the house through the hordes of reporters and television crews, she felt a tight knot of anxiety form in her chest. This could be a very difficult day. The truth was that she had no idea where Tabitha was or whether she was alive.

Tabitha was unhappy. She had wet herself during the night and couldn't make him realise what she'd done. When she'd refused to eat the cornflakes, he'd tapped her bottom. Now he thrust a piece of toast in her hand and she began to suck on it. She grabbed the cup of milk and drank it all. She didn't like the noise and put her head beneath the pillows. She had a rash on the inside of her leg. She started to cry out for her mummy.

Amanda had returned to her room after eating her breakfast and was now lying on her bed. She had thirty minutes before she would be collected from the hotel reception by City Fiction's Paris agent. They had a long day ahead of them, including three shop visits, and a lunch with an important French book distributor and several agents keen to introduce their clients to her.

However, she was thinking about Oliver and Alistair. She generally prided herself on her strength of resolve. She thought back to her decision to part with Zach. She had loved him so much and relished their time together, but had no doubts that she had taken the correct course of action. He had a wife and two children and that's where he had to concentrate his attention. She had had to be firm.

But Oliver was turning her inside out. Days spent apart were only adding to her desire to be with him. But their deal posed an enormous challenge – where was she even with that? She had told him that she was willing to re-negotiate and her intentions could not have been much clearer. Yet now her brother wanted to make her COO and Oliver chairman of City Fiction.

"Merde," she said to herself, as her bedside telephone began to ring.

124

Chief Superintendent Gardner sat in on the seven o'clock meeting where Superintendent Obuma briefed over thirty officers and discussed their responsibilities for the coming twenty-four hours.

The process followed by the police throughout that Thursday was almost exactly the same as the previous day. Calls were coming through from the media exposure and the follow-up process was underway. As yet nobody had seen a green car. The school was searched again. Nigel Brewer, the caretaker, suggested they look at an adjoining warehouse which had already been searched once. They crawled all over it, but found nothing. Tabitha's home and local area were searched again. The police closed the sweet shop and tried to re-interview the Masters. They had searched the shop and accommodation after facing a tirade from Alice Masters, who said that her husband was "out consulting a solicitor".

"So, DCI Rudd. We're not making any progress. We are nearly past forty-eight hours. Is she dead?" Avril Gardner sat back in her chair. "Superintendent Obuma. Your thoughts too, please."

"We go back to square one and repeat the whole exercise again. That's usual procedure." He sighed. "Informants, local intelligence, sex offenders' register visits, house to house working out wider from the high street, local schools... and that's for starters."

"Yes, I know that, superintendent. The list?"

There followed a long discussion involving those engaged in tracing and interviewing the registered sex offenders. An officer provided the details.

"There are sixty-seven on our register within a five mile radius. We've also interviewed six others who should be convicted. Eight are on holiday... with the Far East a popular destination!"

There was a ripple of laughter rapidly hushed by Avril Gardner.

"No more jokes, please. We have a missing child."

"Ma'am," continued the officer, "we've interviewed forty-six of the fifty-nine we believe to be here. We intend to re-interview four of them but at this point in time we do not believe we have a serious lead."

Superintendent Obuma informed the meeting of yesterday's events with Eugene Watson and the subsequent arrest of another registered offender. Several officers suggested further possible cases that should be re-visited, including one man who was under investigation. Each idea was logged and responsibilities allocated.

"DCI Rudd," said the chief superintendent, "please tell me more about Nigel Brewer."

Andrew handed Sara the menu and invited her to make her choice. Somewhat to his surprise, she selected grilled kippers. He relayed this to the waiter, together with his own selection of a full English breakfast with Earl Grey tea and green tea for Sara.

The tables at One Lombard were almost fully occupied. A table of eight gave off the distinct air that they had been working through the night and were now celebrating the completion of a transaction. The bottles of champagne suggested that the professionals were in line for generous fees.

"The City fights back from recession," he laughed. "I hope that you were pleased to receive my invitation to have breakfast?"

"Not really," replied Sara. "You will have a reason, I'm sure. I understand from Abbi that you don't usually ask staff members out for meals – apart from Oliver, I suppose."

He looked at her in surprise. "Straight to the point as usual, Sara."

"I'll make you a prediction," she said. "You're going to give me a paternal chat about making more of an effort to get on with Gavin and Duncan."

He gulped. "Well, that was certainly something I had in mind to cover with you."

"Do you want to know what's wrong with Harriman Agnew, Andrew?"

"I'm sure that your short time with us has equipped you with exactly that information," he replied.

"A few days were ample."

Their breakfasts arrived. The kippers were soaked in melted butter and smelt delicious. Andrew thought his tomatoes were over-cooked but decided to carry on stoically. He wanted to know what Sara thought was wrong with his firm. The waiter arrived with fresh pots of tea and a basket of brown toast.

They began eating. The noise from the table of revellers was increasing and everybody seemed keen to start the working day in positive territory. A journalist from CityAM, the free financial paper distributed at central tube stations, was interviewing a chief executive of an online betting company. Tempers were fraying as the topic of a recent profits warning, made to investors via the market information system, was aired.

"So what's wrong with Harriman Agnew, Sara?"

"Simple. You and Charles."

"I really think what with Charles having his daughter *kidnapped* that we need to be circumspect, Sara."

"Why? I'm sure they'll find Tabitha. The issue here remains."

"So Charles and I are the problem."

"Yes."

"Is that what everybody thinks?"

"No idea. I don't discuss these thoughts with anybody else. I'm raising them now because I've no intention of being treated like a naughty school girl."

Andrew paused as he carefully considered the train of events. He wanted to know the answer to his own question.

"You don't care if you lose your job, do you?"

Sara laughed out loud. "Actually, Andrew, I do. I love it at the office. They're a great set of people and they're desperate to succeed. I was taught in my business studies course that mergers are difficult to make work. Harriman Agnew is working ok."

"So why are Charles and I the problem?"

"Because the company is carrying both of you."

He gulped and spilt his cup of tea.

"While you wipe your shirt I'll explain what I mean. The company is too small for two effective chairmen. I realise that's a result of the merger and I accept there had to be compromises.

But Oliver runs the business and Gavin – ok, we'll talk about him in a moment – runs brokerage. Abbi, Martin, Jody, Melanie and I do the rest. What do you do, Andrew? You're out most of the time having breakfasts and lunches and you go to your club in the evening. When did you last bring in some new business?"

He didn't like this line of questioning at all. "I run the business, Sara."

"No you don't. Oliver does that. He's so decent that he covers up your own lack of activity. And what's Charles done in the last few weeks exactly?"

She was not to know that this was a question Andrew had been beginning to ask himself.

"I'm not going to discuss Charles with you at any time, Sara, and certainly not today when his daughter is missing."

"Let's discuss you then."

"I think not. We'll talk about your relationship with Gavin."

"What's there to say? He's a total arsehole," she said loudly.

As her words echoed around the restaurant, there was a momentary lull in festivities at the neigbouring table.

For DCI Rudd the day was horribly frustrating. On two occasions word came through that the officers interviewing the sex offenders might have a lead. On each occasion it proved negative. The media interest produced a torrent of phone calls and the computerised logging system was swamped. One gentleman from Hampstead caught a tube train to Ealing and presented himself at the police station reception to confess to the kidnapping – not the first he had admitted to, either.

Sarah went back to the high street in the afternoon and stood outside the school. She walked past the Masters' shop but did not go inside, speaking instead to some of the officers who were delegated to question the public. One told her that the Masters had left the shop at lunchtime and that there were temporary staff serving the customers.

Around three o'clock there was a sudden flurry of activity in one of the buildings being searched by the police and council officials – but it transpired it was just a tramp who had converted it into his temporary home.

The tensions were rising. The media coverage was growing in its intensity and the Madeleine McCann tag was sticking. CS Gardner telephoned her every hour and she met with Superintendent Obuma on three separate occasions. Tabitha had disappeared completely. Other police forces were searching for the dark green car without really knowing what they were looking for. There were extra checks at the ports, which all had Tabitha's photograph.

Around five o'clock Sarah went home, where she took a well-earned shower and spent some time with her children. Nick poured her a small brandy which she drank quickly. Their conversation of the previous evening was weighing heavily on both their minds.

"We don't know where she is, Nick," she confided. "I'm running out of ideas and I've looked in every direction."

He held her hand and kissed her on the lips. "The media is saying she's probably out of the country by now."

"No, she's in Ealing, Nick."

"Sure?"

"Certain," she said. "I just have the feeling that I'm missing something."

"Certain is a strong word, Sarah."

"My favourite college lecturer told us that missing children are nearly always found in the most obvious place."

"And where is that?"

"I wish I knew."

She stood up, gave her husband a quick hug and kissed each of her children. She left her home to continue the search for Tabitha.

Charles was walking the streets around his home with a hip flask in his pocket. The police had stopped trying to keep him indoors and he had avoided the press by going through the hedge at the bottom of his garden.

He was telling himself he didn't need a drink because he had chosen a new way of life for himself. But he was carrying the flask just in case he decided he might choose to have one. He thought back to his drinking days. He would plan his schedules so that he always met a client or contact at around noon in a hotel. It was perfectly acceptable to have a gin and tonic at that time – and it never affected his work in any way. But it affected him in other ways.

He was becoming increasingly frustrated with the police. It was their job to find Tabitha and they seemed disorganised. He just wanted his daughter back. His hand rested on the pocket containing the drink. He wondered whether he should demand a meeting with all the top brass. Perhaps a drink now would give him the resolve to assert his rights as a parent. He would go home and talk it through with Lucy. She always backed him and she was suffering so much pain. He would also sort out the reporter who had dreamt up the 'Madeleine McCann' headline. He would never forgive that sensation-seeking action.

Yes, Charles Harriman had a number of scores to settle, once they had found Tabitha.

Sarah reached the Harrimans' home at eleven o'clock in the evening. It was a tense half-hour they spent together. She'd met with her senior officers at eight o'clock. The media-generated responses were disappointing. Nothing but time-wasters.

"You think she's dead, don't you?" accused Lucy.

"We have statistics, Lucy," she said. "They won't help us at this moment but I'll be honest with you – I thought we would have found her by now."

"So why aren't you out looking for her??" shouted Charles. Lucy leaned over and put her hand on his arm.

"We're looking everywhere, Mr Harriman. That I promise you."

"Well, you're obviously not looking where she is because if you were you would have found her!"

DCI Rudd nodded. "I can't counter that," she said. "We're extending out tomorrow by another three miles."

"Why didn't you do that today?!" he said, anger bubbling inside him like lava.

Sarah looked helplessly at Lucy, who stood up and went over to her husband. He immediately left the room without a glance at the police officer.

"Where is she?" pleaded Lucy.

"She's in Ealing." DCI Rudd paused. "We just don't know where."

"What are the chances that you won't find her?"

"As I said, we have the statistics. This is different."

"Different?"

"I'm certain that the lorry crash and Tabitha's disappearance are connected."

"How?"

"In normal circumstances we'd have proved or disproved Mr Masters' green car issue within hours. But there was so much confusion that we simply aren't sure."

"It must be the Masters then."

"There is certainly something a bit odd about them – but they've not got Tabitha. We've searched their home from top to bottom. The dogs would have picked up her scent."

"So, what happens now?" Lucy asked, desperate.

"We keep on trying everything we know."

DCI Rudd looked at Lucy and the pain etched on her face. She so wanted to offer some words from which she might take comfort. The difficulty was that Tabitha had completely disappeared and, despite all the experience available to DCI Rudd, nobody had come up with any suggestion that might break the deadlock.

But she *knew* that Tabitha was somewhere in Ealing.

Earlier in the day, Nigel Brewer had hesitated before making the phone call. He had been out beyond the school gates and watched as a van pulled up. The police were searching the buildings behind the row of shops, most of which were locked up. He had been thinking it was possible that Tabitha might have wandered further afield and he had a suggestion to make to the officer in charge. He had obtained her mobile number from one of the policemen who had visited the school.

He cancelled the call and put his phone away.

He so wanted to be helpful. He felt he had much more to offer but, because he was just the school caretaker, he was not being taken seriously. He decided that the best way for him to make an impact would be to find Tabitha.

Sara was wandering around the perimeter of the Tower of London, now lit by floodlights. It had been a difficult day, starting with a difficult breakfast. She had gone far too far in her comments to Andrew and had been surprised that he had not reacted more strongly. She had then followed up with an almost inevitable clash with Gavin, which had needed Abbi and Martin to sort out. She had then arrived back at the flat to discover that Alex had taken some holiday and would be away for four days.

She had never given too much thought to her style and personality. She was aware that people found her direct and lacking in grace, but she saw things in logical progressions. That was partly why she was proving so adept at her market research projects. She understood the nature of chasing knowledge and was a master at lateral thinking. She had been slightly surprised by the scale of praise she had received for her work on City Fiction. She had simply done the job at hand and gone some way in working out what Andrew Agnew wanted to find out. She realised that, quite possibly, Andrew himself did not fully understand his own thinking on the matter. She wondered if he was using her report as a short cut to making a decision.

Sara had only ever gained job satisfaction from her own subjective evaluations. She was unimpressed by praise when she doubted the motivation of the speaker. In the everyday life of the office she heard, time and again, colleagues saying things they did not mean. It was often the easy way out.

She was surprised that Alex had gone without telling her first. She had tried the mobile but that was switched off. The atmosphere earlier in the day had been fine and they'd cuddled in bed before Sara had departed for her breakfast meeting. She wondered about writing Alex a letter in which she could bring out the hurt she felt over recent tensions and now, with this sudden departure. She decided that she would speak straight to the point when they met up again. She was good at that, after all.

Sarah returned to the police station, sat at her desk and straightened the paperwork. She glanced at a text message from her husband – she knew it was late and she should probably go home, but remained where she was. They should have found Tabitha by now. She was ready to discount the story of the green car. They had put all the pressure they could on the Masters.

"Where *are* you Tabitha?" she said to herself, putting her hands over her face. "I know that you're here somewhere…" She sat back and went over the whole investigation, trying to spot a weak link. She was certain that Tabitha was alive and in Ealing. She was most likely being held in an obvious place. It is not easy to hide a child of four years of age for very long because somewhere something will show. Sarah looked down the list of phone calls received during the day but couldn't see anything out of order. She was looking for a name or something out of the norm that would lead her to the child. She slowly turned the pages of her file.

And then, at long, long last, she realised the truth. It was staring out from the file in front of her. 7.00pm. 8.30am. 11.00am.

"You bastard!" she cried out.

She picked up the telephone and spoke to Superintendent Obuma. Forty minutes later, DCI Rudd, along with two armed officers, went through the front door, and another five police officers, two of whom were female, and two of whom were carrying weapons, broke down the back entrance. The doctor they had on hand was asked to wait until he was called for by the police officers.

They immediately arrested the two occupants of the building, but did not stop to search the rest of the premises. DCI Rudd knew exactly where Tabitha was to be found.

In the early hours of the morning, just after midnight, Lucy had reached a point where she didn't care if her husband opened the bottle of scotch or not. He was sitting on his own.

"Charles," she said, "please have one. It simply doesn't matter anymore. Pour yourself a drink now if it will help you."

Charles stared dully at Tabitha's photograph, which he'd propped up against the side of the bottle.

Lucy was exhausted. She'd found Scarlett's and Lily's questions the most agonising thing to deal with – they'd watched the news bulletins throughout the afternoon and evening and were, naturally, extremely alarmed.

She was suddenly startled from her reverie by flashing blue lights pulsating through the gaps in the curtains. She rushed to the front door and pulled it open. She saw, standing there, DCI Rudd.

And in her arms, the policewoman was holding a tired, but excited and healthy-looking, Tabitha.

As Lucy clung, weeping, to her daughter, she turned back into the hallway. Scarlett was standing at the top of the stairs holding out Tabitha's favourite cuddly bear.

About ten minutes later, a car horn sounded outside their home. It was followed by another and then one more. Suddenly a cacophony of sound erupted and, as Lucy went to the front door, she realised that their friends and neighbours were congregating outside, waving and shouting, many in their pyjamas. The press were trying to take photographs and rushed forward, past the three police officers, to interview Lucy.

As Lucy stood with her daughter in her arms, feeling like she would never let go again, Charles appeared with Scarlett and Lily. The Harriman family was together again.

During the cheering and general shouting, a local reporter found himself being pulled into the bushes in the front garden. As he protested, a fist smashed into his face.

Amanda could not sleep. She had had another successful day in Paris but now her thoughts were elsewhere. She had re-read the paper from her brother over and over again and understood the logic of his proposals. She was also not going to deny that she was flattered by the thought of being chief operating officer. And she accepted the notion of a young and dynamic chairman, for the very reasons put forward by Alistair.

She had only one reservation. The suggested candidate was not available. She had been thinking through her approach with Alistair and how to tell him this news when she received a text. She picked up the mobile from her pillow.

"Want to send you a(nother) text. Ok?"

She hesitated before replying to him. He had never done this before. Had Alistair spoken to him already? Was it a text she would enjoy receiving?

"Providing I want to read it, go ahead."

It was six minutes before the message arrived. She looked at it in total amazement.

"I want to walk down the Mall holding your hand xx."

She read it and re-read it.

She then curled up in her bed, relishing these words. They said everything. He was picturing the two of them, together, strolling down one of the most beautiful avenues in the world. Ahead of them was a palace of dreams, a life together, a partnership of love. She read the words once again. Perhaps she was allowing herself to be carried away with schoolgirl romance. Yet the sheer thought of simply walking together, holding hands, captured for her the essence of their promised relationship.

She pictured the slow, leisurely meander under the trees and alongside the parks. He wanted to hold her hand as they walked down the Mall.

She wanted that too.

It was Friday 17 June. Superintendent Obuma was struggling to contain his anger, even though the Masters' solicitor was being pedantic about the rules. He was threatening a formal complaint about the late arrival of a search warrant, requiring compensation for the damage to the premises and alleging intimidation of his clients.

Gerald and Alice Masters were behaving in a childlike manner, playing with each other's hands and giggling.

"She's a lovely girl," said Alice. "Can we have her back, please? We made her happy. She really liked the peach melba ice cream."

Sarah Rudd was with the chief superintendent.

"They had planned it meticulously, ma'am. Gerald Masters had converted the back of his delivery van into a little home for her. It was, of course, air-conditioned and Tabitha was comfortable there. In the afternoons she was taken about ten miles west to a secluded forest just south of the M4 motorway, where they'd have a picnic together. One of our officers had mentioned that she'd noticed there were different people serving in the shop but I failed to register the significance of this. One was Alice's mother. She must have known."

Sarah rubbed her eyes. She was exhausted. Chief Superintendent Gardner picked up her desk phone and asked for more coffee to be brought in.

"They hadn't chosen Tabitha specifically," continued Sarah. "They had young children in their shop all the time and especially at the end of the school day. When Gerald saw the tanker crash he rushed round to his yard and pulled his van into the side road. He spotted Tabitha wandering outside the school gates looking for her mother and he snatched her. Of course, he later told us his van was at the garage for repairs. We never thought to check that statement. I'm so sorry."

The secretary came in with a tray and Sarah accepted a second cup of strong black coffee.

"Normally he would have been caught within hours but the lorry incident proved decisive. Everybody, including us, was rushing all over the place. Nobody saw him do it. Every time we searched their premises he was out in his van. He showered incessantly so the dogs picked up nothing from him."

"Did we make any mistakes, chief inspector?" asked Avril Gardner.

"Yes," replied Sarah. "I should have found her that first evening. It always had to be Gerald Masters. His story was weak and there was no other suspect. I missed the obvious."

As she tidied up her office, she sent a text to her long-suffering husband.

"Coming home. Oodles of love. S x"

As she left the police station, heads were nodded and hands put together. DCI Rudd was being acknowledged as a truly professional police officer. She had linked the absence of Mr Masters' van with the police visits. He had managed to outsmart the search teams. She had spotted the pattern, found Tabitha and earned their respect.

Later that morning, Nigel Brewer was arrested by Superintendent Obuma. The day before, DCI Rudd had ordered a complete search of his house. She had discovered that, although he lived on the school premises, he had a home in Southall. There had been a delay in obtaining the search warrant.

The police found nothing to incriminate the caretaker. Ten hours later, the technician found 257 pictures of naked girls from the ages of three to fifteen on his computer. He had deleted them two days earlier, but they were recovered from the remnants still available on the hard drive.

PART TWO

Delivery

Chapter Seven

Charles was amazed by the reception he received as he walked into the offices of Harriman Agnew Capital on the Monday morning following Tabitha's return. Several of his colleagues applauded and two of the girls had tears in their eyes.

He spoke a few words of gratitude before shutting himself away in a meeting room with Andrew, who immediately asked about his family.

"Thanks for all your support," Charles started by saying. "Please thank everybody. Tabitha is fine. The hospital cleared her on Saturday morning. There was nothing physical to concern us and she'd been well fed. As far as we can tell there's no mental damage. They didn't do anything intentionally to upset her."

"Is she talking about it?" Andrew asked.

"Mostly to Scarlett. She's simply overjoyed to have her back."

"What about Lucy?"

"She's exhausted. She spent the whole of Saturday with the three children. Scarlett understood everything and wouldn't let Tabitha out of her sight. Lily was Lily, just letting the world go by. The police came on both Saturday and Sunday – and, of course, we had several local newspapers wanting interviews." Charles drank some more coffee and then put the cup down.

"It's Lucy I'm more worried about, to be honest," he said. "She was horribly affected by the Madeleine McCann headline. In fact, the national papers hardly used it and within twenty-four hours we were history. The fault lay with the nursery school in allowing Tabitha to wander out of the gates. The teachers are blaming each other. The local reporter simply decided he had a scoop."

Andrew remained silent and watched as Charles seemed to wrestle with his thoughts.

"Andrew, I need a favour," he said at last.

"Just ask, Charles."

"I'm taking us all away for two weeks. I've hired a boat in the Sporades. We're going to sail the Greek waters. We fly out of Heathrow tomorrow."

"Good idea. Take as long as you wish."

"What about here? Shall we have a management meeting?"

"We had that at seven o'clock this morning. Just go."

Charles looked relieved and turned to leave the office. As he did so the door opened and Sara walked in.

"Oh, excuse me. I have this room booked," she said.

"Sara. You met Charles when you brought in your research report. It was Charles and I who agreed that you should join us."

Sara looked at the chairman.

"How is Tabitha?" she asked

"That's kind of you to ask, Sara. She's recovering well."

"You shouldn't have left her alone."

Charles looked at Sara. His forehead was creased with anxiety.

"Don't you think we don't know that, Sara? We have Tabitha back. At night I lie in bed thinking the unthinkable."

"I'll come back, Andrew," said Sara, before leaving the room.

A few minutes later, Charles left the office and walked slowly to Monument tube station, where he caught the District Line train to Ealing Broadway. He didn't feel particularly well. He wanted a drink.

Sara returned to the office ten minutes later. She'd taken to the daily work in the new business department of Harriman Agnew Capital with an impressive energy and commitment, and was slowly becoming quite popular. It was South African Martin Daboute with whom she really connected. He was seriously bright and could laugh at himself. He questioned everything Sara said. She teased him mercilessly about his weight.

The first points of the day went to Sara, who started the management meeting by announcing that Martin, over the weekend, had invested in some talking scales. They were actually for users with poor eyesight, as they spoke your weight.

"The first time Martin stood on them," announced Sara, "the voice said 'one at a time please'!"

But, jokes aside, it was Sara and Martin who led the way in helping Abbi create the investor story for City Fiction. And now Jody had joined the meeting to give what Sara thought was a superb analysis of the financial position of the company.

"I've prepared two pro-forma balance sheets," Jody declared.

Sara looked at Martin. "Pro-forma?" she mouthed. "Tell you later," he whispered back.

"We are basing the prospectus on a minimum subscription of seven hundred and fifty thousand pounds. Below that amount and we fail. We must return any subscriptions back to the investors. So my two pro-forma balance sheets are based on a fund-raising of seven hundred and fifty thousand pounds and the second one covers two million pounds, which is the amount we hope to raise. For those of you who are interested, the cash-flows follow a similar path. We have to show that City Fiction has enough money for at least a year if only the minimum amount is raised. They do, of course, because we accountants make sure that they do. But it's a useful exercise. We're finding David Singleton easy to work with and we like him."

"Thanks Jody," said Oliver. "Just to remind you that Abbi is away today, Gavin has taken his wife to hospital and Duncan is attending a Securities' Institute course. Martin, you're preparing the document. What progress and why have we not seen a first draft?"

"Good progress, boss. The lawyers are adding their section as we speak. You'll have a first edition later today. It's not a difficult document. City Fiction is an easy story to tell."

"Thanks, Martin. Let's talk about the investor proposition, please. My job, of course, but Ian Bridges will be leading the salesmen. As you all know, Ian works with Gavin and Duncan and runs the private client sales desk. Ian, the floor is yours."

Ian was six foot three, dark and handsome. He was ready to impress.

"Can I begin, Oliver, by thanking Sara and Martin for their help. As you know, we all have a copy of Sara's executive summary and it's a good place to start. Sara says it's a gamble and normally the FSA will shut us down if they think we're offering high risk investments. But what Sara's saying is that City Fiction are building up their annual sales and so, each January, they know they can pay the overheads for the next twelve months. I don't want to use the phrase 'annuity income'. That is for clever people like Jody here."

There was polite applause and Jody and Sara smiled at each other. "We'll refer to 'annual sales'," continued Ian. "Sara's point is the gamble element – so, if City Fiction are to repay their investors with big profits, they must find some winners. Here again Sara helps us. In her full report she has covered Bloomsbury Publishing at some length. There's the carrot. Will City Fiction be next? Don't forget it has the tax incentives for qualifying investors, which is always good news." Ian reached for his glass of water.

"What we must now decide is, what's the investor profile? To whom are we going to sell the shares? Melanie is going to tell us what we can do."

"Good news, guys and dolls." (Sara groaned inwardly.) "There is a full document which means it can go to any investor. But my suggestion is that our files will cover risk and, in view of what Sara has reported, I think we should make this institutional and high net worth investors only. Put it another way. I think this is too high risk as an investment to offer to private shareholders. It can only go to those investors who are very experienced in assessing potential and the possible loss of their money, and to professional fund managers."

"Thanks Melanie," said Oliver. "I talked to Alistair about this. He doesn't want any one significant investor. We're valuing the company at ten million pounds, assuming a full fund-raising." (Sara's eyes widened and again Martin mouthed that he would explain this to her later.) "So we are offering shares that will represent twenty percent of the company. Alistair doesn't want any one institution to have more than eight percent." (Martin looked at Sara and nodded again.)

"The next stage is for Abbi, when she returns tomorrow, and Ian, to write a draft investor presentation. This covers what we can say over the telephone to the clients. Melanie has to approve our script for regulatory purposes, so let her have it, Ian, as soon as you and Abbi have it done, and we'll review it up later this week."

The meeting was adjourned.

Amanda was ready to return to London. She had an unanswered text from Oliver. She had to sit down with Alistair and explain the situation. She hoped that he would understand about Oliver. There must be other candidates – she knew she could not accept the position of chief operating officer if Oliver was the chairman.

As she let the hot shower water run over her, she began to relax. She knew that Alistair would understand. They had always had a superb working relationship, despite being brother and sister.

She sent a message to Oliver:

"Sorry. Been busy. Leaving shortly. Longing to see you. x."

The newspaper reporter realised that by the time he had left his car the police officer would be in his path. The supermarket car-park was full and he had no escape route.

"Sarah!" he exclaimed. "Many congratulations on your..."

"It's Detective Chief Inspector Rudd when you speak to me. In future you'll always use my correct title." She made no comment about the bruising on his face.

"Sar...er...DCI Rudd. Come on. I was following the facts. And we did get you maximum publicity."

Sarah moved so that she was standing directly in front of him. She looked the reporter squarely in the eyes.

"You're a shitty little toad. You messed with a life. A mother who had lost her daughter."

"Just doing my job, DCI Rudd."

"As I am mine. Your tax disc is a month out of date, your front left tyre is bald and I can smell alcohol on your breath."

Jody had double-locked the front door of her Docklands flat, showered and put on a track suit. She tuned in to Capital Radio and poured herself a large vodka, to which she added a splash of tonic water, an ice cube and a slice of lemon. She sighed as the alcohol trickled down the back of her throat.

Her dining-room table was covered with credit card statements. The mortgage on the flat was the subject of a series of letters from the Building Society. Her bank statement was in front of her and she had called off a later statement from the machine on her way home.

Jody was financially astute and that was her problem. She knew how the system worked and, initially, had used it to her advantage.

In the spring of 2005 she had met Xavier Selous. At the time she was well over a separation from a partner of five years and was finding her feet with Andrew in the corporate finance world. She was in her early thirties and thought she looked pretty good for her age. But she wanted children before too long.

She met Xavier at the Barbican Theatre. During the interval, as they all waited for the second part of the Mahler concert, she found herself sitting by a handsome Frenchman. They started talking and went to bed together two weeks later.

Xavier was charming. He wrote music articles for French magazines, and was spending six months in London for work. Jody fell in love and decided to buy a flat. Mortgages were easy to obtain and she completed a self-certified application. It wasn't even checked at the Building Society. They simply validated her personal details and credit record and granted her a one hundred percent mortgage on a four hundred thousand pound flat on the third floor of a block of flats in St. Katherine's Dock. It had a beautiful view of the Tower of London.

Within weeks, the value, as indicated by current selling prices, had increased by thirty thousand pounds. Jody and Xavier would travel, by weekend, to Stratford-upon-Avon to watch Shakespeare plays. Everything seemed rosy.

Michelle Selous, Xavier's daughter, arrived one evening in the late winter of 2006. She appeared to think that the flat was her London home and, initially, Jody tried hard to accommodate her. But, after three months, Jody realised that Michelle was stealing money from her purse. She tried to discuss it with Xavier but he was dismissive. He had no money either.

Meanwhile, the interest rate on the mortgage was increasing as the markets reflected the oncoming financial crisis. Jody found herself paying five hundred pounds more each month. She had a bank overdraft of eighteen thousand pounds which she kept as her rainy day reserve, since her outgoings could suddenly be affected by extra medical bills.

She started using the cheques being offered by the credit card companies. Their 'interest-only' offers (despite the three percent cheque transfer charge) were alluring. Jody was certain things would work out. She found it easy simply to write out a cheque and pay it into her bank account. The usual ten to twelve month's interest free period would never be a problem. She would repay the amounts well within that period by using her Christmas bonus, which Andrew was suggesting could be over one hundred thousand pounds.

But, as finance director, Jody realised that the revenues of the business were falling. A major transaction was lost and the final bonus, the last she was to receive, totalled only sixteen thousand pounds. She used it to pay some bills and to pay off part of her bank overdraft.

When Michelle was arrested in April 2007 for drugs offences, Jody gave Xavier three thousand pounds for legal costs, then a further five thousand, and then said there would be no more money until she could speak to Michelle's defence lawyer. Xavier moved out of the flat and she only saw him again a handful of times.

As the recession took effect she faced two serious issues. In 2009 the Bank of England reduced rates of interest in a series of measures which eventually reduced her mortgage payments to a manageable level. She then spoke to the local estate agents but there was simply no chance of selling the flat without offering perhaps a twenty percent discount on the price she had paid.

It was the credit cards where her problems really emerged. She had six cards from six different companies. As the interest free periods expired, the rates applied at normal levels. That was bad enough, but several of the American providers had started a campaign of dirty tricks. They would stuff their envelopes with leaflets, several of which, if you bothered to search for the information, referred to circumstances where the credit card company had the right to increase the rate of interest. One company had a clause, in small print, giving it the right, in eleven different cases, to raise their rates. One referred to economic conditions. The individual could refuse the increase and repay the balance. Many, like Jody, didn't have the funds to consider repayment. She reached a crisis point with the American credit card where the rate of interest had been put up in stages to over thirty percent. She went to see her bank and they gave her a personal loan. That night she cried with relief. The bank told her they were used to seeing clients with the same problem. She borrowed ten thousand pounds from Andrew, interest free, for ten years. She met with her parents and her father gave her five thousand pounds. She cashed in a life policy for eighteen thousand pounds.

She did not live. She existed. She always tried to be positive. The merger of the two firms and the securing of the finance director job had given her a massive boost.

She studied the summary in front of her:

Mortgage
Balance outstanding £410,000. Value of flat £360,000
Monthly payments, interest only £847.10

Bank overdraft
Limit £18,000. Balance £6,300.00 overdrawn

Credit cards (6)
Total balances £49,231.06
Monthly payments (including capital) £1,733.50

Bank personal loan (over four years)
Balance outstanding: £19,434.67

Monthly payments: £588.55

Jody earned, before bonuses, an annual salary of £96,000. Her monthly take-home pay was £4,688.89. Her financial outgoings were well over £3,000. At least she could walk to work.

The one figure she could not face writing down was the direct debit to her bank account from the clinic for Ben's care. The one for the last month had been for £1,344.43.

She sat on her favourite comfy armchair and drank some more vodka, this time with less tonic.

The following morning, Abbi surprised Sara by saying that she needed to talk. They left the office and went together for a coffee, which Sara bought. She placed the cardboard containers on the table and told Abbi about events yesterday and the progress being made with City Fiction and the writing of the investor story. She stopped suddenly and looked at her companion.

"You're going to tell me. Why not now?"

"Medical tests," said Abbi. "Yesterday. A private clinic."

"You ok?"

"Not me. Jonathan."

"Problem?"

"Try unprotected sex with another woman."

Sara remained silent.

"He told me over the weekend. Usual thing. Office drinks to celebrate a new contract which Jonathan had won for the business. Wine bar. Seemed like a good idea. In Jonathan's business he's a target for the younger girls. One, and she's really pushy, apparently 'persuaded' him to book a hotel room."

"Where were you?"

"You'll love this, Sara. I was visiting his mother, who's in an old people's home in Bethnal Green."

"The tests?"

"Clear."

"Good bye Jonathan?"

"Well, I'm hurt. But I still love him to death."

"Till the next time."

"He's absolutely gutted. I really believe him."

"Want some advice?"

"Yes, please."

"Make him suffer. Separate beds for a week. Get him wanting it so much he'll never forget what the consequences are if he tries it again."

"Bit late for that. Last night... well, I wanted him."

Sara laughed. She stood up and looked at her workmate.

"Back to City Fiction, Abbi. There's work to be done."

Gavin and Duncan were biding their time. They were still confused and pissed off by the way Charles had simply told them that the firm was merging and they were relocating to Queen Street. But, on the other hand, it was year four of the recession and they knew they were doing well to retain their positions as corporate brokers in Harriman's team. It had been a better year in 2010, with some new business opportunities coming in from Asia. They had received bonuses at Christmas but, at ten percent of their salaries, the money, which was taxed at the higher rates, made a minimal difference to their lives.

They had taken an instant dislike to Oliver. And now, though Gavin's language had toned down, his attitude remained the same. It was not the public school, Oxford background issue. That was the norm in the City. It was his air of entitlement and his promotion as head of corporate finance in the new firm that really got to them.

They watched as the City Fiction contract materialised. Abbi really knew her stuff, but they agreed that Oliver and Ian would struggle to raise the funds – and they had no intention of helping them. They'd defend Ian when the time came. Oliver would carry the can for its failure.

Andrew poured Rachel a sherry. He was drinking wine.

"So she's settled in?" he asked.

Her daughter, Bryony, had arrived in Australia two days earlier and was preparing to backpack up to Queensland before crossing over to South East Asia.

"Yes. The whole party seems to have found its feet. How about you? Have you had a good day?"

"Charles came and went." He told Rachel what Sara had said to him. He also told her that he had received a letter from the

150

regulator saying that they were happy with the merged firm and Harriman Agnew would retain its permissions.

"Meaning?"

"Clean sheet again. We're back in business."

"We've not made much money over the last three years, Andrew. Are things going to get better?"

"It really is a stronger team now. Our difficulty is there is so little business in this country. I voted for Cameron and I applauded Osborne's budget. The deficit has to be reduced… But, I'm beginning to think that they've cut too much."

She moved around to settle beside him more comfortably.

"You know you were talking about Gordon Brown's book, *Beyond the Crash*? Well, you left it lying around so I read it."

"And?"

"Well, if I understand his position, he is saying that America and the UK, and large parts of Europe, are fucked with crap currencies and unsustainable budget deficits. Global growth depends entirely on consumer spending in China, India and the rest of East Asia."

"Don't forget about Africa, Brazil and Canada, but yes, that's a great analysis." He smiled and poured some more drinks.

"So what are you going to do about it?"

"I'm planning a two week trip: Singapore, Hong Kong, China and South Korea. Will you come?"

"Not India?"

"I've never been comfortable trying to do business in India. Their commitment to their investors never seems to be at the level we expect. No, we'll start at Singapore."

"I'll come," she said. "You can leave me in Hong Kong and pick me up on the way back."

"Agreed," he said. "I'll confirm the schedule with the lads tomorrow."

The waters around the Sporades, to the west of the Aegean Sea, were warm and tranquil. There were twenty-four islands from which Charles and Lucy could choose but only four were inhabited. They had chosen to moor up at Skopelos. Their forty-two foot boat, which they had picked up off the Greek coast, was

151

designed for eight to ten people. Charles had passed his coastal navigation exam and was a careful skipper. Lucy managed the winches and they both knew the knots for the ropes. The girls wore safety jackets at all times when they were on deck and were attached to safety harnesses. Scarlett and Tabitha delighted in pretending to navigate the wheel while Lily played with her games console.

On their third evening, at around six, they were dressed and ready to go into the local town. Charles secured the cabin locks as they climbed up the ladder and walked over to the quay side, ready to choose a taverna.

Lucy managed to order various dishes, all with chips. Scarlett was next to Tabitha and Lily was sulking because she'd now decided that she didn't like her bunk bed. But an ice-cream feast improved her mood at the end of the meal and, before long, all three girls were back on the boat and fast asleep. Before she finally shut her eyes Tabitha was aware that Lucy was applying more aftersun cream to her left shoulder. As a doctor, she was obsessive about protecting her daughters' skin.

Lucy and Charles sat on the deck, drinking the coffee Lucy had brought from England.

"Ok?" he asked.

"Fine. Another lovely day. I think we need to find a beach tomorrow and let the girls have more time on land."

"Good plan. I have Wilbur Smith to keep me company," he laughed.

She smiled, though she found she couldn't concentrate long enough to read a book. She occupied herself instead with magazines and medical journals.

"You were telling me about statins."

"Yes, I was. It was an article in *The Lancet* that caught my attention. We dish statins out like Smarties. They're supposed to be this wonder drug. I think that doctors in Ealing between them have half the population worrying about their cholesterol levels."

"Is that not a good thing?"

"Well, who am I to argue with the experts?" she replied. "Obviously with today's fatty foods people are clogging up their arteries and statins will save lives."

"So what's your point?"

"Just instinct, really." She drank some more sherry. "The longer I'm a doctor the more I wonder at the workings of the human body. I have learnt that time after time, if you give the body a chance, it will sort itself out. Take me prescribing statins. I have patient after patient worrying themselves about their cholesterol reading. 'Mrs Smith. I am pleased to tell you that your cholesterol reading is 4.8.' Mrs Smith has no idea what I'm talking about. She's been brainwashed to believe that this one reading is going to determine her future health."

Lucy was warming to her subject. "I could help Mrs Smith so much more if I had the time to advise her on her diet. What will she go and do? She'll be elated about the reading I've given her and she'll rush to the bakers and buy some cream cakes."

"So why prescribe her statins? Just give her some diet sheets."

"I do that, of course. But the answer to your question is professional indemnity."

He looked puzzled. "What's that got to do with Mrs Smith's cholesterol?"

"It means that if Mrs Smith drops down dead with a heart attack, my records will show that I provided the correct treatment. I can't be at fault except I didn't prolong her life."

"So what was in the article that excited you?"

"There's some research out showing that statins may cause diabetes. It confirms what I suspect but I cannot practise on my gut feelings..."

"So Mrs Smith will continue to get her statins," he laughed.

"Yes, and her cream cakes!" Lucy smiled at her husband.

Suddenly the atmosphere between the two of them changed.

"I know you want to ask me," he said.

"You don't have to answer," she replied.

"I want to say that I wouldn't have opened it, Lucy, but that third night was bloody difficult." He paused. "When I saw you suffering with the paper headlines, I suffered with you."

"It may not get much better. You drank too much alcohol for such a long time."

Charles told Lucy what Sara had said in the office.

"Was it our fault, Lucy?" he asked his wife.

Lucy put her glass down and went and sat at her husband's bare feet.

"Charles," she said. "I need to tell you something."

"What do you mean? That sounds serious."

"Well… I'm pregnant."

Charles looked at Lucy in complete surprise.

"Have you seen the doctor?" he asked, at last.

"Charles, I am the doctor!"

He laughed too.

"Any chance of a boy?"

Jody read the letter from the clinic with a growing apprehension in the pit of her stomach. It explained that Ben had suffered two seizures during one night and they needed to change his drugs regime. The doctors wanted to attempt a three-month trial, which would cost Jody an extra three hundred pounds a month. They thought that Ben was suffering from scoliosis.

Amanda landed at Heathrow Airport late on Thursday afternoon, where she took the express train into London and the Jubilee Line to St. John's Wood. She reached her flat, unpacked, showered and drove straight over to Alistair's house. She had with her a bottle of Châteauneuf-du-Pape, which she knew was one of his favourite red wines.

She was nervous and hoped she would be able to explain her concerns without upsetting him. When she arrived, he was working at his desk and seemed pleased to see her, thanking her effusively for the wine. After she'd sat down and made herself comfortable, they discussed her sales figures which, in these recessional times, were remarkable. He was even more pleased with the results of her foreign rights negotiations. Europe was developing into a united market for financial services and Alistair was sure that this improved the potential for his finance-based titles.

"We must discuss this with Abbi and put it in our presentation," he said.

"So… that paper you wrote," she said. "It was very interesting. But are you sure that I'm right for the position of COO?"

"You're the perfect choice. It's a dream team. Me, the publisher, you the COO, David as FD and Oliver as chairman."

There was a long pause. "Have you asked him yet?" she asked.

"Of course not. We must have a board meeting first."

"It's just, Alistair, I've got some doubts about Oliver."

"Why? He's ideal. Young, talented, experienced… just what we need. You've been raving about him for ages. Why the doubts?"

"Well… isn't he a bit young?" Amanda was clutching at straws.

Alistair looked at his sister with narrowed eyes.

"What's really going on here, Amanda?"

She cast her eyes down to the floor and sighed.

Alistair knew from experience that his sister's moods were often influenced by her relationships. He decided to test out his theory.

"What happened to Zach? I liked him."

She told her brother about the decision she'd made, about her concerns over Zach's seeming lack of interest in his wife and children.

"So there's no man around at the moment?".

"Er… well… not quite. There is somebody."

His face broke into a smile. "Great, that's great news. Who is he?"

Amanda took a deep breath – and began to tell her brother about her relationship with Oliver; how it had started, how cautious she had been, why she had put the affairs of City Fiction first and how cleverly she had thought up the basis of 'the deal'…

At which point Alistair exploded. She had never seen his face quite so red.

"A deal?! What the hell were you thinking? How dare you go around doing some sleazy 'deal' on my transaction? Oliver is raising the two million as a professional corporate financier, not to gain access to your knickers!"

"Alistair! How dare you talk to me like that? You make me sound like a..."

"Yes. A what, Amanda? Like a what? Oh for god's sake – I told Sara you seemed to always be in trouble with men... but this, this is something else!"

"So, that's where her comments came from, is it? How dare you discuss my private life with a teenage researcher!"

"She's twenty-four, Amanda!" He was raising his voice now. "And it's hardly bloody private when you're making sick deals based on my business! Just think. Please think about what you've done. You shouldn't be involved in any way with Oliver. More importantly, you've totally belittled my work. And all because you two just couldn't wait to jump into bed together!"

"Stop it. Stop it, please, Alistair. Stop talking like that. Stop making me sound so dirty. We love each other."

"You what? You're an idiot. Love? That's not love, Amanda."

"'Oliver'," he mimicked. "'I can't open my legs for you, even though I love you, until you've raised two million pounds for me.' Well, am I wrong? Is that not how it is?"

Amanda couldn't hold back her tears, or reach the door fast enough.

"End it, Amanda. Tonight!" he shouted at her departing figure.

She took a deep breath, wiped her eyes, and turned to face her brother.

"We may have a big problem, Alistair, if I'm forced to choose between the two of you."

Once she was sitting safely in her car, she sent a text message. *"I know it's late but can I come round? xx."*

Her heart leaped as she read the immediate reply.

"Is Rachmaninov ok – or would you prefer the Arctic Monkeys?"

But, for reasons she was later unable to explain to herself, she instead returned to her flat in St. John's Wood.

Alistair spent the next day at City Fiction in a tidal wave of indecision.

156

He picked up the phone to speak to Oliver and then put it down again. He went back and forth into the main office, picking up files and putting them down again, merely to see if Amanda had arrived. He decided to text her and then deleted his message. He thought about phoning her but suspected when she saw his name on her mobile screen she wouldn't answer. He relived their row and bitterly regretted some of his words. The other members of his team sensed his mood and kept their heads down.

At lunchtime he left London on the M4 motorway to drive to Exeter to meet an author whose script he had enjoyed reading. He turned his phone off and decided to let events take their course.

Amanda finished unpacking their picnic basket and handed the bottle of wine to Oliver. St. James's Park was crammed full of Saturday tourists enjoying the sites of London. Many would end up at Buckingham Palace hoping to see the Queen, as the Royal Standard was flying.

They had talked things over in great detail. Oliver was still a bit miffed that she had not arrived at his flat after texting him and she'd revealed her brother's plans and their subsequent row. Oliver then told her about the warning Andrew had given him at their lunch.

"So you agree, right? We have no choice but to wait for events to sort themselves out. Better still if you can finish raising the money."

"Perhaps."

"No perhaps about it. We would have regretted it."

"So there's no re-negotiation of the deal?"

"Well, we've a new set of circumstances."

"Good god, I never knew that going to bed with a woman could be so complicated."

She sighed. She'd spoken to Alistair earlier that morning. He'd discussed the proposed publication of his Exeter author and avoided all other subjects. She went with the flow and they'd agreed to talk again on Monday.

"I'd like to think about things," Oliver said.

Amanda sat up. "Second thoughts?"

"Let's meet for breakfast on Tuesday. Chez Gerard. Bishopsgate. Eight o'clock."

"But we're here now. Let's talk now."

"No. I need to think. Tuesday. Breakfast."

"Why Tuesday?"

"I need to think on Monday as well."

Amanda slammed the top of the picnic basket closed.

Jody allowed herself one night out a month. She particularly loved the Raymond Gubbay music programmes on a Sunday night at The Royal Albert Hall, which often ended with the 1812 Overture written by one of Oliver's rejected Russian composers. When the cannon fire shook the dome of the auditorium she always experienced a surge of excitement.

On a Sunday evening in June she was in the upper circle bar at the interval. She ordered a large vodka and ice and played around with a packet of salted peanuts, before managing to find a table in the crowded room with one empty seat. She nodded to the two other people as she sat down and they made no objection to her presence.

She was replaying some of the earlier music in her head. She wouldn't have objected if the whole programme had been devoted to Elgar. His enigmatic variations managed to transport her to a different place as she remembered the Malvern Hills in Worcestershire where the composer lived out much of his life.

She was suddenly shocked from her reverie. "You enjoy your vodka?" said a deep, foreign voice.

She regained her composure and turned to see a well-built man sitting with a younger woman.

"My name is Dimitri. You are drinking my national drink while you wait to listen to one of the greatest of our Russian composers," he said, smiling.

They were cut off by the first of the bells announcing the imminent start of the final part.

Dimitri surprised Jody by inviting her to join him for another vodka after the concert. Jody surprised herself further by accepting. They agreed to meet in the foyer.

Later, with the sound of cannon fire ringing in her ears, Jody met the Russian and his companion in the theatre entrance. Further surprise ensued. Before she knew what was happening, she found herself being driven in a large black Mercedes, with smoked windows, to the Hilton Hotel in Park Lane. Dimitri occupied the short journey by speaking on his mobile phone in fast, indecipherable Russian. His dark-haired companion sat silently. After they arrived in the lounge bar she disappeared and Jody did not see her again. She made an excuse to visit the cloakroom where she checked her appearance. She had retained her figure through childbirth and maintained a frugal diet, though there were now specks of grey in her hair. She had a bearing that, together with her sparkling eyes, made her attractive, with an immaculate sense of dress. She hurried back to her Russian host.

The waiter knew Dimitri. He brought a bottle of vodka, a bowl of olives and a bucket of ice, set up their table and left them alone.

The next hour flew by. Dimitri was a lively companion. He owned several companies in Southern Russia. But he also wanted to know about Jody and was visibly concerned when he heard about Xavier and his daughter. It was such a relief to speak to someone who really seemed to care, and Jody poured out her problems to this unfamiliar man.

The evening drew to a close when Dimitri said he had more calls to make. Jody was driven back to St. Katherine's Dock by the chauffeur. As she watched the lights of the Thames Embankment, she recognised the music playing in the car. Bach.

When she returned home from work on Monday evening there were flowers and a bottle of vodka awaiting her on the door step. After the day she'd just had at Harriman Agnew Capital, she particularly appreciated the liquor.

Andrew slammed the copy letter on his desk. Oliver blinked at this unusual display of anger from his chief executive

"He's just walked out. Gone to – and I quote – "bigger and better things". The bugger had this all planned out, Oliver!"

They were absorbing the rather important news of the loss of Ian Bridges, who had seen Andrew over the weekend to tell him he would not be returning to the office.

"Melanie is seeing the lawyers this morning and we can, of course, make it difficult for him over the transfer of his FSA registration."

"But we both know that we'll not do that," said Oliver.

"True. I'm just a bad loser," said Andrew. "It just means it's now up to Gavin and Duncan to raise the money for City Fiction." He paused. "There is actually something else I need to talk to you about too."

Andrew explained about his proposed trip to the Far East and they considered some of the implications for the business. The chairman would be back from his holiday and overall Oliver was supportive.

"Don't give up on Britain yet, Andrew," laughed Oliver. "We still have City Fiction."

At ten o'clock, in the main office, Oliver started the meeting to discuss the next steps for City Fiction.

It began badly. Gavin was recovering from a heavy weekend, spent significantly in his local pub.

"Lost golden boy, have we?" he sneered. "I suppose it will now be nice to Gavin and Duncan time. You won't raise the money, Oliver. You need us."

"Where is everybody?" asked Sara.

"Andrew is away for the rest of today," said Oliver. "Melanie is at the lawyers. Jody is not needed for this meeting."

"And the head salesman has gone awol. What a fucking joke!" shouted Gavin.

"The only joke in this meeting is you, Gavin," said Abbi.

"No. There's another funny thing in this meeting," Gavin replied.

"And what's that?" asked Martin.

"Fucking City Fiction. That's what I'm talking about. You'll never raise anything for them."

"Why not?" asked Sara.

"Because they're crap publishers. Duncan agrees with me."

"Can you justify that statement?" asked Abbi.

"Yes I can, Miss Marketing Manager. You see, I have read one of their books."

He reached down and took from his briefcase a copy of the City Fiction title, *Imperfect Storm*.

"I'm quite surprised you actually bought it," said Sara.

"Don't be daft, Sara. It was on Abbi's desk so I pinched it."

Gavin wiped his nose with his jacket sleeve. "This Simon Watson. He can't write for shit."

"It's Simon Wilson and it's a wonderful book, Gavin," said Abbi.

"Why don't you give us a synopsis?" suggested Sara.

Gavin cut across her. "Actually my wife Martine read it. The whole book at my request. I wanted to know what nonsense this company is getting involved in. It's my career as well."

"It's a wonderful story, Gavin. If I may say so, perhaps Martine might prefer Martina Cole," suggested Abbi.

The recent simmering tensions were close to boiling over. Gavin stood up and moved towards Abbi.

"What are you suggesting about my wife?" he hissed.

"What Abbi was suggesting," said Sara, "was that *Imperfect Storm* is beyond her intellectual grasp. Any woman marrying you must have serious questions to answer."

"You lippy bitch! Let me show you what happens to girls who don't know their place," shouted Gavin. He advanced towards Abbi.

Martin stepped in his path but was pulled back by Duncan. Gavin reached Abbi only to find Sara blocking his way.

"If you want to lay a finger on Abbi, Gavin, you will have to go through me," she said quietly.

Gavin hesitated, thought carefully and then backed down. He was later to tell Duncan that he could never hit a woman.

At long last Oliver took control. He ordered the room to clear except for Gavin and Duncan. Thirty minutes later the two brokers left the office and went to the pub.

Oliver reconvened the meeting and within the space of twenty minutes he had managed to galvanise the Harriman Agnew team. When he'd finished they were convinced that City Fiction would become their best ever client. He revisited the basic investor proposition and said that he would personally take responsibility for the fund-raising. He was very convincing.

Sara put her arm around Abbi's shoulders and whispered in her ear.

"Cometh the hour, cometh the man."

Abbi nodded in agreement.

That evening Oliver re-read an email from his father.

He wrote that he was running out of ideas and perhaps Oliver should just listen to the radio until he heard the piece of music again.

"I do have one thought, son. It seems to be the mixture of the music which so impressed you. The combination of a piano, the violins and the trumpets, which is unusual. You mention mountains being climbed. The range of the piano can produce that effect.

I think your composer was predominately a pianist who composed. Son, it has to be Rubinstein. Listen to his piano concertos."

Oliver emailed back thanking his father but saying he hadn't yet given up his belief that the composer was Russian.

He received an immediate reply.

"Rubinstein is bloody Russian. Off for my lunchtime gin and tonic."

Chapter Eight

She was wearing a pink two-piece outfit. Her fair hair hung softly around her face. She had added little make-up after her early morning gym session and, for jewellery, wore only a gold crucifix around her neck. She kissed Oliver on his cheek and they sat down at the corner table, which allowed them some privacy. She ordered yoghurt, fresh fruit and granary toast; he requested a full English breakfast. They asked for green tea and coffee, respectively.

"This is a first. I'm not sure I've ever met for breakfast to negotiate a relationship," she said.

He didn't reply. The tea and coffee were served, but he continued to look around the restaurant, avoiding her eyes. Amanda's fruit arrived and shortly afterwards a full English breakfast was placed in front of Oliver. Amanda called the waitress over and prompted her about her granary toast; Oliver then decided he wanted some brown sauce. He never ate black pudding without brown sauce. Amanda then decided she wanted another serviette and asked for a second bowl of yoghurt. When that was produced she again reminded the waitress about her granary toast. Oliver asked for his coffee cup to be refilled. The granary toast arrived. Amanda asked for a tub of butter. When that was served, she said she would like some jam. She was offered strawberry or damson. She wanted raspberry. That wasn't available. She decided she didn't want jam after all. There was a long silence.

"So… how are your thoughts progressing?" she asked, eventually. She had spent two further lonely evenings in her flat with far too much time to think about their situation. She found the whole thing frustrating and annoying. A relationship by negotiation? It was all so unnatural, so unspontaneous. But then she would remember that she had introduced 'the deal' in the first place. She was hurting for her brother too. His words were lost. She'd simply misjudged the whole situation.

She was allowing her emotional stability to be rocked by her loyalty to her brother and her desire for Oliver. She kept thinking back to the river bank and remembering those moments with him. And that message he'd sent…

"*I want to walk down the Mall holding your hand.*"

No words had ever captured for her what she really needed in a relationship before. She desperately wanted to make that same walk. She was ready to give herself to Oliver, to one man. She didn't want to be alone any more.

Oliver looked across the table.

"If I'm completely honest, I'm not enjoying what's happening."

"To us?" she asked.

"No. Not in the specific sense. I like to live my life by making each day as fulfilling as possible, but at the moment I'm finding the tensions at work quite difficult to deal with."

He went on to explain about the conflicts with Gavin and the lack of support from Andrew. He mentioned that Charles had gone on holiday.

"I feel I should be dealing with matters better but I just can't control the meetings."

She looked at him. Why was he talking about work?

"But are you finding our situation difficult?" she asked.

"That's why I wanted time to think," he said. "I've been wondering if we've been complicating matters."

In his own mind the situation was clear. He had two objectives: to raise two million pounds and to get closer to her. Both were proving less than straightforward.

"Complicating how?" asked Amanda

"I'll raise the money for City Fiction. That's my job."

"But you're not the fund-raiser, are you?"

"Gavin and Duncan are the lead brokers but I've raised money in the past."

"So are you saying that I'm the problem?"

"We have to think about Alistair, yes, and your commitment to him. But I've come to a conclusion."

Amanda tried to look less anxious than she felt.

"Only one thing matters," he said.

She gazed back, heart beating.

"You," he said.

"Me?"

"You are simply the loveliest woman I've ever met. I find it impossible to put it into words."

"Well, you could try," suggested Amanda.

"Every few moments I find myself thinking about you. I can't get you out of my mind. Your beauty. Your vitality. I never thought a woman would do this to me. I know that the moment I have you in my grasp I'll never let you go."

She listened to his honeyed words. A lot of men had expressed desire for her – Zach had been particularly eloquent. But this was different. A new level.

"But there are issues," she said. "I have to make my peace with Alistair. You must talk to him. You must complete the fund-raising."

"There are no issues," said Oliver, "apart from one." He looked directly into her eyes. "Do you want what I want, Amanda?"

She placed her hand on top of his.

"Very, very much," she said.

The mid-morning phone call took Jody by surprise – but she immediately accepted Dimitri's invitation to lunch at the Dorchester Hotel. His chauffeur picked her up in Queen Street at around 12.30pm and, with a clear drive along the Embankment and right to Trafalgar Square, through Mayfair and into Park Lane, she found herself sitting down with her host at 1.15pm. A glass of champagne was placed before her and then the waiter appeared with a dozen red roses, which were presented and then taken away.

It had been her intention to ask him how he knew her business telephone number, as she couldn't recall naming Harriman Agnew Capital during their first drink together.

But instead she pointed out to Dimitri that she did not know his name or anything about him. Then, without any formality, she was served a plate of fresh grilled sardines with a mustard sauce and a glass of cool Chablis. Dimitri continued to drink vodka and take calls on his mobile. Despite her confusion, she could not keep the huge grin off her face.

"My full name is Dimitrius Illyor Petraffus," he said. "I am proud that you have joined me for lunch. I have asked about you in the City. You are highly regarded as finance director of Harriman Agnew Capital. I like the new partnership. I'll meet Andrew. He will want to meet me."

She put her knife and fork down and looked at him. She wanted to ask him why he had changed hotels but the moment passed.

"So this is about business," she said.

"You are a lovely lady. We have many, many beautiful women in Russia but I always think that a wonderful English lady is more alluring. My English is good, no? Alluring, yes! This is about my coal mines, but if I can do it through you, it will be good. I'm very generous and I always reward those people who bring me what I want."

Jody smiled, in what she hoped was an alluring manner. "Tell me about your coal mines, please…"

Dimitri waited while the grilled Dover sole was served, off the bone. The next glass of wine was a Riesling. He continued with his vodka.

In the next fifteen minutes he built a picture of his family background in Leningrad, his time at university and his early days working for the energy regulators out of Moscow. As he began to talk about his days as a businessman, she put a hand on his arm.

"Dimitri," she said. "I want to hear everything about you in much greater detail, but I must get back to work. Will you allow me to cook for you in my home one night?"

She surprised herself with this suggestion, but she wanted to understand him better without the constant phone interruptions. She instantly liked him. He had charm and personality and he carried himself as a leader of men. She had no idea where it might lead, but she knew she must get to know him better.

Oliver was in a sombre mood. He had met with Alistair. They'd agreed the schedule for the preparation of the draft share subscription document, the meetings with the lawyers and the accountants, the key role that David Singleton would play in preparing cash-flow forecasts and the work that Abbi would be undertaking in preparing Alistair, Amanda and David for the investor presentations.

At no stage was Oliver alone with Alistair and he'd given no indication that he wanted to talk privately.

He had returned to the office to meet another prospective client and worked at his desk for the remainder of the afternoon. At around six o'clock he was leaving the building to catch the tube home to Clerkenwell when he found himself in the lift descending to the ground floor, together with Sara.

She accepted his offer to buy her a glass of wine and soon they were standing on the cobbled path outside The Golden Lion in Tabernacle Street, among several hundred other early evening drinkers. A table came free and they sat down. They exchanged pleasantries and he decided that a bottle of wine was needed. When he returned to their table he noticed that she was dressed in a light green top and jeans. She was not physically demonstrative, preferring to sit fairly still, just occasionally using her hands to emphasise the point she might be making. She was a good conversationalist and seemed interested in what Oliver was saying. He slowly moved to his interest in her adventures on joining Harriman Agnew Capital and her thoughts on City Fiction.

"I'm amazed how I've been seduced by the attractions of City Fiction. The people involved seem almost like disciples. They love their books and the authors. They take fantastic care over the production of each title."

"Yes, but it's whether they can sell the books that matters."

"eBooks are changing everything. But you know, Oliver, I think I got it right. They must find some winners."

There was a pause in their conversation after Oliver made a clumsy attempt to pry into her private life. Sara admitted to living near to the Tower of London and little else. He made only one attempt to introduce a more personal element which she

167

rebuffed by standing up and returning a few minutes later with a second bottle of wine.

He decided to tell her about his search for the composer of the piece of music that he wanted to trace. She insisted he explained it to her from the start. He tried humming the theme but she guided him back to the start of the story. The playing of the piece on the radio, the girl cyclist and her accident, hearing the music again at The Westbury, his search through the Russian composers – Rachmaninov, Shostakovich, Tchaikovsky, Medtner and Rubinstein.

"Sara," he said, "it's so frustrating. My father suggested that I listen to some of Anton Rubinstein's music. I'd never heard of him so I did some research."

He noticed that she seemed interested so he told her what he had discovered.

"Anton Grigorevich Rubinstein was born in 1829 and died in 1894," he said. "He was a Russian Jewish pianist who founded the Saint Petersburg Conservatory. He was renowned for his sarcasm and a prolific composer. Twenty operas, six symphonies and works for chamber ensembles."

"Wow," she said. "And I thought that Andrew Lloyd Webber had done pretty well."

He laughed and drank some wine. As the evening progressed the noise outside the pub grew louder. He moved his chair nearer to her.

"He was one of Russia's greatest ever pianists," he continued, "but it was for his five piano concertos that he is best remembered. It's these that are mainly played today, including the fourth that was said to have influenced Tchaikovsky's own concertos."

"Very impressive," exclaimed Sara, clapping her hands together. "You know your Russian composers!"

"Thanks. I've always had a capacity for memorising information. It's putting it to use that's my challenge," he laughed.

"Take me through the music again," she asked.

"Right. Piano start. Da-de-da with the emphasis on the first da." He repeated the start. "Da, that's long, then de-da."

"Which octave?"

"Pardon?"

"Which section on the keyboard?"

"Oh. Lower down. The left hand."

They looked at each other and laughed.

"This could be a long night," she said. "Da-de-da. Then what?"

"Violins and piano together going up the scales right to the top. Then the brass section with the trumpets and drums. Then dum,dum,dum,dum."

"Then what?"

"I think the theme was repeated. Da-de-da and so on and it may have been twice."

"Did you hear the whole piece?"

"Yes, I think so."

"How long?"

"Perhaps eight minutes."

"So have you heard any of Rubinstein's works?"

"It's unlikely to be him. Not that much of his music is played on the radio these days. I went through the Classic FM schedules for the last six weeks and couldn't find his name at all." He poured some more wine into their glasses. "I managed to download one of his piano concertos from the internet. It's not Mr Rubinstein who wrote my piece."

She seemed unconvinced.

"But your father identified him," she said.

"And when I heard his music last night I knew it wasn't him."

They played with the idea of having a final glass of wine, but reluctantly agreed that tomorrow was a working day. They left the wine bar, parted company and went their separate ways.

At three o'clock in the morning, Oliver was awoken by a beep on his phone. It was a message from Sara.

"Used all search engines. No music with title 'Ascent'. U heard 'mountain': could b European. Father right. U say piano dominates. Must b pianist who composed and who's popular. It was Liszt. Listen 2 Liebestraum - 1 of the greatest pieces of piano music composed. U should play Mephisto Waltz No.1. That's the sound U described 2 me."

He put his head back on the pillow, touched by her efforts.

The following evening Dimitri cancelled his dinner engagement with Jody. With an hour to go, and as the hostess prepared to put a rack of Welsh lamb into her kitchen oven, Dimitri telephoned to say that he was delayed because of an extended meeting. He was sending the car to pick her up at eight o'clock. He'd cut the call before Jody had uttered a word.

She arrived with the chauffeur at the Dorchester Hotel at eight-forty and was soon tucking into a glass of white wine and canapés with a verbose Dimitri. He spent a shorter amount of time on his more usual charm offensive and quickly launched into extended detail about the contract he had negotiated for the exporting of his coal production into the Ukraine.

"Jody," he continued, as he drank some more vodka, "they tried to re-negotiate the price of the coal fifty minutes before my representatives were due to sign." He slammed his fist on the table. "Jody, big mistake. Nobody tries it on with Dimitri Petraffus. They received a call from a friend of mine in the Ukrainian trade association. It was a short phone call, Jody. They signed fifteen minutes later. It is worth fifty million dollars. It is only the start."

"That's a lot of coal, Dimitri."

"I own very big mines, Jody."

He picked up her hand and kissed it.

"Me and my team will present to Harriman Agnew Capital tomorrow."

She raised her eyebrows and asked with whom he had organised this.

"You will speak to Mr Andrew Agnew," he roared. "We'll arrive at eleven o'clock. You'll raise me ten million pounds and I will be saying a very generous 'thank you' to my friend Jody!"

As can happen in the Sporades, the afternoon thermals disappeared and the Harriman's boat drifted southwards towards the Greek coastline.

They were all together on the upper deck. Lucy had covered herself in sun block and applied a surgical approach to her three children. Scarlett was already becoming conscious of her figure and directed her mother carefully during the procedure. Lily was playing with her games console and laughing. Tabitha was feeling the heat and hiding under a huge straw hat. After speaking on the radio, Charles rejoined his family. He told them that the winds would pick up in about an hour's time. It was very hot. Lucy checked everybody again. She was absolutely paranoid about skin cancer.

Charles poured everybody a glass of fresh fruit cordial and then, to Lucy's surprise, announced to Scarlett, Lily and Tabitha that they were going to have a new baby.

He laughed. "It might be a brother!" he said.

Lucy looked at him in surprise.

"Charles," she hissed. "I haven't seen my doctor yet."

"You are the doctor, Lucy. Remember?" her husband replied, beaming.

Scarlett hugged her mother, Lily scored a record number of points and Tabitha said "a brother, ugh".

Charles wrapped himself around his wife and they lay down on their cushions as the sun beat down on them.

Lucy had been watching her husband with some intensity. She could see that he was, for much of the time, lost in his thoughts. But he was showing no further signs of struggling with his battle against alcohol. She knew herself that the abduction of Tabitha had given him every reason to give in to his demons. Time and again he had agonised over the bottle of scotch he placed in front of himself. His temper was frayed and his nerves were tested. He did not give in. He kept talking about the fact he was making a choice about how he wanted to live his life.

She suspected that he was thinking through something else. She realised that she was better advised to leave him alone. He would, in due course, tell her about it.

"Andrew, you've been saying that we are short of new market opportunities. I'm convinced that Dimitri could be a good client."

"But you know nothing about him, Jody," Andrew argued.

"But that's your job. Every month I send salary slips to that lot out there. Let them perform."

"They will. Of course they will, but ten million pounds, for us, it will absorb all our resources."

Civil war broke out at Harriman Agnew Capital at lunchtime. During the preceding two hours, Dimitri Petraffus, his accountant, his lawyer and a woman who was never really identified, gave – what was accepted by those present – a dazzling presentation on his coal mines in southern Russia.

Dimitri did most of the talking. The accountant gave an impressive speech about international accounting standards and focused on Jody throughout. The lawyer produced a document which he said was a copy of the contract signed the previous evening with the Ukrainian customer. It was in Russian. Dimitri showed a final slide indicating that the required fund-raising was ten million pounds. He then announced that the valuation of the company would be sixty million pounds. And in a year's time the shares could have a value of three hundred and sixty million pounds.

He looked directly at Andrew. "Read your financial pages, Mr Agnew. What are the deals the markets want? Mining. Look at Glencore. I'm bringing you a wonderful opportunity."

"Dimitri," Andrew said, "Glencore is the world's largest commodities trader. It was valued by the market at over six billion pounds on its flotation on the London Stock Exchange in May. It's Swiss-based. It had all the heavyweight finance houses behind it. Its competitors are Anglo American and Rio Tinto."

Dimitri roared with laughter.

"You catch on well, Mr Andrew Agnew," he laughed. "Now let's talk about money." He took some papers from his briefcase.

"I pay you a fee of three hundred thousand pounds and four percent of the funds you raise. That will be another four hundred thousand pounds. On the day you pay ten million pounds less your costs into my bank account I give you free, Mr Andrew Agnew, shares in my company. I will give Harriman Agnew eight million shares representing about three percent of the total of our shares. I am sure you can work out what that will be worth when our shares go to the London Stock Exchange."

Oliver was the first of those present to calculate the answer of nearly eleven million pounds.

Dimitri, his accountant and lawyer, and the unidentified woman, left the offices soon after this exchange.

In the conference room Andrew was seeking the opinions of his colleagues. The tone was set by Gavin.

"Brilliant. Jody, you are a star," he said. "It'll take every waking hour we've got but Duncan and I can raise the money. Jody, you are going to see the accountants this afternoon. The lawyer has agreed to meet with ours tomorrow morning. Melanie, Martin, will you get the regulatory matters underway. Abbi, Dimitri will go down a treat with the fund managers. You should start preparing the institutional presentations immediately. As Dimitri said, after the success of Glencore, they're all looking for mining deals."

The whole room turned towards Gavin in complete surprise. He had spoken at some length without using a single expletive.

"Would you like me to research his mine and the Russian coal industry?" asked Sara.

"Why?" snapped Gavin. "It's all here in the presentation. Why do we need you?"

"Andrew!" Oliver slammed his fist on to the table. "I'm head of corporate finance. I knew nothing about this deal. I accept that Jody was right to seize the opportunity but we are rushing headlong into a transaction we know nothing about. I don't like the way it's being done and how you're all being dazzled by the money."

"If that's what public school taught you," shouted Gavin, "I suggest you fuck off and become a professor of knitting! Bloody City Fiction. 'It's a gamble'," he mimicked as he glared at Sara. "Crap. Raising two million pounds for that will exhaust our contacts. The institutions will bite our hands off for this coal mine." Gavin looked at Oliver. "Stuff your publisher. Let's do some real business."

"Andrew," Oliver pleaded. "You can see what's going to happen. If you allow the deal to go ahead, I can see City Fiction being pushed aside. I can't do it on my own."

"Not on your own – with me," said Martin.

"Thanks, Martin," said Oliver. "With Martin. But we need our client base. That has to include Gavin and Duncan."

"Forget it, fairy feet!" shouted Gavin. "We're going to raise ten million pounds and make this company a fortune. Jody, what's my commission on ten million?"

"Far too much," she smiled.

"I really do think you should allow me to have a look at the background and the industry." Sara turned to Andrew. "I can have a report on your desk in three days."

Gavin looked at her with undisguised menace.

"I don't know what you're fucking doing here, Sara. I never wanted you interfering with our deals. I could have researched City Fiction standing on my arse."

"I think you mean head!" roared Duncan.

"What I'm trying to say, Sara, is keep your fucking face out of our business. Got it?"

Oliver turned to Andrew.

"Andrew, you must step in. This is unacceptable behaviour."

The chief executive tapped the table. "Meeting closed. Dimitri's transaction goes ahead. Jody, my office please."

That evening, Sara, Martin and Abbi decided to catch the tube train down to Embankment station where they walked a few hundred yards to find a pub. They wanted to be away from Queen Street.

Martin put their drinks on the table and looked at his two companions.

"This isn't going to be easy," he said. "How are we going to split our time between these mines and City Fiction?"

They remained silent for a few moments.

"Oliver's out on a limb," said Abbi. "Andrew is the boss. We have to go with Dimitri."

"Gavin and Duncan are capable of raising the funds and it'll boost our company performance," said Martin. "I accept he was rude to Sara today – but we're used to that."

They sat together quietly in the dark interior of The Royal Oak in Witham Street.

Abbi was the first to speak again.

"We must try to complete both deals. We can't leave Oliver on his own."

"I worry that his mind's more on Alistair's sister, to be honest," said Martin.

The two women looked at him in surprise.

"I didn't know you were a gossip, Martin," laughed Sara.

Abbi left the table and made her way to the crowded bar. She returned with another round of drinks.

"Any further thoughts?" she asked as she placed the glasses on their table.

"She's pretty hot," said Martin.

"No, Martin," chuckled Abbi. "About us helping to complete both deals."

"Let's face facts. Gavin is deciding everything."

They turned and faced Sara.

"She's right," said Abbi.

"But I smell something. Dimitri's not right. He's bought Gavin, I reckon."

There was a pause while they reflected on Sara's statement.

"And Jody, perhaps," said Martin.

"I think I'm going to have to help you all out," Sara said, in a quiet voice.

Andrew poured his partner a glass of sherry and reached for his gin and tonic. They were sitting on the twelfth floor balcony of their flat overlooking Regent's Park.

"As days go, Rachel," he said, "today was up there with the best."

He then explained in some detail about the appearance of the Russian entrepreneur, the deal and the fund-raising involved, and the clash between Gavin and Oliver.

"It's unusual for Jody to be involved, isn't it?" Rachel observed.

"In the sense that finance directors do not normally generate new business, very unusual. But her role is very important. She seems to have Dimitri's confidence and that will be helpful in obtaining all the financial information we will need."

"I get it about the possible earnings and how it could be a great result for you. But why Harriman Agnew and why are you so sure you will raise the ten million?"

"Two good questions. The first is simple. Ten million pounds sounds a lot but it's below the radar of most of our competitors. I suspect Dimitri has been doing the rounds and has found he is too small in City terms. Secondly, and this is so important, markets follow trends and at the moment, with the buying from the Far East, the price of energy and minerals continues to rise. There is virtually no new business activity within Britain because of the state of the economy. The institutions desperately need to invest their funds if they are to make returns for their shareholders. I share Gavin's view. We can raise this money."

"Yes, and make yourselves good bonuses... What about Oliver? I'm worried because I sense that he's really your main back-up."

"He was damaged today and he didn't deal with matters very well. He never saw Gavin coming and if I'd intervened it would have diminished Oliver's authority. My hope is that he can still complete the transaction for City Fiction."

"I think one more small sherry is in order," decided Rachel. She replenished her glass and sighed.

"I don't know what really goes on but my suspicion is that Oliver is the front man. He is good with clients and staff. The dirty business of fund-raising is for Gavin and his pal. What's his name?"

"Duncan Hocken, and you're right, especially since we lost Ian Bridges."

Andrew relaxed back in his chair. Rachel had hit on his major worry. Gavin and Duncan had no intention of helping to raise the funds for City Fiction.

Oliver closed the curtains, lay back in his Clerkenwell lounge, and listened to the music of Franz Liszt. "Not Russian," he thought to himself, "but Hungary is pretty close."

As the sound built up he read the CD cover notes:

"He was the greatest piano virtuoso the world has ever known. He literally redefined what ten fingers were capable of, and such was the

sheer force of his musical personality that it took just a single touch of the piano keys to have adoring women collapsing at his feet in a swooning feint."

He decided that the next time he entertained Amanda, the background music would be Franz Liszt.

The CD started with the Hungarian Rhapsody No.2. He read more of the cover notes:

"This piece features exuberant emulations of the cimbalam, 'rubato' violins, and the driving syncopated rhythms of the contemporary gipsy band."

This was followed by Sara's chosen piece, Liebestraum No. 3, a number of attractive compositions, and then the Mephisto Waltz No 1, described in the notes as:

"A no-holds-barred depiction of the tavern scene from Goethe's Faust, in which a bored Mephisto decides to inject a bit of pep into the rather drab proceedings by grabbing a violin and playing havoc with the local band's waltz tune. The dancers are then encouraged to abandon the formality of the waltz for a ravenous orgy of love-making."

Oliver was struggling to connect his memory of 'ascent', 'mountains' and Russian piano music, plus the drums, but Sara had been compelling with her recommendation.

He listened to the nearly twelve minutes of the Mephisto Waltz. He replayed it and replayed it again.

He picked up his mobile and texted Sara.

"Mephisto Waltz. Great try. See what you mean. Not my music. Back to the Russian composers. Thanks for trying. O."

Sara read the message quickly and threw her mobile back on to the bed. She returned to her screen and acknowledged with her thanks some information which had come in from Moscow.

She didn't go to bed at all that night. She spent nearly two hours pulling the documentation left by the Russians apart. She ended up with three lists. The first was names, the second had country breakdowns and the third was a series of random thoughts.

She began a series of emails to her contacts and several replies came through almost immediately. Sara was quickly

177

puzzled. Most of the responses confirmed the accuracy of the information that was given in the client proposal.

She realised that the task ahead was likely to be more complex than she had first thought.

She was certain that Dimitri Petraffus was a fake. She owed it to her employer to find out his true background. She was also determined to damage Gavin.

Oliver arrived at Elm Tree Road as Laurence Llewelyn Bowen was reaching the half-way stage of his Sunday morning programme on Classic FM. He had selected Elgar, Chopin and an obscure Austrian composer. There was no Russian music and no 'da-de-da'.

Amanda appeared at the front entrance to her flat looking radiant in a white track suit. Oliver was sitting in his car waiting for her. She put her bag on the back seat, joined him in the front and kissed him lightly on the lips. They drove to her fitness centre where they changed and attacked their schedules on the various computer-based machines. Amanda discussed her latest printouts with one of the trainers, the conclusion being that she was very fit indeed.

They returned to her flat just before one o'clock. Amanda put a chicken in the oven and poured them both a glass of cold white wine. They sat down on the balcony chairs and looked out towards Lord's Cricket Ground.

At this point in time, and somewhat unexpectedly, their relationship began to go wrong. In fact, it began to go very wrong. She wondered later whether it was her fault for having too high a level of expectation.

Amanda was starting to wonder whether she should go to bed with him. For some reason, he chose this moment to tell her about his discussions with Sara over the possible composer of the piece of music he was trying to identify.

As an exercise in romantic tactics, it was a disaster.

"I hope you didn't talk to her about us," Amanda snapped.

"No, no," he spluttered. "Anyway, what's your problem with her? Her report on City Fiction really helped you out at our end..."

"You're the head of corporate finance. Why did you need some immature, scruffy girl to make the decision?"

"She's not immature. In fact, she's pretty together for her age. She's just uncomplicated. She speaks her mind."

"So I've experienced," said Amanda. "Anyway, I don't want to talk about her. When are you going to speak with Alistair?"

He was flustered by her question and tried to disguise it by going back into the kitchen to fetch the bottle of wine. He returned and refilled their glasses. He then took a deep breath and told Amanda about Dimitri Petraffus and his coal mines. She wanted to know everything. She realised the threat to City Fiction almost instantly.

Oliver sensed the growing tension. He therefore sat back, picked up his glass of wine, and took her through the various issues.

"Amanda, Sara is just a researcher working for the corporate finance team," he said. "I like her and I enjoy her company. She took an interest in trying to help me identify the piece of music I'm seeking. But that is all and there is no need to discuss her any further."

He looked at Amanda but she was not showing any facial expression. She spoke suddenly.

"Let's get this right, Oliver. Ian Bridges, your key salesman, has walked out. Duncan and the other bloke are going to raise ten million pounds for some Russian who has walked in off the street. Abbi is now concentrating on the investor side instead of coming to us – and Sara is texting you in the middle of the night about the source of some piece of music. When are you going to make progress on raising the money for City Fiction?" Her face was stony cold.

"And," she continued. "What the hell is going on with us?"

"I won't let it fail," blustered Oliver. "I won't let you down, Amanda."

She put her glass down hard on the table top.

"I need to talk to Alistair," she said.

When she returned to her flat, two hours later, the chicken was slightly over-cooked.

On Monday morning, Dimitri and Jody met for breakfast at Simpsons-in-the-Strand. Jody had spent a great deal of the weekend trying to analyse the accounting information Dimitri's team had delivered to her.

The Russian was in an ebullient mood and ordered a full English breakfast. She selected the bowl of fruits. He talked non-stop and, somehow, the key issues that she wanted to discuss passed them by.

Dimitri suddenly announced that he had a meeting at Coutts. He would walk west along the Strand and the chauffeur was therefore available to drive her to the Harriman Agnew Capital offices.

As they stood outside the restaurant, Dimitri opened the passenger door and took out a small bouquet of flowers, which he handed to Jody. He kissed her lightly on her cheek.

"Remember, Jody. I always thank the people who help me."

When she arrived at the office and entered the conference room she realised that the meeting was just starting. She sat down next to Andrew.

Gavin banged the table and distributed several small piles of papers.

"OK, people. Much to do."

"Where's Duncan?" asked Andrew.

"On a plane," replied Gavin. "Let's go through my progress report. It starts..."

"So you're chairing this meeting?" asked Oliver "I thought that would be my job. Seeing as I'm head of corporate finance."

"You are, yes. But this is my deal. You stick to City Fiction. The draft document is taking shape. Thank you, Martin. Melanie, you are still finalising 'know your customer' and money laundering checks."

"They're certainly supplying what we want, Gavin. There are five directors and we have a file on each. The only problem is that much of what we have been given is photocopied material. I'll stretch a point but on passports I must see the originals."

"I took that up with Dimitri when I met with him on Saturday morning," said Gavin. "He's arranging for copies to be certified by the lawyers. So that's one thing sorted out."

"You met Dimitri on Saturday?" queried Oliver.

"I'm more than willing to coach you on customer relationships, Oliver," Gavin replied.

"Lawyers who are in Russia?" said Melanie.

"Bloody lawyers, Melanie. Look them up on the website. They're a big firm. If you're going to keep on bloody asking for things, we'll lose Dimitri as a client."

"Actually, I'm having the same difficulty with the accounts, Gavin," said Jody.

"Oh for fuck's sake!" cried Gavin. "Martin. The draft document?"

"Is in great shape, Gavin. They've supplied some marvellous sections, including photographs of the Donetskii Basin, geophysical reports, drilling surveys – just what we need."

"Ok. Abbi. How is the investor presentation shaping up?"

"Well, Gavin," she replied, without any warmth, "they'll come across strongly. Dimitri will want to dominate but, as he's the key strength, we'll let him have his lead."

"Where's Duncan?" Andrew asked again.

"He's on a plane to Russia, Andrew. The seven mines are south of Moscow. If you look at page fifteen of the presentation you'll see the various locations."

"What will he do while he's there?"

"It's really down to me, Andrew," said Jody. "I told Gavin that I was struggling with the accounts and he asked what would bring me the most comfort. I replied that if I could substantiate the amount of coal which the reports suggest is present I would feel much happier. If the coal is there, the strength of the balance sheet is effectively underwritten."

"Ok, thanks, Jody. Sara – are you doing anything useful?"

"What do you mean?" responded Sara.

"I mean – are you playing a fucking part in this deal? Bring some of your brilliant research ability to help Martin with the document."

Sara looked towards Abbi and then back to Gavin.

"Make up your mind," she said. "You said you didn't want it."

Gavin looked at the table and then at Martin.

"Martin," he ordered "I want a draft of the document by lunchtime on Friday. You have five days. We can then all work on it over the weekend and we'll call in the lawyers to comment on it next Monday."

"You're sure you know who you're dealing with?" asked Sara.

Gavin exploded and told Sara, in between the expletives, to mind her own business.

"Just asking," she said, as she stood up and walked out of the room.

Oliver met with Alistair at lunchtime. It proved to be a difficult conversation as he was unable to conceal his frustrations. Abbi was due to be visiting City Fiction to discuss further progress on the investor presentation but had phoned to postpone. Martin had been scheduled to email a list detailing all the professional firms and their addresses and the draft EIS document. These had not been received. David Singleton was ready to meet with the reporting accountants. Jody had insisted on being present but had emailed to cancel the meeting.

Alistair was telling Oliver about the success their eBooks were having, but suddenly he stopped and picked up his phone. He punched in a number. "Can you join us please?" he asked.

Amanda entered the room, avoiding Oliver's eyes.

"Amanda told me about your conversation yesterday. Please take me through it again," Alistair asked.

Oliver told him about the Russian deal, leaving very little out.

"But you're head of corporate finance, are you not?" Alistair said.

"Well, yes, I have to keep reminding myself of that," replied Oliver.

Alistair asked him to leave the room while he talked to Amanda in private. After twenty minutes, he was called back in.

"You'll understand, Oliver, that we aren't happy. But both Amanda and I still retain our confidence in you. We suggest you sort matters out and get our transaction back on the rails."

On his way out, Oliver tried to approach Amanda. She turned away.

"The problem is still the same," said Martin. "Andrew is going along with it. He is transfixed by the fees and he really does believe that Gavin and Duncan can raise the money. All ten million pounds of it."

"It's a great presentation we've got ready," said Abbi. "Really strong. The photographic stuff on the mines is compelling and Dimitri is a natural. He scares me to death."

"I think he might have scared the living shit out of more people than just you," said Sara. She looked at her watch and said she had to leave.

She later met her Liberal Democrat MP friend. The sex was quite enjoyable. The foreplay, which involved a tirade against the party leader Nick Clegg and other cabinet members, bored her senseless. But she needed access to certain files.

Chapter Nine

Duncan arrived at Moscow Domodedovo Airport at eight-thirty on the Monday evening. He was met by a dark-suited middle-aged man who told him that "Dimitri sends his apologies. He cannot be here. He will meet you in the foyer of the hotel at seven o'clock tomorrow. He says he has to fly out on Wednesday morning and therefore we will need to visit all the mines tomorrow".

The next morning, after breakfast in the hotel restaurant, Duncan was waiting, as instructed, in the foyer. He knew they had travelled to the south of Moscow but he had little idea where he was exactly. When he arrived, Dimitri was in an expansive mood and hurried Duncan into the back of a black Mercedes, where he handed him seven folders. Each, he explained, represented one of the mines, which collectively made up Dimitri's businesses.

After about thirty minutes Duncan was aware that they had entered a courtyard through an entrance in high brick surrounding walls. After exiting the car, the party went into an administration centre and on through three heavy doors before reaching a conference room. There were six quite youthful people, three male and three female, sitting around. As he sat down, the Russian members of Dimitri's staff applauded him.

Quite quickly several more men arrived, the lights went off, a screen descended from the ceiling, and a coloured picture of the headquarters appeared.

Dimitri stepped forward.

"Mr Duncan Hocken from England, we welcome you," he said.

"We are going to tell you about our businesses. There will be eight speakers, including myself. The first is Stanislav Viddor, who is my deputy, and who will tell you about the mine here, our biggest producer of thermal coal. This will be followed by a further six presentations about our six other mines. This will take us forty minutes. We will then visit each of the mines, one by one. I understand that you wish to measure how much coal we have underneath the ground. I gave this information in London. However I have asked my technical manager, Spirio Mustov, to present an analysis at the end of this session."

The deputy chief executive duly made his speech and then handed over to the first of the six other speakers. Each used a panorama of slides to show their mines before handing over to the next speaker. All spoke in Russian and were translated by a fair-haired, middle-aged woman, who never once smiled. At the end, Spirio Mustov put up slide after slide of figures and told Duncan that their estimate of the total volume of coal in the seven mines was three hundred tons. Duncan knew that one ton of coal was valued at two hundred thousand pounds – so this meant the value of the coal was over two hundred million pounds.

Following the serving of coffee, Duncan was whisked away by two of the Russian workers, who took him out of the office block and across the courtyard into a changing room. There appeared to be two groups of miners: the first, who occupied the left hand rows of benches and who were changing into their overalls, and the second, who had just arrived at the surface at the end of a nine hour shift. They were rather quiet. After stripping off their clothes, they were heading for the showers and toilets. Many had congregated in an adjoining area, where they were smoking cigarettes.

A man approached Duncan and indicated that he should change into the green clothing that he was holding out for him. Duncan thought about the security of his briefcase and laptop but decided that he simply had no choice but to follow the sign language and change. He was then provided with a pair of high sided boots, tight fitting but just about wearable. When the two workers saw that he was ready he was led out of the changing rooms and down a breeze block passage towards what was clearly the entrance to the mines.

He was given a safety helmet and it was indicated that he should wear it immediately. They passed through two steel doors and into a lift entrance. Three other people followed them.

The cage was secured and down it went. Down and down until it stopped with a jolt. During the next hour, Duncan estimated that they walked perhaps three miles. The pace was unrelenting. At times they stopped as a railway engine towing trucks loaded with coal passed them and twice he was instructed to shelter in a specially constructed safety recession in the rock face. He was told to face the wall and then he heard an explosion and smelt the stench of cordite.

He observed that every miner was working very hard. There seemed to be no talking. He saw several coal faces where men using electric drills were loosening the rock and others were extracting the coal. This was then being shovelled into trucks on the narrow gauge railway line. There were dual track areas where the outgoing and returning transport passed each other and the shafts were lit by main lights attached to thick cables housed above the tunnels.

The pace was intense and Duncan realised the pathways were following an upwards gradient. The sweat was pouring off his face and he could feel that his underwear was soaked. But still they went on and on. At one point, Duncan was offered bottled water, which he drank greedily. When he needed to relieve himself he just stopped and peed into the side of the rocks like everyone else.

As he was seriously beginning to wilt in stamina, they reached the entrance to the lift cage. The door was closed and within minutes Duncan was back on the surface. He was taken to the changing rooms where he stripped and showered gratefully. A man appeared with fresh underwear and laughed. Fifteen minutes later, Duncan was reunited with Dimitri in a cafeteria. He accepted a large mug of tea, but declined toast and jam.

"You see my beautiful mine!" bellowed Dimitri. "Your Jody. She keeps emailing me. How much coal is there? Now you can tell her!" he yelled, as he slapped Duncan on the back.

They were soon away, with Dimitri leading the party to what immediately seemed to Duncan to be a series of loading bays.

"My new fleet of Yarovit trucks," explained Dimitri. He then called forward Spirio, who was accompanied by an interpreter.

"Mr Mustov wants to tell you that each truck holds..." He stopped and engaged in an intense dialogue with Comrade Mustov, "...er...er... thirty tons of coal." He paused. "Yes, thirty," he concluded. They exchanged further words. "We have seventeen trucks of which you can see eight waiting to be loaded." They spoke again. "We turn the trucks around...around...back and forth." Duncan nodded to indicate he understood what was being said. "Around...yes...three times a day. We move..." Further conversations took place. "We move one thousand five hundred and thirty tons of coal a day." There was now quite a pause as the interpreter listened to Spirio. He began talking again. "This is our largest mine. The other six produce, working six days each week...er...yes...produce...between five hundred and a thousand tons of coal a day."

Duncan tried hard to stay on top of the maths of Dimitri's coal production but, at this point, he simply gave up. He knew that his task was to verify the value of the coal deposits but a combination of Russian hospitality and an avalanche of statistics was exhausting him.

Meanwhile, back in London, Sara and Abbi decided to have lunch together. Sara was pale and quiet. She was wearing a bright yellow dress which even Andrew had said was inappropriate for the office. Gavin had commented that if she wanted to impersonate a budgerigar, then that was her choice.

Abbi was neat, perhaps a few pounds over the doctor's weight chart, but she wore it well. She was wearing a dark striped business suit which had thin white lines running vertically in the material. She was fair and kept her hair short and didn't wear much make-up. She was continuing to live with Jonathan, and continuing to forgive him for his one stray night.

"Gavin is driving everybody crazy today," Abbi said. She was eating a Mediterranean vegetable pizza and drinking white wine. Sara was nursing a large gin and tonic and nibbling on some mixed nuts.

"Jody," continued Abbi, "is rushing around London having meetings with accountants, Melanie is shouting down the phone at her lawyers, Martin is on version seven of the document. A normal day!" She laughed.

"How is the presentation going?" Sara asked.

"Dimitri is in Russia. He's back on Thursday. Don't tell anyone, Sara, but it's a doddle. It's so easy to put together. The mines look great."

"If it's all genuine," said Sara.

"Yes. But we're checking everything out. Duncan's counting the coal as we speak!"

Sara looked down at her phone. She was waiting for an email. She left the table and returned with fresh drinks.

"Tell me what you think about Oliver."

Abbi smiled. "Any particular reason?"

"He can't cope with Gavin."

"He's not getting any support from Andrew. I've had a difficult morning with City Fiction. They're pretty angry. Oliver's over there now. What does he say to them?"

"It's just about money, isn't it?" said Sara. "Dimitri's seduced them all."

"Yes, Jody included – and she's influencing Andrew."

Duncan would have preferred to travel in an open truck so he could see the countryside, but Dimitri had other ideas and the black Mercedes was soon transporting them to the second mine. After about half an hour they stopped and Duncan found himself in a road-side restaurant. He later realised that Dimitri drank nearly a third of a bottle of vodka during their stay. He tried hard to limit his own consumption of Russian beer. They had been joined by Stanislav Viddor, Spirio Mustov and an interpreter. The atmosphere was ebullient, with Dimitri hugging everybody. The new member of the group was a dark-haired woman in her early twenties, who spoke very good English. Duncan was vaguely aware that she was using the various gaps when the others were taking toilet breaks to move closer alongside him.

"My name is Yolanda," she said to Duncan. "I'll be with you for the rest of the day."

189

Duncan turned and noticed that she was indeed very attractive. She was wearing a dark trouser suit and a simple necklace. Her skin was flawless and her perfume was provocative. Duncan was, however, trying to resist a further glass of Russian beer.

They were soon travelling again and the interpreter joined Dimitri and Duncan in the car. Yolanda described the countryside they were travelling through. "We're now arriving at Mr Petraffus's next mine," she announced after a short while.

They turned into an open cast mining area in which there were three pitheads and about fifteen miners milling around. At the base of a pile of coal, several were shovelling it into a truck which was almost full. Behind it were another five trucks, all already fully loaded.

Dimitri indicated they were leaving. Duncan turned to Yolanda and said he would like to have a closer look and to go down the mine. Yolanda talked to Spirio who shook his head and pointed to his watch.

Yolanda put her arm around Duncan. "We have much to see," she said. "Mr Mustov says you will go down the next mine."

Twenty minutes later they stopped at what seemed to Duncan to be a road-side tavern. The drink flowed and Yolanda continued to interpret the conversation.

"Mr Petraffus is happy today." She paused as she searched for the English words she needed. "Tomorrow he will sign a big contract and on Thursday he will go to London where you will raise him lots of money, Duncan. You are a lovely man." At this point she kissed her English guest on the cheek.

They were soon travelling again and quickly reached the third mine. Duncan looked down at his file to try and identify which of the other six mines they had seen. Yolanda told him the name but he had trouble reconciling it with his list. Dimitri grabbed Duncan, pulled him out of the car and together they almost ran around the work area. It was another mine, with cranes and piles of coal. The usual loading of his fleet of Tarovit lorries was taking place.

"Look!" cried Dimitri.

"Mr Petraffus says you are impressed, Duncan," laughed Yolanda. "There are seven lorries here. We have a big fleet."

The cavalcade moved off again and Duncan noticed that there now seemed to be four vehicles. Yolanda remained attentive.

They arrived at another mine and this time Yolanda told Duncan that a schedule of underground explosions was about to commence and that it was not safe to enter the compound. Duncan told Yolanda that this was not satisfactory and that he must see the mine. Dimitri became annoyed and there was a hurried conversation with Stanislav.

Suddenly Duncan was asked out of the car and he, Stanislav and Yolanda walked towards three lorries being loaded with coal. Dimitri remained in the car making phone calls. Duncan insisted on taking a photograph of the logistical operations.

They were soon travelling again. Within the next hour the same exercise was repeated at the next two mines. It was now getting dark. Duncan grabbed Yolanda's arm and pulled her to one side.

"Yolanda. I must see the next mine, please. I must go down the mine shaft. I must see the coal."

"Of course you must, Duncan," she acknowledged. She spoke to Dimitri, who roared with laughter. They boarded their vehicles and left the area.

They stopped after ten minutes and Dimitri led the way into a house just off the main road. They all sat in a lounge and tea and cakes were served. Before they left, a bottle was brought out and the Russians applauded. Small glasses were filled and Duncan groaned as he felt obliged to take part in the toasting of the health of Mr Petraffus.

An hour later they arrived at the next mine and before Duncan knew what was happening he was stripping down, putting on overalls and descending down a mine shaft extremely fast. When the lift hit the bottom Duncan exited the cage and was violently sick. Nobody took any notice.

He soon found himself in the car with Dimitri and Yolanda. Comrades Viddor and Mustov were no longer with them. He asked the interpreter what was happening and he was told that they were on the way back to the hotel.

He glanced down at his notes.

"Yolanda," he said, "we've missed a mine out."

191

"No, silly Duncan, you have seen seven mines. You fell asleep in the car. We woke you up and told you we were passing the opencast mine. Mr Petraffus pointed out the lorries, if you remember."

They arrived back at the hotel and Dimitri rushed round and dragged Duncan out of the car. He hugged him. "So. See you in London on Thursday. We raise the money. Yes?"

Yolanda went with Duncan into the hotel, saying she needed to speak with him. He went to his room, checked his emails, showered and changed, before rejoining Yolanda in the lounge. She had also changed into a tight, white cocktail dress.

She had ordered a bottle of wine. Duncan sat down and she poured a glass for him. As she handed it over, she placed her hand on his arm.

"Mr Petraffus says I am to answer any questions you have and to make sure that you enjoy our evening together."

Duncan drank some wine.

"Yolanda," he said. "I need to meet with Spirio. I'm in a muddle with the figures. I must list each mine and provide London with an estimate of the coal reserves. It is essential."

"Of course, Duncan. I will organise for Mr Mustov to join you for breakfast tomorrow morning. But now we must enjoy the evening."

He lifted her hand from his thigh.

"And I must go and work, Yolanda. Thank you for your help today."

"But Duncan," she protested, "I have a pleasurable evening organised for us. A pleasurable night..."

Duncan smiled and stood up.

"I'm sorry. I'm off to my room to write up my report."

As he reached the lifts, he turned and saw Yolanda was talking urgently into her mobile. She looked very concerned.

Both Lucy and Charles decided after a week that it was time to return home. The three girls all agreed – seven days sailing the Sporades was enough. They wanted to get back to their friends in Ealing. Tabitha rarely left Scarlett's side and Lily grumbled about the food.

But there was another reason. Lucy and Charles had, in principle, reached an important agreement, which had had a big impact on both of them.

Charles did not have an alcoholic drink once during the holiday. On the evening that he and Lucy realised they were both thinking in a similar direction he was very tempted to break his newly found self-discipline. But he and his wife had now decided on their future together. He was choosing the way of life he wanted to follow. He was in control. His old friend, the bottle, had long departed.

Duncan had ordered a taxi for eight-thirty in the morning. He was due to leave Domodedovo Airport at one o'clock. Spirio Mustov hadn't appeared at breakfast but Duncan had a far more pressing matter to worry about.

When he woke up in his bedroom he found a parcel on the table. He opened it to discover ten thousand pounds in English fifty pound notes. He repackaged the money and took it to reception, where he left instructions that it was to be returned to Mr Dimitri Petraffus. It only occurred to him later that the receptionist never questioned his instructions or asked for any further details.

He had sent an email to Jody earlier in the morning.

"Jody. You want 300 cubic tons of coal. I know just where to find it!"

He was gambling that when he reached London and completed his calculations the coal deposits in the mines owned by Dimitri would justify the valuation of the company.

As his plane levelled off at thirty-five thousand feet above Russia, Duncan smiled to himself and thought about Yolanda. He wanted to tell his wife about how strong willed he had been. On second thoughts, he decided that was not such a good idea. He accepted a drink from the stewardess.

"It's the Russian way of doing things," he laughed to himself as he relaxed back into his seat.

The key document reached Sara through the post. She texted the Liberal Democrat MP:

"Got it. Let's meet up soon. S x"

193

As she studied the papers she began to realise that the only solution she could think of was decidedly risky.

Gavin banged the table.

"Brilliant, Duncan. What a report. OK team. We have a client with seven mines and millions of tons of coal. Martin, you are a star. What a document. Brilliant. Melanie. Don't you dare let me down. You get the fucking documents from the lawyers or you don't come back to this office. Abbi. Great, great, great. The best presentation we have ever produced. Oliver. You have said nothing. Right. We spend the rest of the day signing off. If anything is unfinished then fucking finish it over the weekend. Dimitri was delayed but he flew into Heathrow earlier this morning. He has meetings over the weekend but is all ours from Monday morning onwards. Abbi, we have six institutions to see on Monday, right?"

"Right, Gavin," she replied.

"Ok, we will raise ten million by the end of next week," he announced.

Andrew sighed inwardly and texted Rachel to confirm that their trip to the Far East was looking quite probable. The money for Dimitri would be raised and the fees, commissions and shares would make the directors of Harriman Agnew Capital rather wealthy. He could go East without any worries.

"Sara. What the fuck are you still doing here?" asked Gavin.

Abbi was reluctant to postpone their trip to France – she and Jonathan wanted to stock up on French wines and cheeses. But there was something about Sara's tone of voice that worried her. They met on Saturday morning at Abbi's flat and Jonathan joined them after an hour. At first they dismissed Sara's plan as idiotic. But as more and more detail emerged Abbi began to waver. It was, however, Jonathan, as an outsider, who eventually made their decision.

"Are you really sure, Sara?"

She nodded without words.

"There are other ways," continued Jonathan, "and if it goes wrong you'll be in real personal danger. I'm not sure that we could reach you in time."

There was no response.

"Right, ok, we're with you," stated Jonathan.

"Are we?" said Abbi, looking intently at Sara. "You realise that you'll have to be Sara Flemming. There's no time to create a false identity."

But Sara just nodded. She had Gavin in her sights.

Could it be, thought Oliver to himself, 'Night on Bold Mountain'? Was this the piece of music that was proving so elusive to identify?

He was still reeling from the week's events and, in particular, the putdown administered by his colleague during the Thursday meeting. He had tried to discuss events with Andrew, but the chief executive seemed dazzled by the potential earnings from the Russian deal.

Ascent, he thought. Could 'night' be mistaken for 'ascent'?

He had spent his lunch hour in the Barbican music shop, discussing his mystery music with the manager. He couldn't get it out of his mind. The piano start, the strings, the move up the scales, the trumpets and the drums.

"It could be one of 'The Five'," the manager suggested.

Oliver was then introduced to this group of Russian composers, sometimes also referred to as 'The Mighty Handful' or even 'The Mighty Coterie'. The manager became expansive, as was usual when he found a rare, willing listener. He managed to deliver the following information in about two breathless minutes.

Their formation began in 1856. Two Russian composers, Mily Balakirev and Cesar Cui, met and were joined a year later by Modest Mussorgsky, and then by Nikolai Rimsky-Korsakov in 1861 and Alexander Borodin in 1862. In that year all were in their twenties, apart from Rimsky-Korsakov who was only eighteen. All were self-trained amateur musicians. Their nationalistic approach to composing, based in part on village songs, Cossack and Caucasian dances, church chants and church bells, created their reputation for reaching out for the "soul of Russian music".

Looking down the list of works by Mussorgsky, it was Oliver who spotted 'Night on Bold Mountain'. He could barely contain his excitement. "Ok, that's enough history," he said. "I've a feeling we might have identified the composer!" However, disappointment immediately followed when this proved to be an orchestral piece without piano.

Nevertheless, as far as Oliver was concerned, Mussorgsky could well be the composer of the music he sought. On the advice of the manager he purchased a CD containing 'Pictures at an Exhibition'. Perhaps the most famous of Mussorgsky's piano works, this was composed in 1874 following the sudden death of the composer's friend, the artist Viktor Hartmann. The music was written as a dedication and to celebrate an exhibition of over four hundred of the artist's works in the Academy of Fine Arts in Saint Petersburg.

Late on the Friday evening, in his Clerkenwell home, Oliver turned down the lights, poured a glass of white wine and let the music wash over him. However, he only heard the first few bars of the two Promenades which introduced the main sections. As he nodded off, he missed Mussorgsky's depiction of the motion of walking through the picture gallery.

At around ten past nine in the evening of a glorious July day, Dimitri was smiling to himself in the lounge bar of the Dorchester Hotel in Park Lane, and pondering whether to telephone for an escort to entertain him during the night ahead. The usual charge was one thousand pounds, and there were no limitations. He drank some more vodka. He was pleased with the day's work. Tomorrow in his hotel bedroom he would rehearse for the start of Monday's presentations. He was frustrated that he had been unable to contact Abbi, whom Gavin had found out was in France. Nevertheless, Dimitri was ready for Harriman Agnew Capital to raise ten million pounds, which he anticipated he could double in about three weeks.

The waiters were busy scurrying between tables to answer the demands of some impatient guests. The pianist was playing a piece by Debussy which she followed with 'God Only knows', made famous in the 1960s by The Beach Boys.

Dimitri was tired, but enjoying the adrenalin that came with the anticipation of making money. He needed a woman and had a number of ideas on how he would spend his time with her. He refused to wear a rubber. The agency knew that and charged extra, without any protest from their client. He decided that he would make the call.

He had already noticed the two women two tables away from him. The redhead he didn't fancy but the skinny girl with the crop top and leather skirt took his attention. As he raised his glass to his lips, the two women suddenly stood up and the redhead began screaming at her companion.

"You slut! You whoring slut! Touch him again and I'll fucking..."

She didn't finish her sentence, instead swinging her open hand hard into the other girl's face. The girl was knocked backwards, stumbled and then fell across the next table and right into Dimitri's lap. He instantly held her to him, enjoying the feel of her in his arms, and stared in amazement at the attack. The management arrived in force and took hold of the redhead. They asked the girl, still being held in Dimitri's arms, whether she wanted to press charges. Between her tears she managed to shake her head. The manager asked her if she needed medical assistance, but Dimitri announced that he would look after her. Another member of staff brought a bag over and placed it by the girl. The redhead was led away and the tables were straightened.

Dimitri had now positioned the girl into the space beside him. He snapped his fingers and, following a terse order, a brandy was served. She gulped it back. There was a reddening weal across the side of her face. She located her bag and took out some tissues and a tube of cream which she applied to her injury.

"What's your name?" asked Dimitri.

"Sara."

"What was that incident about? Why did she hit you?"

"She thinks I want to steal her boyfriend. They're breaking up and she needs an excuse. I was in the way." Sara looked at her rescuer, wiping her tears away with her hand. "May I have another brandy please?" He snapped his fingers at a waiter. The drink was served and once again Sara finished it rather quickly.

"My name is Dimitri. Dimitri Petraffus. I own coal mines in Russia. I am here on business."

"You're on your own?" asked Sara.

"I have staff here," replied Dimitri, "but tonight I'm on my own."

Sara picked up her bag and said that she needed to go to the cloak room. Dimitri followed her with his eyes and decided not to telephone the agency. When she returned she'd put on a white top.

"Are you married?" asked Sara.

"Three times," roared Dimitri. "I like you."

Slowly she began to feel comfortable in his presence. She soon recovered her poise and when Dimitri invited her to have dinner with him, she accepted. She said she had to make a phone call. She went outside and returned eight minutes later.

After they'd finished their meal, Dimitri asked Sara if she would care to join him in his bedroom for drinks. She refused. They carried on talking and Dimitri asked her many questions about herself, her work (she was a researcher for an MP) and her male friends. Again Dimitri suggested they should go to his room for the evening. He offered her one thousand pounds. This time Sara accepted his invitation.

They reached the tenth floor and entered his suite. Dimitri disappeared and took a shower, before reappearing in a white towelling robe. Sara handed him a large vodka from one of the four bottles she'd found by the ice bucket. She'd switched on the music system and the sound of Beethoven filled the room.

"Now, Dimitri," she laughed. "Why don't you tell me why you're really in London? You haven't told me the truth."

"You're a clever girl, Sara," he said. "But why should I tell you?"

"How about because every time you reveal something interesting I'll remove a piece of my clothing?"

"Ok. Good. I like that game." Dimitri re-arranged the table so that they sat opposite each other with the bottle of vodka between them. Sara had put some ice in a small bowl. While Dimitri stood up to take a phone call, she slipped a pill into his drink.

"Good, we start our fun." He undid his robe, but Sara stretched across and pulled the two sides together to cover his masculinity.

"I am raising ten million pounds from some people in the City. What will you take off?"

"Nothing. That's not enough. I want something much more interesting. Who are these people?"

He was beginning to slur already and Sara realised she had to slow the process down.

"OK. I will tell you. I am raising money on my mines south of Moscow in the Donetskii Basin. A firm called Harriman Agnew. They are getting it for me. Now, you take off your top."

"No. Not yet. You must try harder. Why's that interesting?"

"Because I only own one mine. They think I own seven!" Dimitri roared with laughter and Sara took off her top. She was wearing a pink, low cut bra. She had neat, full breasts and her nipples were pressing against the material. She poured Dimitri another drink.

"Dimitri. You're a naughty boy. But how, if you own one mine, do they think you own seven?"

"You English. You love paperwork. All I do is understand what you want and give it to you. They keep telling me 'it is FSA regulations'."

"FSA?"

"Financial Services Authority. They scare them all. Not me. Rules make it easy. I read the rules. Me and my lawyers, we work out the answers. You take off your clothes, Sara."

"You make it sound far too easy," said Sara, as Beethoven continued the evening concert in the background.

"As I say, you clever girl. I tell you what happened. You take off your clothes."

"We'll see, Dimitri. What happened?"

"They sent a nice man called Duncan to see us. He was a tough guy. We tried with him with a woman. She was a beautiful Russian hostess. He said 'no'. We gave him a lot of money. He gave it back."

Sara took off her bra and Dimitri's erection shot out from under his towelling robe.

"Wow," exclaimed Sara.

"You remove your skirt," ordered Dimitri.

"So how did you fool this…what did you say his name was... David?"

"Duncan. We planned it carefully. We showed him our mine. My only mine. We then take him to see another five mines. He could not hold his drink. He thought he visited six mines. But before we arrive at each mine, my lorries reach that mine before us. Sara," he roared out, "he counted the same seven lorries five different times!"

Sara took off her skirt.

"Even better, Sara…We don't even own the other six mines!"

"Dimitri, you're a clever man, aren't you?"

Sara took off one of her hold-up stockings.

"Two mines owned by my competitors. I had to take some armed guards for a little… persuasion."

Sara took off the other stocking.

"You take off your knickers now, Sara."

"Dimitri, you fooled this man but it can't be as simple as this. You laugh at our rules but it can't be that easy."

"Take off your knickers," ordered the Russian.

Sara's heart rate was now in excess of one hundred and twenty. She knew she was entering into dangerous territory. She removed her final item of clothing. Dimitri stared at her.

"Open your legs!" he commanded.

"Dimitri. I want you to fuck me as hard as you can."

He took off his robe and displayed an amazing amount of body hair. He went round to Sara, pulled her out of her chair, and dragged her to the bed.

She grabbed his penis and encouraged him to lie beside her. She went down on him and began sucking, but sat up suddenly.

"Dimitri," she cried. "One more vodka." She leaped off the bed and went to the bottles. She poured two glasses and into one she dropped a pill which she had hidden earlier at the back of the refrigerator.

"Dimitri. We can fuck each other. But first you must tell me how you fooled them."

"Simple, Sara," said Dimitri, fondling himself. "Money. It is always money. There's a firm of lawyers in London. For a million pounds they prepare everything. Title deeds, directors' forms. Everything. At Harriman Agnew there is a man called Gavin Swain. I have never found anyone so ready to believe anything I tell him. Money, Sara. Money money money. Now we fuck."

Sara knew that the pill needed one minute to act. But she had miscalculated Dimitri's body weight and the dosage supplied by her former graduate boyfriend, who was now researching bio-chemistry drug development, was ten grams short. Suddenly, he pulled her underneath him, pushed her legs open and tried to enter her. She screamed and he slapped her. She pulled her nails down his face, but he punched her and bit into her left nipple, refusing to let go. She squeezed his testicles and he roared in pain. He punched her in the stomach and while she was winded he turned her over and tried to enter her from behind. He used his body to hold her down and pushed his finger into her anus.

Sara was reaching the point where she could resist no more but, suddenly, the pill worked. Dimitri started to moan and rolled off her, onto his back. He began to snore.

Sara rushed to the bathroom and was violently sick. She was bruised and bleeding. She sat on the toilet for ten minutes and cried, before returning to the bedroom and checking on the snoring Russian.

She then splashed water over her face in the bathroom, dressed and collected her things. She also located three small recording machines from around the bedroom which she had positioned earlier when Dimitri was in the bathroom. She switched them off and put each in to her bag.

From inside the fridge she extracted a small jar which she had deposited earlier when she was serving Dimitri his vodka. She then took a pair of latex gloves from her bag, went over to Dimitri, opened the jar and pulled the foreskin down his penis. She slowly rubbed the cream – which contained a substance her ex-boyfriend told her would "do the trick" – over his glands and pulled the skin back up. She then applied the cream to his testicles.

Her final act was to go through his briefcase and find a number of documents with the name of a London firm of lawyers on its heading.

She left the bedroom and pressed the 'Do not Disturb' button.

Dimitri Petraffus spent the next three days in a Harley Street clinic as his private doctors tried to ease his burning pains and to identify the sexual disease they assumed he had contracted. He made several frantic calls to a firm of London lawyers.

Lucy and Charles Harriman were safely back in Ealing and the girls were all asleep. Tabitha was in bed with Scarlett.

"No doubts?" he asked.

"I'm certain, Charles. It gives us a future."

They had reached a point where neither mentioned the issue of alcohol. She felt that if her husband could stand firm during the abduction of Tabitha it was likely that he would continue to rebuild his life without drink. Their decision to change their way of life was the security they needed for the future.

It was Jonathan who first spotted Sara across the foyer of the Dorchester Hotel. He and Abbi had decided to wait just ten more minutes before calling the police.

He rushed across and caught her as she began to fall. Abbi arrived shortly after and took Sara in her arms. She had now discarded the red wig.

"Get the car, Jonny," she said.

"I'm ok, Abbi. I've got it all on tape." Sara clung to her friend. They struggled over to the entrance and attracted a number of stares. When Jonathan arrived with his car, Sara slumped on the back seats and they quickly left Mayfair, arriving at Abbi's flat at one-thirty in the morning. Jonathan took the tapes from Sara and promptly drove off.

Abbi helped Sara into the lift and up to her flat. She took her into the bathroom and switched on the shower. She then helped Sara undress, turned on a powerful hot water spray and soaped her from top to toe, before gently pulling her out of the shower and drying her with two warm towels. She led her to a guest room and helped her into the bed, closing the door behind her.

At eight o'clock the next morning Sara and Abbi were in the kitchen drinking freshly percolated coffee. Jonathan arrived at eight-thirty. He handed Sara two discs.

"The first one, Sara, has everything on it. The second we can listen to now. It's the one you can play to your colleagues. There are two bits I had to leave in. I'm sorry. I wish I hadn't but it was the only way to relate Dimitri's confessions to what you were trying to prove." He paused. "I've destroyed everything else and I've forgotten everything I've heard. My suggestion is that you throw the first disc into the Thames, but that's your decision."

At eleven o'clock Abbi and Sara were sitting in the conference room at Harriman Agnew with the chief executive.

"I think, Abbi, you have some explaining to do. Why is this so urgent?"

"Andrew, I'll let Sara tell you, but you need to understand that she has made an immense personal sacrifice to get the information you are about to hear."

Sara took a deep breath. She began by explaining that she had immediately distrusted Dimitri Petraffus, but that Gavin had rejected all her offers to research him. She had obtained information on his background from a private source and discovered that he was a fraudster.

"You can prove this?" asked Andrew.

She said that she could but she'd realised she'd need more if Gavin and Duncan were to be persuaded about the truth of the situation. Sara continued by saying that she also knew that Jody was very supportive of the transaction and, again, she would need extremely strong evidence if she was to prove her case. She explained the plan put together by her and Abbi.

"I'm not able to tell you everything that happened Andrew, but what you are about to hear is a recording I made in Dimitri's bedroom last night."

"Is this serious?" asked Andrew.

She switched on the CD player and watched as Andrew listened to the shorter, but equally as devastating, disc. On two occasions Abbi gasped as she realised what Sara had been through.

When the recording ended Andrew sat there saying nothing. After a period of utter silence he asked to listen to it again. Abbi went to the kitchen and made a fresh pot of coffee. Sara sat looking out of the window and watching the traffic on the Thames.

"What," asked Andrew, "do you think Dimitri will have done when he regained consciousness this morning?"

"I think he'll have needed to talk to his doctor," said Sara. She refused to explain why.

Oliver was puzzled by the phone call from Andrew. He was told that they were to meet tomorrow morning in Andrew's office at eight o'clock. Andrew refused to say why.

He spent Sunday morning at the gym, had lunch with some friends and, by the evening, was feeling utterly miserable. The text message arrived at just after nine o'clock that evening.

"Feeling rather low. A x"

He read and re-read it. He thought about his reply. He was increasingly worried about raising two million pounds for City Fiction.

"We're being tested, aren't we? O x"

The reply was immediate.

"No. Not you. Me. I'm so sorry. There were no issues. I just... sorry, Oliver. I'm crying which is not like me. A x"

Oliver groaned and poured himself a scotch. He read her latest text again. This girl most certainly knew how to play on his heart strings.

"I'll be joining you if I don't raise £2m. O x"

He thought that she wasn't going to reply. He waited for twenty-two minutes before the bell rang out from his phone. His heart skipped a beat.

"I just want to share everything with you. A x"

He responded immediately.

"You do have mood swings, don't you? O x"

The reply came within seconds.

"Guilty. A x"

Chapter Ten

Sara was dressed in a dark blue top and knee-length skirt, a more conservative look than usual. Her hair was swept across her face and she wore very little make-up.

"His real name..."

"I don't care a fuck what his real name is supposed to be!" shouted Gavin. "Andrew, how come this bloody woman has got us all in here? We have a huge week ahead and we're going to raise ten mil and make ourselves a lot of fucking dough. Got that, you little shit? Now shut the fuck up."

Melanie was the first to react to the outburst.

"Gavin," she advised. "I met with Andrew an hour ago. Take my advice and listen carefully to Sara."

"To that fucking skinny little... who fucking employed her anyway?"

He stopped speaking because Martin had left his chair and had his left arm around Gavin's neck. He was whispering in his ear. The room went silent.

Andrew asked Sara to re-commence her report.

"His real name is Sergei Villich Andropov. Dimitri Petraffus is an alias he has been using for the last three years. He does own the mine at Donetskii but he is heavily in debt and is said to be involved in arms shipments into the Ukraine. If we had raised him the ten million pounds it's suspected that he would have negotiated another weapons deal with the Somali pirates based in North East Africa.

"He was born in Eastern Russia and joined the army at an early age. During the military conflict in Afghanistan he was accused of raping three women and discharged from the army. For the past three years he has used the mining business as a front. He has money but he generally uses violence to achieve his aims."

"Prove it," snarled Gavin.

"I realised that it would be difficult to convince you of the truth. Dimitri – let's call him that for now – is clever. He has all the paperwork and my suspicion – and it's a trick he's pulled before – is that if we had withdrawn from the deal, say because Melanie was unhappy with the directors' documentation, he would have sued us. His lawyers usually win. We would have had to call on our professional indemnity insurance and put a report in to the regulators. Usually he allows the firms he sues to survive but it's expensive and disruptive."

"Prove it," repeated Gavin.

"My sources are reliable," continued Sara. "In fact, one is particularly helpful, but to get the information I had to give my word that I would not release the photocopy documentation I was given."

"I knew it – you can't. Meeting over," announced Gavin.

"The easy thing about you, Gavin, is that you are so wholly and pathetically predictable," said Sara. "I knew that however certain I was you would dismiss my findings. So last night I took the precaution of spending the evening with Dimitri in his bedroom."

"Ha! She's nothing but a cheap slut!" shouted Gavin, looking around him, his face contorted in a grin of pure malice.

"Sit down," said Andrew, as Martin stood up. "Sara, please continue."

"I tape-recorded what he said. I used my mobile and two separate machines. I have two discs. One captures the whole evening and I'll only allow that to be replayed under special conditions. The one I'm going to play you has been put together by an IT expert. He will swear an affidavit if necessary. It captures what Dimitri said about the mining transaction."

"Who's this 'expert' you refer to?" asked Duncan.

"Jonathan, my partner," said Abbi. There were looks of surprise around the table.

"Are you involved in this too?" asked Duncan.

"Jonathan and I were with Sara last night at the Dorchester. I think you should listen to the recording."

Sara pressed a button and for the next twenty minutes the voice of Dimitri Petraffus filled the room. Jonathan had found it difficult to extract his words alone and occasionally the circumstances under which the recording had been made became all too clear. As Duncan listened to the revelations about his trip to Russia he looked extremely agitated, but the air seemed to go out of him suddenly. He'd refused the girl and the money. Melanie sighed with relief on hearing this passage. She liked Duncan. He'd tried hard to see all the mines.

As the recording reached its climax and Sara was desperately trying to find out the truth about the scam, her agonies became all too obvious. She just stared ahead. The disc came to an end.

Andrew looked at Gavin.

"Gavin. You are suspended on full pay. Go home. I'll call for you in a few days. You are to make a full statement and email it to Melanie by twelve noon tomorrow."

"Go fuck yourself, you pathetic wimp!" Gavin yelled at Andrew. "You let all this happen! I walked all over you. Do you think I want to stay with this load of crap? I already have another job. I was going anyway. Two weeks' time I will be with..." He named a broker in the East End of London which – unbeknownst to him – was already under investigation by the FSA.

Gavin left the room.

"He has forgotten that I'll have to put in a report to the FSA," said Melanie. "He may find getting a transfer of his registration more difficult than he thinks."

"I suspect Gavin is heading for different waters." It was the first time Oliver had spoken.

Andrew now took charge. Melanie agreed on the work necessary to meet all the compliance issues and agreed that her full report should include the name of the London solicitors at the heart of the scam. Jody was asked to provide a financial analysis of the costs involved, including Gavin's severance package.

"He gets paid for being a total shit!" exclaimed Sara suddenly.

"That's the way it works," replied Jody. The room went quiet.

"So what happens now?" asked Abbi.

"I suggest we raise two million pounds for City Fiction," replied Oliver.

"I've been fighting alcohol for some years," said Charles.

Andrew sat opposite his partner in the lounge of his Mayfair club. He wondered if he should continue with his gin and tonic.

"I stopped about eight weeks ago. My family are behind me. When Tabitha was stolen I reached rock bottom and nearly gave in. You know that Lucy's a doctor. She's spoken to a consultant on my behalf. He's told her it's likely that I'll have to fight it for the rest of my life."

"Do you want to fight it, Charles?"

"When we lost Tabitha, in a strange way, I found out a few things. What really matters. That's what I want to talk to you about. The consultant said I can help myself by avoiding stress. Lucy and I independently reached a similar conclusion. Lucy is pregnant, by the way. She's going to return as a full-time doctor. Under Lansley's health reforms, her earnings are expected to exceed two hundred thousand pounds a year. She'll take eight weeks off for the baby. I'm going to become a house father. My career in the City is over, Andrew."

"Well, in that case… we have a conundrum, Charles," said Andrew.

"Conundrum?" asked Charles. "It's pretty clear to me. I want you to buy me out."

"And that's the issue, Charles. Rachel's father died last year. We knew he was financially astute but we recently had the full valuation of his estate. He picked the right dot-com stocks and stayed with them. Rachel will inherit around seven million pounds. We've decided to live in Hong Kong. Bloody Cameron. He's ruining this country with his liberal pals. We're off."

Andrew then updated Charles on recent events at Harriman Agnew Capital.

"If I'm honest with myself I've not dealt with events too well. I've allowed Gavin to run riot." He looked at Charles. "After all these years I'm still dazzled by the money." He smiled ruefully.

"I had a feeling you were leaving us, Charles, so I've invited Oliver to join us." Andrew explained the basis of his proposed offer to Oliver, which Charles supported immediately. It would mean that he and Lucy would have financial security.

On cue, Oliver had entered the club and was shown over to where his two bosses were sitting. He was provided with a scotch and water. He listened in total amazement.

"So there it is, Oliver. We are offering you the opportunity to complete a management buy-out of the firm. The price is three million pounds. Charles and I each get half a million now and the balance is interest free and payable as fifteen percent of post-tax profits until the debt is cleared. We'll both sign sub-ordinated loan forms so that this does not impact your capital adequacy requirements. We must keep the FSA happy. This is the name and number of a London banker who'll back you. You'll have to sell yourself to her but the facility is agreed."

"Is that Eliza Montegray who we just happened to have lunch with recently?" asked Oliver.

"By an amazing co-incidence I think it is," laughed Andrew. "She rated you."

Oliver stood up, walked away from his chair, ran his hand through his hair, turned round and sat down again.

"That's it?" said Oliver.

"Have you any questions?" asked Andrew. "Here's our offer in writing."

Charles went to say something and then realised that Andrew had worked out his situation some time ago.

After Oliver left the club, still in shock, Andrew telephoned Jody. He finished the conversation by telling her that if she wanted it, he would lend her one hundred thousand pounds, interest free, over ten years. He would also write off the ten thousand pounds which she owed him.

"Why?" she asked.

"Because," Andrew replied, "Oliver's going to need you."

Amanda was sitting in her favourite chair in the lounge of her flat. She was drinking a cup of fresh coffee. She had read the letter three times and even then she needed to spend more time thinking it through.

It was a long, carefully written missive. The first part was, for her, sheer poetry. The style, the individually crafted phrases, the stirring emotions… it all combined to create a wonderful

209

sense of destiny. It had not been necessary – but if the writer's intention was to dig deep and recapture past feelings, the result was a success.

The second section came as a complete surprise to her. She followed through the police involvement and their consequences. She read the long sentences and felt the man's underlying pain. Even though every word, each sentence, every paragraph had clearly been reviewed and carefully edited, there were more questions she wanted to ask and to which she needed answers. She accepted a woman might have written certain parts in a different way.

She stopped reading, stood up and went over to the full length mirror in her bedroom. She stood in front of it, turned round and looked at herself from top to bottom. She then studied her face. She wiped her eyes and went back to her chair and to the letter.

Her telephone rang and she allowed the answer-phone to click in. She listened to Alistair's request and decided to return his call a little later in the evening.

She read the penultimate paragraph again: it carefully summarised recent developments, the outstanding issues and their possible solutions. She paused again and thought through each of the proposed answers. She was, at this point, neither agreeing nor disputing any individual matter. They all led to one over-riding proposal, which completely overwhelmed her.

The final paragraph asked her to think things over and, when she was ready, to text a reply. She already knew her answer. She was not scared to respond or to find the right words. She was overwhelmed by a sense of responsibility. This wasn't a knoll in Regent's Park or a picnic by the side of the Thames. Her decision could, and almost certainly would, affect five people's lives.

An hour later she texted a short reply. It was neither "yes" nor "no". It was, however, much nearer to the positive.

She then thought briefly of Oliver, but decided to move on.

Oliver finished explaining the circumstances to his colleagues. He said that he had met with the bank director and they had agreed a loan of one million pounds. That would be paid out to Charles and Andrew. Their balances would remain as subordinated loans.

"What's subordinated?" asked Sara.

"I'll explain later," whispered Martin with a smile.

"In addition the bank will advance us an overdraft facility of another million, but I think it's too much borrowed money. I suspect that Charles and Andrew are underwriting it. We need to find a million ourselves. I can put in half a million." He had spoken to his father, who had objected quite strongly to being woken up in the middle of the Australian night.

Abbi rushed from the room and made several calls from her mobile phone.

"I'll put in one hundred thousand pounds," said Jody. They all looked at her.

"I'll talk to my husband," said Melanie. "I think we're good for fifty thousand."

"I haven't got any bloody money," said Martin. "How about I invest fifty thousand from my future commissions?"

"I'm in for ten thousand pounds," said Duncan, "providing I can do the same as Martin up to forty thousand pounds."

"So. We have seven hundred and fifty thousand pounds," said Oliver. "It's still not enough. We need a million."

"You'll give up and not complete the deal because we are a little short of the sum required?" exclaimed Melanie.

"Look at what our clients go through, Melanie. So many of them are under capitalised. It will be hard enough without worrying about cash flow. We have a reputation to rebuild. The market will know about Dimitri Petraffus. I must have a million pounds."

"We need to think about changing the name," said Sara.

"I've already searched the register," said Jody. "Chatham Capital is available. I've already registered it and all the web names."

"We still need to find two hundred and fifty thousand pounds," said Oliver. "I'm not committing without the extra money. Let's meet again in an hour's time."

For several of the potential shareholders in Chatham Capital, the next sixty minutes passed slowly. A few hurried and furtive phone calls were made.

Oliver asked all his colleagues to return to the board room.

"I'm sorry," he said. "I need another twenty-four hours. I can't find the extra money. The bank has said no and both Andrew and Charles have told me to find it myself."

"It's like the bloody dealing floor," said Duncan. "The last tranche is always the hardest because you've asked everybody."

"But you always find it," said Martin.

"There's always the one person you've forgotten about," added Duncan.

Abbi coughed and moved her coffee cup.

"Jonathan will invest two hundred thousand pounds," she said, "and my mum is lending me the rest."

There was a stunned silence.

"Jonathan has one condition," continued Abbi.

"Condition?" asked Oliver.

"Sara stays with us. If not, he's out."

"Can I have some shares, please?" asked Sara. She looked at her watch. She was going to her doctor for an examination and didn't want to be late.

Friday went well for Oliver. He had consecutive meetings with his lawyers, accountants and bankers. He met with each of the team, discussed their individual investments and answered their questions. Melanie continually texted to keep him appraised of her progress with the regulators. He made a phone call late in the afternoon. Sara had agreed to his proposal.

She stretched out and undid two of the buttons on her shirt. She had enjoyed their meal together and was gazing around the lounge of his flat.

"I was surprised to get your phone call, Oliver," she said.

The new head of Chatham Capital laughed. He explained that he wanted to share the evening with the person who had made it all possible.

"To be honest, Oliver, we all think you have the hots for Amanda Wavering," she said.

"Never believe a rumour," he laughed. "Surely I don't have to tell you that, Sara."

"I must go home," she said. "Can you call me a taxi, Oliver, and can you pay for it?"

He tried hard to persuade her to stay but she was determined to leave. As she reached the door she turned and looked at him.

"Oliver, have you read *The Girl who Played with Fire*?" she asked.

"The Stieg Larsson book?" he replied. "Alistair keeps going on about the series. I've read *The Girl with the Dragon Tattoo*. Why do you ask about the other book?"

"*The Girl who Played with Fire*..." Sara began. The phone rang and the taxi driver announced that he was waiting downstairs.

"You should read it," said Sara and she was gone.

Oliver poured himself a drink and felt a sharp pang of disappointment. He would experience another when he decided to play Mussorgsky's 'Pictures at an Exhibition' again.

As he slumbered on his sofa he realised that this wasn't the music he had heard on his car radio. The piano was wrong, the orchestra was wrong. He sighed. How many bloody Russian composers were there?

The five days, which began on Monday 18 July with a full meeting of the Chatham Capital team, were to prove exhausting for all those involved. The euphoria of the management buy-out was dissipated somewhat by the endless meetings with the bankers, the accountants, with Charles and Andrew and with the individual members of staff who were completing their financial arrangements. Melanie wondered if she should move into the offices of the Financial Services Authority in Canary Wharf, such was the amount of time she was spending with the regulators. One requirement was that any shareholder owning ten or more percent of a regulated business has to be individually approved by the Authority, which meant much more paperwork. Oliver was simply being pulled from pillar to post.

But, even in these tense and demanding circumstances, almost all his colleagues were watching their new leader mature. It was accepted that he had been undermined by Andrew and

213

the extreme behaviour of Gavin during the now aborted Russian mining transaction. He'd tried to assert himself as the then head of corporate finance, but the riches of Dimitri's deal had seduced them all. Jody, in a private moment, wondered if she had let Oliver down. Now it was in the past. Oliver had bought two new suits and had his hair re-styled. He walked around with an authority no one had seen before.

The one person who watched him more closely than anybody else was Sara. Oliver was lost in admiration for her resourcefulness and courage in undermining Dimitri Petraffus. He'd managed to retain the disc for a night before handing it back to Melanie and had played it in the privacy of his flat. He had been horrified by the muffled sounds of violence and overwhelmed by the lengths to which Sara had gone. Sara, for her part, just loved his growing authority. He reminded her of her late father and had several of his mannerisms. She had always thought of him as a decent, sporty, serious man but now she noted an inner fulfilment beginning to emerge. She'd asked him what his father thought about the buy-out and he'd taken an email out of his inner pocket and allowed her to read it.

It was not only Oliver who was growing up on the spot. Martin was showing increasing leadership qualities and it was he who insisted that everybody stopped whatever they were doing and attend a meeting in the conference room. He took the lead and Oliver was more than happy to allow him this latitude.

"Abbi, Sara and I met with Alistair and his colleagues at City Fiction this morning," he said. "There is some good news. Over the weekend, Abbi has worked on the investor presentation and this morning the lawyers have approved the document. We're ready to roll."

"And the bad news?" asked Melanie, fresh back from Canary Wharf.

"I'll let Duncan tell you," said Martin.

"Bottom line, market conditions are dire," he said. "I don't want to stir up issues but the reason Dimitri's business so appealed was that even in these times of recession there's always an investor demand for mineral and natural resources." He paused and drank some water; he knew that he was rebuilding his reputation with his colleagues. "That's obviously because demand from China, the Far East, South America and Africa is holding up prices." He paused again and picked up Abbi's presentation package. He waved it in the air.

"This is a great piece of work by Abbi, Sara and Martin. We've got clearance from Melanie and the salesmen's script has been approved. We're ready to sell the shares."

"So what's the problem?" asked Jody.

"There are two. City Fiction is in publishing. It's not oil or gas. It's much more speculative. Please read Sara's original report. It's all in there."

"I'm lost," said Oliver. "Sara's recommendation was positive."

"Agreed. But it focused on the risks involved and how Alistair needs to find winners. Sara's decision was to back him."

"No," said Sara. "That's not what I wrote and it's not what Abbi has put in the presentation. We focused on the annuity income." She stopped and turned to Martin. "Hey, look, fat man, I'm learning the lingo!" Everybody laughed, which helped ease the tension.

"Abbi and I are saying that the business is solid. Alistair is first class and Amanda is vital to the operation. What Duncan, I think, is talking about is that extra quality which makes an investor write out a cheque."

Oliver smiled. "You really are catching on, Sara. I had a pal who called it 'sizzle'. He'd say to me, 'Oliver don't show me a deal until it has sizzle'."

"So where's the sizzle in City Fiction?" asked Jody.

"That's the only problem," said Duncan. "The brokers are ready and keen to try to sell the stock."

"Ok, but you said there are two problems?" said Jody.

"The economy is in dire shape. It's continual bad news from America where Obama is fighting the Republicans on his budget deficit reduction proposals. The Eurozone is in stress with Greek debt, and now Italy, and add in Spain and Portugal. But I think the issue with our clients is the lack of growth. The second quarter's figures were awful. Cameron seems to want to

215

save the world and Osborne says we can get our bonds away. They're like headless chickens."

"No, I won't have that," said Oliver. "Cameron is showing himself to be a very decisive leader and Osborne has the confidence both of the City and the bond markets."

"Cameron is going to wreck the NHS."

The meeting stopped as everyone around the table absorbed the vehemence of Jody's statement. "Five bloody pledges," she said. "He has no idea what he's doing. He thought it looked good to sideline Andrew Lansley. The great Prime Minister giving another wonderful speech. He should try getting the NHS to work now."

"You sound as though you're talking from personal experience?" asked Melanie.

"No, no. It's just a friend of mine has had another bad experience. Just look at the reality. The closing down of the PCTs and the LHAs was supposed to cost one and a bit billion. The latest estimate is three and we know it'll be five. And, as yet, the bill is stuck in Parliament receiving the Liberal Democrat treatment and there are no savings." She slammed her fist on the table. "It's crap government."

There was silence in the room. Her colleagues were not to know that her outburst was based on the five page letter she had written to her MP at the weekend.

"Duncan," said Oliver. "What you're saying is that the sales team will have problems selling the shares."

"Yes. With respect, I don't really understand what Jody's talking about, but I do know that the clients are reading the newspaper headlines and watching news programmes. They're more risk averse than at any time since 2008."

"So what are you doing?"

"We're starting this morning. We'll have four of us on the phones. Let's meet at six tonight and I'll summarise what we've achieved. But I'm telling you not to expect too much."

The meeting closed a few minutes later. Sara nodded to Martin and Abbi and suggested they went out for a coffee. The range of drinks at Starbucks seemed more appealing than that of the staff room.

Amanda settled back on the park bench and sighed with contentment. Two hours earlier she had been rather nervous. She had thought through each person's point of view. She had carefully selected a modest, pastel coloured dress. She'd tried hard to listen to the others, but she'd also wanted to make an impact. As they had walked away to be taken home she knew she had achieved her aims. She was asked by the remaining person present if she had any further thoughts.

"Thoughts," she said. "Thoughts…" She paused and reached for a hand. "It's funny. What I'm thinking about now is so different to what I expected to be pondering over in my mind."

"OK. Develop that for me."

"I had a checklist in my mind and I was ticking the boxes. I expect that you were doing the same."

"No. I've only got one box to tick."

"Yes. I get that. It's easier for you. I have to think about my personal responsibilities."

"Why? I've done that already. You'll be wonderful. Just think what they've been through."

"But it's more complicated than that."

"So which boxes still remain unticked, Amanda?"

"I'm not sure there are any left," she said and smiled.

Charles Harriman opened the front door. He had been at the kitchen sink washing up the breakfast dishes when he'd heard the front doorbell ring. He looked at the visitor with a sense of concern.

"Mr Harriman. DCI Rudd. I was in the area and thought I would call in to see how Tabitha is getting on." Sarah paused. "Is Mrs Harriman in?"

Charles invited DCI Rudd into the house and she followed him into the kitchen. There was fresh coffee in the percolator and she gratefully accepted a cup, but refused the offer of a ginger biscuit.

"I know how busy you must be, so I appreciate you calling in," he said.

"You're obviously working from home today," she said. "You're in the City if I recall?"

217

"I was," replied Charles. He explained to DCI Rudd about his decision to change the way he lived his life; how the work of corporate finance no longer attracted him.

"The abduction of Tabitha made us re-evaluate our lives," he said. "Lucy has a good position as a doctor and I managed to sell my business. We've been very fortunate." He stopped. "What is going on at your end – what will happen to the Masters?"

"The slow wheels of justice are turning now," said Sarah. "He'll probably get a short prison sentence. The family are running the shop." Sarah paused. "So, your daily routine must have changed quite dramatically, Mr Harriman?"

"Being a house husband is pretty hard work," he said. "To be honest, I quite enjoy having more time with the girls. Scarlett is maturing all the time. She's the only one who talks about the kidnapping." He laughed. "And I certainly have the best kept garden in the area."

"Do you not miss the buzz of professional work?" she asked.

"Not really. I'm taking a greater interest in politics and I watch the news programmes during the day. The Eurozone crisis is keeping me occupied at the moment."

"My reason for calling was actually not just about Tabitha," she said. "I don't know whether you know, but the police these days are putting greater emphasis on our community work. We have several advisory groups and I was wondering whether you and Dr. Harriman might be interested in joining us. For all the wrong reasons your experience makes you very well placed to help us." She paused as her coffee cup was refilled. "We want to know if we could have handled the abduction of Tabitha any better – as an example of what I'm trying to say."

"You found her. What else mattered?" said Charles.

"What I'm trying to suggest – " DCI Rudd stopped speaking and took a call on her phone. "I have to go," she said. "May I call back one evening to pursue this further?"

"Probably not," said Charles. "Please don't misunderstand me. We'll always be grateful for what you did, but this isn't for us. I'll leave others to worry about the community."

Their eyes met as DCI Rudd stood up and prepared to leave and she saw something in his expression that concerned her.

She decided afterwards that Charles hadn't listened to anything she had said. He was, in her opinion, scared of something, but what that was she did not know. As she drove away, she saw Charles pulling up some weeds from his front garden in her rear view mirror.

Martin put the three lattes on the table.

"Is mine with skinny milk, fatso?" asked Sara.

He ruffled her hair and smiled.

"Duncan's not going to raise the money. I found his attitude pretty unconvincing," he said.

Abbi took a long gulp from the cardboard cup before replying. "I think he's feeling the pressure. He had rather aligned himself with Gavin."

"He did come out well after showing his strength of character in Russia," said Martin.

"But he said this morning that he can't sell the shares in City Fiction," said Sara.

"That's what I heard," he replied. "But let's wait until tonight."

"No," said Sara. "The atmosphere was bad this morning with Alistair. He and David Singleton are nervous. We have to demonstrate some progress."

"How?" asked Abbi.

"Well," said Sara. "Let's ask ourselves another question. Who put the money into Bloomsbury, for example?"

"We can get a list of the shareholders," said Martin. "But we can't approach them. They're not our clients."

"But," enthused Abbi, "what about the institutions which invested? We can present to them."

"If they'll see you," said Martin. "They're both public companies so holders of three percent or more are a matter of public record. Sara, just go onto the AIM and PLUS websites and look up the individual companies. It's all on there."

At six o'clock, in the conference room, Duncan reported that his sales team had placed fifteen thousand pounds of shares in City Fiction. The mood around Chatham Capital was decidedly dejected.

219

As Martin left the office with Sara and Abbi he recounted a conversation he'd once had with Ian Bridges. He told them that Ian had said that the key to raising money was getting the first investor. "Get a fund in and the others will follow."

Sara heard this and tucked it away. Her plan was already well under way.

"Coming for a drink?" asked Abbi.

"No. Things to do," replied Sara.

The additional commitments at Chatham Capital and the financial aspects of the buy-out of the business meant that, for Jody, time was at a premium. She reached the home in West London and immediately found herself in a meeting with the nurses and a doctor. The change in Ben's drug regime was reviewed and a nurse said she had already noticed an improvement. This was offset by their concerns that earlier in the day he had experienced a minor fit that was quickly halted.

After the meeting was concluded she spent an hour with Ben, who was not himself. She had been warned that the change in prescription might have a short-term effect. She talked to him nonetheless about England's winning cricket match against the Indian tourists but he curled himself in a ball and seemed unresponsive. He would not have understood much of what Jody was saying, but the doctors had taught her that the repetition of her voice would give Ben more security.

As she left the ward and looked at the other beds with their occupants, she experienced an awful sinking feeling.

Sara had listened carefully to the discussion on shareholders' lists. She spent the rest of the day downloading information on several publishing companies from the official AIM and PLUS Markets websites and from the individual businesses.

By three o'clock in the afternoon she'd identified seven London-based funds which had made investments into the sector. She then investigated each of the funds – she was particularly interested in the lists of directors.

It wasn't until an hour later that she made her discovery. It was exactly what she was looking for. She checked her facts one more time – he was a Peer in the House of Lords and a Liberal Democrat, and the fund of which he was a non-executive director had made investments into two publishing companies.

Sara sent a text message and she received a response almost immediately. At six o'clock that same evening she met with one Liberal Democrat MP – her former bed partner.

She'd decided that the only way she was likely to make progress was to tell the truth. She gave her companion a complete package of information on City Fiction and made her proposal. She said that she would be most impressed if an introduction could be made to a certain gentleman in the Upper House.

Sara had struck gold: the MP and the Peer were to meet later that very evening. The package of information was handed over and the MP himself was surprised at the enthusiasm with which it was received.

What neither Sara nor the MP could have known was that the Peer, now into his seventies, had spent the last two years writing his memoirs. He'd been a City Investment Manager and felt that he had some interesting tales to tell. He had found an agent who had, initially, taken the book to the two publishing houses in which his fund had invested. Both companies had rejected his submission.

As the Peer read the information on City Fiction he became more interested. The following day he visited the offices of his fund in Old Broad Street and met with the chief executive. The head of investments was called in and within an hour had distributed the information to his team. At five o'clock that afternoon a complete analysis of City Fiction was given to the chief executive.

A day later a decision was taken to consider an investment in City Fiction. A call was made to Oliver Chatham who, initially, couldn't understand how the fund was involved. At this point, Sara had picked up the news and met with him to explain what she'd done.

Twenty-four hours later, Alistair, Amanda and David completed a superb presentation to the analysts at the offices of the fund. They then had a private meeting with the chief executive and his non-executive director, and were asked to return in the afternoon. By five o'clock they were advised that, in principle, the fund would make available one million pounds. Alistair was elated and Oliver breathed a huge sigh of relief.

As they left the building they found that the Peer was waiting for them and swiftly invited them to join him for a drink at his club in King William Street. Once they had settled comfortably into their Edwardian surroundings, their host told them that he thought that he and several of his associates might be willing to invest in City Fiction.

"Of course it's not a condition of our investment," he said. "I just wondered if you would have time to consider my book?"

He handed Alistair a brown paper parcel and ordered a further round of drinks.

Duncan's sales team went into action the following morning. The news that the fund was investing opened the doors and by lunchtime Chatham Capital had provisionally booked the two million pounds for City Fiction.

"Three days' hard work ahead but we'll get there," he announced.

Alistair had spoken to his main freelance editor and overnight they both speed read the Peer's book. By lunchtime they had completed a four page critique and had delivered their report by courier to the House of Lords.

To their surprise, it was not bad at all.

Later on, when Oliver was to reflect on the events of the summer of 2011, it didn't escape his thinking that 'the deal' all started in the Polo Bar of The Westbury. He could recall with absolute clarity the early stirrings of his attraction to Amanda.

It was in 'the Haven for Lovers' of that same hotel that he found himself on the Wednesday evening following his fraught meeting with Amanda. He needed company and he was looking forward to seeing his colleague again. He'd never disguised his affection for Sara. They'd been thrown together by the City Fiction transaction, and it was her research report that had led to Harriman Agnew accepting the client. And it was now to be her analysis of the shareholder groups which would be the springboard to the successful fund-raising.

It was, however, her exposure of Dimitri Petraffus and her willingness to suffer personal abuse and danger which so affected him. She was beautiful, too, in her own way, but it was more her air of mystery that tantalised him. Men the world over will always chase what they cannot have.

He looked at his watch. She would be joining him in thirty minutes. Popular jazz played out around him and Louis Armstrong was suggesting that it was a wonderful world. Oliver smiled.

The ending with Amanda had come suddenly and unexpectedly. She had been in the offices of Chatham Capital delivering a package of documents to Melanie. Somehow she had heard a reference to Sara. The speaker had said he thought that she was meeting Oliver later that evening. It was a chance remark and it was not conclusive but it was enough for Amanda. She'd asked if Oliver was in the office and was told that he was out at a meeting. She'd returned to City Fiction and texted Oliver, asking that they meet in the Threadneedles Hotel in Lombard Street for a drink at five o'clock.

He'd said that was fine and she'd arrived at the bar area wearing a business suit. She went straight in for the kill, but he'd held up his hand and suggested he bought some drinks. He'd ordered two glasses of wine and allowed Amanda to explode. She'd told him that she'd always been suspicious about his attraction to Sara.

"Are you seeing her tonight?" she'd asked.

"Yes," he'd replied. "But it's just a business drink. She's a member of my staff."

"How many other people will be present?"

"Just Sara."

"Where are you meeting her?"

That was a more difficult question because Oliver had realised that The Westbury would suggest more than a business meeting. But Amanda had already moved on.

"Well, you'll find out soon enough but I'd rather tell you myself." She'd stopped and sipped some wine. "Zach has

223

obtained custody of his children. Apparently his wife had been stalking the headmaster at her school and the police became involved." She'd taken another sip. "Their divorce is going through – Zach has the boys and I'm moving in with them."

He'd wondered whether to tell her that this breached the terms of their deal, but decided this might not be the best move.

"Let's be honest with each other, Oliver. We've never really settled into a relationship. You're everything a woman could want but perhaps I've been looking for something different." She'd paused. "I'm fed up of the uncertainty."

"Are you ready to be a mother to two boys?" he'd asked.

"Zach and I have spent time with them. I'm their friend. Their new friend. Their mother will always be Zach's ex-wife. She's having therapy and is expected to recover. Zach has bought her a house."

They'd sat in silence for a few moments.

"We'll be a family and we'll add to it in due course. It's what I always wanted."

He wanted to say the right thing – somehow to indicate his genuine pleasure at her news and also his frustration that their relationship could now never be fulfilled. He achieved neither, because Amanda stood up, kissed him and walked briskly out of the hotel.

It took him some time to collect his thoughts. He had watched one of the most beautiful women he had ever known walk out of his life. Even as she left the hotel her vitality gave her the most seductive aura. She had simply said "goodbye". There had been no discussion, no appeal and no chance to change her mind. Oliver was still confused about his true feelings for her and, now he'd been rejected, was unable to decide what he really thought. He had wondered whether, if they had become closer, he might find that Alistair had too much influence. He wondered what Zach thought of her brother. She was going off to look after two boys and co-operate with a soon-to-be ex-wife – her feelings for Zach must be true.

He went back to his office and attended to his emails and phone calls. Both Charles and Andrew had called him, wanting the completion of the buy-out as soon as possible. When he left, only the salesmen remained as they debriefed with Duncan on the day's activities and results.

Now, two hours later he was waiting for Sara at The Westbury. He was surprised how excited he was feeling. He knew they were growing close, but felt some vague resistance on Sara's part. Tonight he intended to tell her how he really felt about her.

He wondered if he should tell her about developments with Amanda before deciding that this was not a good idea. He found his mind drifting away and recalling their times together.

Sara arrived twenty minutes late. It was the first occasion he could recall seeing her in a dress. She looked beautiful. Unfortunately, she was also holding the hand of a petite dark-haired girl.

"Oliver," she said, "this is my partner, Alex."

He looked at Sara and he studied Alex and his mouth dropped.

"I did try to tell you," she said. "You should have read *The Girl who Played with Fire.*"

"Of course," Oliver said to himself. "Steig Larsson's second book. Lisbeth Salander was a lesbian."

A smile played on Sara's lips.

"We're not staying," said Sara. "See you tomorrow."

He was staggered at the way Sara had come out to him. It was typical of her style. Her attempts to deflect his attentions suddenly made a little more sense.

He watched them leave and then ordered a large scotch. He would get a taxi home. He suddenly felt rather deflated. Nothing was going right. The music system was now offering, for some strange reason, Frank Sinatra and 'Strangers in the Night'.

He was that individual and he'd managed to lose the woman he had really wanted. How on earth had he allowed Zach to re-appear on the scene? He suddenly desperately wanted to contact her.

As he continued to ponder miserably on recent events, he realised that he could hear a familiar piece of music. He turned to his right, where he found a dark-haired woman with ear phones attached to her iPlayer. He could just make out the sound, 'da-de-da', and the violins and trumpets. It was his piece of music.

He smiled and introduced himself. She said that her name was Christina and, when he asked whether he might listen to the music himself, smiled and put the machine on the table. She turned up the volume. It was what Oliver had been searching for. He felt his spirits slowly begin to rise.

He told her about his search through the Russian composers.

"You want to know the composer and the title?" she said.

"Yes, more than anything," said Oliver. "Do you know them?"

"Oh yes," replied Christina. "But let's get to know each other first."

She was from Finland and worked for the Helsinki Tourist Board. She loved her subject and soon Oliver knew that her country had a population of five and a half million people, was a member of the United Nations, the European Union and the Eurozone and was considered one of the most peaceful countries in the world.

She called the waiter over and ordered vodka and tonics for both of them without consulting him.

"There are four countries with borders attached to Finland," she said. "If you can name them, then I might be willing to tell you the details of the music you want."

"You speak perfect English," he said.

"I do many things perfectly," she replied. "Now, the four countries that border my country."

"Sweden, Norway…er…Russia."

She clapped her hands. "One to go," she laughed.

Oliver clawed his memory for his school geography lessons. There had been some boundary changes. He could visualise the land masses and felt certain it was on the eastern side. Suddenly he had the answer.

"Latvia!" he announced.

"Oh, so close," she said. "I'll allow you one more go."

"It's south."

"Yes, yes, come on Oliver, you can get it."

"Estonia," he said.

226

She gave him a congratulatory kiss on the cheek.

"You are so clever, Oliver. That was difficult!"

Oliver glowed with pride. "Come on, Christina, please, the composer and the title."

"Oliver," she said, "I'm on my own tonight. I like you and I think I would enjoy your company."

He took a rapid drink of vodka and noticed that she'd signalled to the waiter for further supplies.

"We could make love listening to the music and afterwards I could tell you the composer." She had carefully hidden the screen of her iPhone so he could not see the name of the composer.

Oliver looked at her, gulped and burst out laughing. An hour later they walked together towards the lifts. Once they had reached floor five and entered the room, Christina closed the curtains and began to undress. She sat on her bed and indicated to Oliver that she wanted him to join her. He made a false start and she had to tell him that she expected him to take his clothes off as well. She turned up the music.

"Oliver, when it reaches the third movement there is a magnificent moment when violins, trumpets, piano and drums combine. First – we'll make love for an hour. Then we'll play the music. It takes seven minutes to reach that point. I want you to give me my orgasm at that exact moment."

"And then you'll tell me the composer?"

"No, then we'll start all over again!" She laughed. "But I promise you, Oliver – fulfil me and I'll tell you what you want to know."

And so their evening of passion began and soon their naked and perspiring bodies were rolling around the bed. 'Da-de-da' filled the room. They went through the first and second movements when, suddenly, Christina put her hand on his chest and pushed him away.

"Please put on your towelling robe," she instructed.

Oliver struggled to understand what was happening but before he could protest, Christina had slid off the bed and made her way to the bathroom. A few moments later she came out with a large fluffy white towel wrapped around her. She sat

227

down on the side of the bed and patted the space next to her. Oliver joined her and sat submissively.

"You're not making love to me, Oliver."

"Er...I'm doing just that, Christina. What more do you want?"

Christina smiled. "You are thinking about somebody else."

"How the hell did you know that?" he exclaimed.

"Is she as pretty as me, Oliver?"

Oliver's defences collapsed. "She's a golden beauty, Christina, but she's with another man."

"You love her?"

"Very, very much. I've only just realised. But it's too late."

"It's never too late."

"If only that were true."

Christina stood up. "I have a busy day tomorrow, Oliver. You must leave now. Go and find her."

He dressed and went to leave, but noticed she was checking her mobile phone.

"I don't suppose you're willing to tell me about the piece of music. The composer, perhaps?"

She picked up a cushion from the chair and threw it at him.

"No. Thought not," murmured Oliver, as he escaped through the door.

Chapter Eleven

Jody was simply overjoyed. The revised drugs' regime was having a real effect on Ben. He was a day away from his fourth birthday and he knew that his mum was going to make him wait before he could open the parcels lying at the bottom of the bed. She had called in at the Arsenal football club shop because she wanted to be sure that the shirt she bought was the latest being worn by the players. It had cost her an arm and a leg, but was worth every penny.

There were two other children in the ward. One was sleeping and the other had his parents with him. She started talking to her son. She told him about the formation of Chatham Capital and their success in raising the money for City Fiction. Oliver had pulled a masterstroke by suddenly announcing that everybody would get a bonus when the commission payment was received by the company. She was to get just under three thousand pounds after the savage deduction of George Osborne's taxes. That's how she looked upon it. She hadn't received a reply from her MP about her views on the NHS, but he was a Cameron supporter so he could do what he liked. She knew that there was a Boundary Commission report due in September which would recommend that the number of MPs was reduced by fifty, in line with the coalition agreement. She hoped that he might lose his seat.

She had had fun deciding how to spend her unexpected windfall. She was going to put one thousand pounds in her 'Ben' fund. She would pay off a similar amount from a credit card, buy a new outfit for the office and use the balance to help pay the latest utility bill.

She was on fire. She had been to the hairdresser and asked him for a different style. She had cleaned the flat from top to bottom. She had removed several framed photographs and stored them away. She was rebuilding her life. She loved the atmosphere at Chatham Capital. Martin was the central figure commanding the office, teasing Abbi, bullying Duncan and suffering at the hands of Sara, who never failed to bring his bulk into the conversation. One day he had found a package from Weight Watchers on his desk.

There was talk of a new client and the brokerage team had placed an AIM stock, raising over fifty thousand pounds.

Oliver spent a lot of his time with Jody and Melanie – they were the 'inner circle'. This was initially inevitable, such were the financial and regulatory demands on their time. But somehow, as the days moved ahead, it became the ethos of the company. Oliver was always available to anyone but their ownership of the business seemed to result in the individuals taking more responsibility. Their meetings were shorter and better focused. Duncan remained on the defensive but was concentrating his efforts with the sales team. Abbi and Sara were working together nearly all the time and, recently, they had surprised Jody by taking her out for lunch.

Ben was gurgling away and she wiped the spittle from his mouth. They had now talked together for thirty minutes and Jody sensed he was gaining in strength. She could resist no more. She reached to the bottom of the bed and picked up one of the parcels. She handed it to him. He tore it open and ripped off his top. Within seconds Ben was playing at 'No. 8' for Arsenal.

His sense of fun was returning, evidenced by several toothy grins. She noted from his chart that he was putting on weight and, when he held her hand, his grip seemed firmer.

She stayed at his bedside for three hours. He slept for much of the last hour, but then opened his eyes and became lively again. Finally, Jody kissed him goodbye and hugged him. As she left the clinic, she prayed that the birthday card that arrived every year would be delivered to her son on his special day.

Nick Rudd pulled his wife towards him and kissed her. He had relished their evening together which, in itself, was unusual. He told her about his teaching activities and a particularly gifted pupil who was being pushed too hard by her parents. He looked at his wife and stroked her face. He was deciding whether to ask her a question.

230

"Bit unusual for you, Detective Chief Inspector Rudd," he said.

Sarah loved it when her husband used her full title. Their opportunities for intimacy were limited by their dedication to their children and her crazy hours. When she had arrived home after finding Tabitha she had cried in his arms.

"What's unusual?" she asked.

"Why did you tell me all about this Charles Harriman? He's not done anything wrong, has he?"

Sarah hesitated before deciding on her reply. Her husband had this great gift for identifying her inner thoughts.

"It's what he might do, Nick. It just *felt* all wrong to me…" she replied.

"What might he do? He's adjusting to a new way of life. Give the man a chance."

Sarah hugged him and snuggled into his arms. She spoke into his chest but he heard every word.

"He was a coiled spring, Nick. He never looked me in the eye once. He's fighting something."

"Are you worried about the children?"

"I've filed a report to the family liaison officers and they're going to find a reason to visit the two schools. I think it's unlikely, though, that anyone's in any danger. Lucy Harriman would almost certainly pick up a problem if there was one." She kissed his neck. "No, I sense the danger is coming from within."

"So what are you going to do about it?"

"I've done all I can. My job is to solve crimes."

"Well said, Detective Chief…"

She interrupted by placing a finger across his lips.

"Perhaps not for much longer," she said.

He shot upright in bed and took her face in his hands.

"Spill the beans," he ordered.

"It's not confirmed yet, but I've been told to expect some good news any time."

"Not…?"

"Yes. Superintendent!" She beamed with pure happiness. "I just hope the new title doesn't affect your libido…"

He proceeded to squeeze the living daylights out of her.

"Well, I think it might be time to check, don't you, Superintendent Rudd?" he laughed. "Now, where are the handcuffs?"

Alistair sat at his office desk and sighed with contentment. He had finished reading a long report from Melanie Reid at Chatham Capital. It set out for him the details of the fundraising, the sources of the money, the new shareholdings, the procedures to be followed, the involvement of the company's lawyers and the date the two million pounds less costs would be received. She had set these out at some length and they totalled over three hundred thousand pounds. Alistair refused to be annoyed. He knew that this was the way the City operated. He mentally had £1.7 million pounds to spend and he began to allocate the resources to realise his dreams. He had received a report from David Singleton and several suggestions on how the additional money might be spent.

His first priority was to recruit a chief operations officer. He wanted to strengthen both the editorial and sales team and David needed a qualified assistant. He also wanted a new chairman. At this point, his thoughts turned to Oliver and Amanda.

He'd been briefed on developments at Chatham Capital and now realised that Oliver was not the right candidate for chairman. He would speak to him about it, but had also decided to take independent advice on the matter. As one door shut so another opened and he realised that the Peer whose book he was now publishing might well provide the answer. They were to lunch at the House of Lords the following week and he was planning to use the opportunity to raise the idea.

The more difficult decision he was facing concerned his sister's future. He was perplexed by her sudden decision to move in with Zach and even more surprised at her willingness to take responsibility for his two boys. She'd said it wouldn't affect her work but she was already arriving later in the mornings, even though she and Zach seemed to share the responsibility for collecting the boys from school.

And he was staggered by the almost immediate change in her. She had gone from being a fun-loving free spirit to a domesticated woman within weeks. As he'd once remarked to Sara, he found her relationships with men hard to understand and never really understood her 'deal' with Oliver. The only thing he knew was that she would make her own decisions.

He was nervous about raising these matters with her too. Their argument over Oliver's 'deal' and the hurt they'd caused each other with their intemperate words still cut deep.

He closed his file and prepared to go home. He knew, in his heart of hearts, that his sister was unlikely to be part of City Fiction for very much longer.

Duncan pushed his way through the crowd at the bar and bought two beers. He returned to the table where Gavin was subdued and not himself.

"So what gives?" he asked.

"Can't find any fucking work, Dunc."

"I thought that you were joining..."

"Never got there, Dunc. I had a letter from the regulators saying my registration was being suspended and I was not to undertake any brokerage work until I was recommended by an approved firm. I've visited all my mates but the markets are dead at the moment."

Gavin wanted to know what was happening at Chatham Capital and laughed ruefully when he heard about the role Sara had played in the fund-raising for City Fiction.

"Got her wrong, didn't I, Dunc?"

He finished his beer and stood up to go to the bar.

"Got it all fuckin' wrong, really ... as Martine never stops telling me."

Zach was away for the day filming in Wapping. He was completing a documentary on the black economy. It had started with a chance remark from a friend at a dinner party who was advocating that the twenty percent VAT rate was equitable. His argument was that the Revenue was taxing Middle England out of existence because they could reach them. However, millions of people trade daily in cash outside the tax system. Much local activity is now for 'back of the pocket' payments and the rise in VAT had increased the demand for non-tax payment deals. But the one tax that cannot be avoided is VAT and the dinner guest suggested it should rise to twenty-five percent. He countered the concerns of several of the other guests that it would hit the poorest by saying that the benefits system must help them. Zach had found several informers in East London who were willing to 'spill the beans' on the cash society. One was a middle-ranking drug dealer. Zach was due to arrive home at around six o'clock.

His two boys were spending the day with their mother. She wouldn't acknowledge Amanda, who simply took them to the front door and made sure they were safely delivered. She would collect them at four o'clock.

After dropping them off, Amanda went straight to the gym and completed a full programme of exercises. Her personal trainer told her she had let her regime slip. She settled into the steam room and enjoyed the heat and the perspiration as it gradually seeped from her pores down her skin. She left after twenty minutes, showered, completed thirty lengths in the pool, showered again, changed, had a fruit drink and then caught the tube into London and walked down Oxford Street. When she reached Regent Street, for some unconscious reason, she turned left and then right down Conduit Street. She reached The Westbury, entered the Polo Bar and ordered a glass of wine. She promised herself that she would drink only one glass because she had to collect the boys later in the afternoon.

The memories flooded back. She missed Oliver. He was still seeing Alistair on a regular basis and she was aware of the developments at Chatham Capital, but she made sure that they didn't find themselves together. Zach had encouraged her to talk about him and on occasions she did just that. But she could never really capture the roller coaster events of 'the deal'. And now here she was with a soon-to-be-divorced married man and two small boys for whom she was responsible. She could have been with Oliver.

What was it that Zach offered that had led to her sudden decision? He was charming and brilliant with words, spoken and written. He was serious and successful professionally. He was fun. He was smart – that much was certainly clear. His boys now had a future and his ex-wife would rebuild hers.

She'd re-read his letter on a number of occasions. It almost improved with each session. Had he seduced her? She thought about her own parents' early demises and her love for Alistair. He had said little about Zach. She sensed he was completely baffled by her choice, but they had settled back into a solid working relationship at City Fiction and she would soon be travelling again.

She and Zach had exchanged views on only one occasion about whether they should have children together or, rather, when they should start the process. Amanda had privately decided to wait at least a year because she wanted to develop her relationship with the boys.

As she finished her glass of wine and listened to the overture to 'Porgy and Bess' being relayed on the music system, she had a sudden jolt of realisation that she was not completely at ease with herself. She paid her bill, left the hotel, caught the tube home, collected her car and drove to collect the boys.

As she reached the path leading to the house, the front door opened and Zach's sons were pushed out of the porch and towards her. Their mother appeared and gave Amanda a strange look, something half way between a smile and a grin. She quickly disappeared indoors again and as Amanda buckled safety belts around the boys in the back seat of the car, she thought they seemed rather subdued.

Andrew and Rachel simply could not agree. For her, it was the shopping malls of Hong Kong that she adored. She spent hours in the air conditioned auditoriums, going up and down in the lifts and viewing shop after shop stuffed full of the latest global fashions. Hong Kong oozed money in every direction. She loved catching the ferry over to Kowloon. The shipping lanes were very busy and it was fun watching the junks trying to avoid the cargo boats. She was furnishing their flat with the latest designs because she had no restrictions on her budget. After the gloom and austerity of Britain this really was the new world.

For Andrew, it was the complete absence of graffiti. Every street was clean. There was no litter. There were no drunks. There were police everywhere. There was no violence. He knew that if he went behind the scenes where the eight million residents lived it would be different, but the Chinese authorities wanted Hong Kong and Macao to be showcases. The transport system was one of the best in the world. The Chinese were flooding in by plane, boat and train. This was where the growing rich from the People's Republic spent their money. The Hong Kong financial markets were booming; the West, Europe and America were a million miles away.

They had arrived and Hong Kong was their new home. Everywhere they went people were smiling. The service in the restaurants was immaculate and they'd been eating out most evenings. The old colony was much in evidence and there were many expats indulging in its financial success.

They had intended to try and stay in touch with their old life but within days they were being seduced by the adrenalin of the territory. Andrew was already speaking to the English finance houses and was planning to accept a consultancy before too long. Rachel was awaiting the arrival of her daughter from Laos and had surprised Andrew by asking if he minded if she flew to Australia with her. He had questioned whether she would be able to get the necessary visa but accepted the position. He would miss Rachel hugely but was already looking forward to seeing her in a few weeks' time.

Andrew had one more task to complete as he arrived at the post office. He had bought the card two days earlier and made sure that Rachel had not seen it. The carefully written salutation read:

"To my beloved son, Ben..."

Abbi clung to the railings of the cross-channel boat. She and Jonathan were getting their day in France at last. They'd decided to leave the car at Dover and travel as foot passengers to Calais, where they would spend four hours before returning.

Jonathan was taking his responsibilities as a shareholder in Chatham Capital very seriously. He was regularly emailing

Oliver with questions and on several occasions had offered some suggestions. He had used his IT skills to devise a transaction monitoring software program and, when Martin came across it, he immediately met with Jonathan and they were ready to start trial runs a week on Monday.

Abbi was surprised when Martin, their guest for the day, had arrived at the harbour with an attractive black woman at his side. She was his wife, Annette, and nobody at Chatham Capital had known about her. The reason soon became clear. She was a lawyer at the FSA, the regulatory body which covered Chatham Capital.

"We met at a Securities Institute evening," explained Martin. "Annette was giving a talk on regulatory procedures and we began talking afterwards. She's never stopped since."

Annette slapped his arm and laughed. "No business talk," she said. "It's so kind of you to invite us. The section I work on doesn't cover Chatham Capital, so don't worry, we'll have no problems today!"

As the ship left the harbour and reached the calm waters of the channel, Jonathan and Martin went for a beer, leaving Abbi and Annette to talk over coffee and Danish pastries.

They discussed their individual work and Abbi was surprised at how realistic Annette was in her approach to regulatory matters.

"Our problem," said Annette, "is that we only seem to meet the wrong-doers. In my section we have responsibility for over two thousand firms. I only get involved when there's a problem. When Martin talks about his work it seems like another world to me."

She paused, went to the counter and bought more coffees and pastries. She returned with her tray and smiled at Abbi.

"I try not to eat these things when Martin's around," she said. "Hey, by the way, who's this Sara that Martin talks to me about?"

Abbi told her about her colleague and Sara's teasing of Martin about his weight.

"Well, it's working," said Annette. "He's bought an exercise bike and gets up at five every morning. He spends an hour on it. Mind you," she laughed, "I can't complain about the results!"

Charles Harriman refused to wear an apron. Lucy had been forced to bite her tongue on several occasions when she'd found the linen baskets overflowing with dirty tops and trousers. They had agreed that Charles would take part of the washing to the local cleaners.

The rot began to set in with Lucy's promotion to an equity partner at Whiteoaks Practice. She was working longer hours and becoming more involved. When she told her husband that she'd agreed to join one of the new Budget Commissioning Groups, and that it would entail some evening work, Charles began to struggle. He recalled his conversation with DCI Rudd and remembered that she'd sent him details of some voluntary opportunities.

That was not the issue. He was proud of his wife. He relished taking and picking up his daughters from school. Their finances were solid and he loved the house. He thought that he was at ease with his battle with alcohol and accepted that City life wasn't for him anymore.

No, the daily problem he had, which he could not talk about with other people, was the stares he received from some of the other mothers when he collected his daughters from school. As they all stood waiting, he sensed their looks of curiosity and, he thought, judgement. There were other fathers around but they seemed somehow more at ease. He felt that he stood out. He started dressing down, trying to look more casual, but it changed nothing. There was a group of three women who centred their attention on him.

It was becoming more and more of an issue for him and he found he was dreading the afternoon task. He tried arriving a little later and then had a problem parking his car. One day he was late and the girls seemed upset when he reached them. They told their mother and Charles and Lucy exchanged some harsh words.

But the day his world imploded was provoked by such a simple event. As he arrived in the playground the trio of mothers laughed out loud and he was convinced it was about him. He took the girls home and they went to their rooms to change out of their uniforms, as was their routine.

He collected a bottle of scotch and a glass and went to the bottom of the garden where there was a table and two chairs. He placed the bottle on the table top and rested the photograph of his family against its side. He poured some scotch and picked up the glass. He brought it towards his lips and repeated, yet again, all the reasons why he would resist – as he always did – breaking his resolve. The definitive argument was that he was making a life choice. But they had laughed at him. They had laughed at his choice.

And on this occasion he didn't take the glass away. He knew that he was now strong enough to drink in moderation. If he was going to relapse he would not have survived the abduction of his daughter. He had said "no" time and again and proved to everybody that he had rejoined the human race. Now he just wanted the freedom to have a glass of wine at lunchtime. He longed to share time with Lucy free of this constraint. He had conquered the demons and alcohol could now be his friend.

As the first few drops of whiskey trickled down his throat, he sensed an exhilaration and relaxation he had longed for over many, many weeks. For Charles, the battle was over. He put the glass back down and looked at it.

"I know that if I so choose, I'll not drink any more today," he said aloud. He stared at the glass for over five minutes. He lifted it to his mouth.

"This is, as Lucy says, a life choice," he said. "Charles Harriman is back. And in control."

He had been thinking about starting another corporate finance business and had a list of people to phone. His mind was now in overdrive. He was alive. The nightmare was over. He allowed himself one final glass of scotch. He would spend the evening writing his business plan. Tomorrow he would buy the girls presents to demonstrate how happy he was. He would take them all out for a meal tonight and announce his new business venture. He would employ an au pair to take care of the new baby. When was that due? Lucy was now three months, or was it four? He was thinking that a woman is pregnant for eight months and eight times four is thirty-two weeks. And add two weeks for those months that have thirty-one days. He laughed aloud in sheer happiness. He was on the way back. He felt like himself, his best self. Therefore, if she was sixteen weeks now the baby would be born in four months, which would be December. No, November. He'd need the au pair in October. That would be interesting. Would Lucy let him have a pretty girl? He had a pal who had one from Sweden. He loved Lucy so much. She had helped him to make a life choice. He owed it all to her. He was on his way back. He had beaten the demons. He was Charles Harriman. He knew that no woman would ever laugh at him again.

When Lucy arrived home she found her husband lying semi-conscious in the grass at the bottom of their garden. Scarlett was crying and trying to wake him up. She immediately called the emergency services for an ambulance and telephoned the A & E unit at the hospital. After Charles had been initially treated by the paramedics and taken by stretcher into the ambulance, she arranged for her neighbour to look after the girls. She then telephoned the manager at the Priory Grange Clinic in Hemel Hempstead before driving to the hospital. She knew from past experience that her husband would recover from his drinking binge within twenty-four hours.

She also knew that life for the Harriman family would never be the same again.

Oliver had always been capable of enjoying his own company. He spent most of his time surrounded by people and so the haven of his flat allowed him quality time. He was looking forward to an evening of solitude, wine and music. He knew that he would think about Amanda. It was now a week since her abrupt departure from the Threadneedles Hotel, which had not allowed him any time to wish her well or ask any questions. It made no sense to him at all. He had always known that her relationship with Zach had been serious, but he had succeeded in occupying her attention without too much difficulty.

She was now proposing to become a guardian of two small boys with a soon-to-be divorced man. Had he imagined the growing passion between the two of them? He had always accepted the basis for 'the deal' and then watched as Amanda struggled with its restrictive terms.

As he wondered what might have been, the bell rang on his mobile. He picked it up and read the message on the screen. It came as some surprise to him.

"Free tonight. Do you fancy my company? Sara."

He had responded without any hesitation and was now awaiting her arrival. Nearly an hour later, she rang the intercom and, a few minutes later, was standing outside his front door holding a bottle. She now lay on his sofa with a glass of champagne in her hand.

"So where is Alex tonight?" he asked.

"Not with me."

He knew from experience with Sara that she had no intention of elaborating.

For some reason he decided to tell her about his aborted liaison with Christina and how near he had come to finding out the answer to his music riddle.

"So, you've still not solved it," she said. "And you've tried so very hard."

He paused at hearing the unexpected praise. He smiled. "It's been a long journey and I felt at times I might be close."

"Take me through the composers again," said Sara.

"All of them?"

"Every one."

"Right," said Oliver. "We started with Rachmaninov. My brother-in-law, Edward, suggested him and, of course, I love his music. But I decided he wasn't the composer. Since first thinking it might be him I've replayed the second piano concerto many times. Obviously he's produced quite a wide selection of other music. But I'm certain it wasn't Rachmaninov.

"I then asked my father, who suggested it could be Shostakovich. He thought I should listen to the 'Leningrad', which was marvellous, but convinced me that this wasn't the composer of my piece either."

He wandered over and refilled her glass. She stretched out her legs and rested them on the arm of the sofa.

"My brother-in-law became involved again and this time suggested Medtner. I enjoyed his music but knew immediately it wasn't him." At this point he sat down and looked Sara directly in the eyes.

"Then came Amanda," he said.

"Who's Amanda?" she asked. "Oh, of course, Alistair's sister from City Fiction. I've heard all about her."

"Let's move on," said Oliver. "She suggested Tchaikovsky. He was never in the frame because his style is so different." He paused again.

"Then my father put forward Anton Rubinstein. I hadn't heard of him but I'm still playing his music. Not him either."

He looked at her. "Who came next?"

She laughed. "Did someone perhaps suggest Franz Liszt?"

"It was a good idea and I thank you for it, but not my man. I liked 'Liebestraum', which I'd heard many times before, but your suggestion of the 'Mephisto Waltz' was fun."

He poured them both some more champagne.

"The final thought came from the music shop – Mussorgsky. His music is great and his piece 'Pictures at an Exhibition' made me wonder whether it might be him. But no."

"So you met this Christina in a hotel and she was going to tell you what the piece of music is called, but it didn't work out?"

"Something like that."

Their eyes met.

"Would you like to stay the night?" he asked.

She looked at him and shook her head. She then stood up and put her arms around his neck, kissing him lightly on the cheek.

"I'd love to stay and talk until the early hours, but then I have to go home."

"Home to Alex?"

"Yes. She'll be waiting for me, Oliver."

Chapter Twelve

He was sound asleep and dreaming. The images he was seeing were fuzzy and a constant banging sound resounded in his head. He wanted to continue in his reverie but the noise would not abate. Finally he gave up the battle and opened his eyes – and immediately realised that there was someone knocking on the door of his flat. He turned over and looked at his watch. It was 6.54am. He had fallen asleep on his sofa in the early hours of the morning.

He struggled to get up and, having risen reluctantly from his comfy base, crawled slowly towards the sound. He undid the lock, grabbed the handle and pulled the door open.

"I have a taxi waiting," she said.

It was Amanda, looking dazzling in a pink summer dress. Her eyes looked tired but, as she saw him, a smile melted over her whole face.

"A taxi?" asked a bemused Oliver. "Why, where, what's this all about? Where's Zach?"

She stood completely still and made no attempt to enter his apartment.

"Go and put your jacket on please, Oliver. The meter is ticking."

"I need five minutes," he said. "Come on in. There's coffee in the kitchen."

She stepped inside but waited as he went into the bathroom, shaved at a record speed, splashed water over himself, combed his hair, went back into the bedroom, and changed his clothes. They left the flat together without speaking a word and, within a few moments, he found himself in the back of a London cab travelling through Holborn, along Oxford Street and on to Trafalgar Square. Amanda asked the driver to drop them off at Admiralty Arch on the south side of the monument. They got out of the cab and Amanda paid the fare.

Oliver had remained quiet during the journey from his flat but as they stood on the pavement, he spoke.

"Amanda, what are we doing here?" he asked.

"What do you think? We're going to walk down the Mall holding hands."

He looked at her in complete amazement. He ran his hand through his hair and undid the middle button of his jacket.

"Hey, that's my line," he laughed.

"And, when we reach the end, we'll decide whether to complete our deal."

Oliver hesitated before speaking. Why was she raising the issue of the deal again? He had thought that events had overtaken it. He could not understand why she was at his side so early on a Sunday morning. She had been resolute. They were to walk down the Mall and then what? They were to make a decision. But first, he assumed, they would talk to each other.

One kilometre to discover the outcome of their deliberations.

They started the walk down the Mall. As they passed under the Arch, they gazed up at its structure. Once used as the residence of the first sea lord and the heads of the Royal Navy, it now functioned as government offices. They took the south side, passing Horse Guards Parade and walking parallel to St. James's Park. There was no traffic as it was a Sunday. There were already a number of people enjoying the summer morning and there were horses being exercised in Green Park on the north side.

They walked slowly together. Amanda moved her right hand towards Oliver's and then took it away.

"Zach has gone back to his wife," she said in a quiet voice. They had covered over two hundred yards. "I suppose they always do."

Oliver stopped and turned towards her.

"How did he tell you?"

"He was pretty specific. There was no discussion. I already knew something was wrong because of the look his wife had given me when I had collected the boys from her house." She paused and wiped her hand over her face. "He put them in the car and told me that she had made an amazing recovery and

244

they wanted to be a family again. He said I could stay in the house as long as I wanted, but I've already moved back to the flat." She paused and looked at him. "Funny that. I'd not even thought about putting it on the market. Perhaps I'm not such a dumb blonde after all."

They continued walking together.

"I never stopped thinking about you – but I know you won't believe me," she said.

"Does Alistair know?"

"Yes. He laughed at me."

The air was still and yet Oliver noticed that she was perspiring slightly. Neither of them slackened their pace. They were now half way down the Mall and Buckingham Palace was looming ahead. They could see the Queen Victoria Memorial looming before them.

"So I'm back in favour?" he said.

"You were never out of favour, Oliver. I got myself in a muddle over Sara and then Zach wrote me this letter… I suppose I'm a bit of a romantic at heart. I fell for it. To be fair, I think he meant it when he wrote it." She hesitated before continuing.

"If his wife has recovered and he wants the boys to have their rightful family home, I suppose I can't really complain about being unceremoniously dumped…" She laughed softly.

"So you decided I might just be there waiting for you in my flat?"

"It seemed worth the cost of a taxi fare." She smiled.

"So, at the end of the Mall we kiss and make up and then go to bed together?"

"Well, we do still have a deal to complete."

"Until Zach's wife harasses somebody else and he decides he made a mistake and wants you back."

Amanda maintained her stride and took Oliver with her. The trees were in full leaf and early morning birdsong crooned around them. A helicopter buzzed overhead and the planes were taking the eastern route into Heathrow.

"We became very close," she said.

"We did."

"Tell me you don't love me."

"Is it that simple?"

"Perhaps not," she replied, "but it's not a bad starting point."

Oliver tried to slow the pace but Amanda carried on without hesitating.

"Your dream is coming true, Oliver. You texted me in Paris saying you wanted to walk down the Mall holding hands."

She continued to look straight ahead as they maintained their pace. Buckingham Palace filled their vision as they looked up.

"Relationships are much more than just holding hands."

"Are they? We're together. We've always wanted to be with each other. We've wanted to go to bed but I was trying to help Alistair. You've been distracted with your new business and with what's-her-name, Sara. I've been charmed, foolishly, by Zach." She paused and turned to face him. "I was needed and it was seductive. I loved the boys but they never really wanted me. I'm not sure why Zach came back. His wife recovered so quickly and he started going round to her house more and more often."

"It serves no purpose, Amanda, going on about it," said Oliver. "This needs to be about us now."

"Yes, it is about us. It was always about us, really. So, do we begin again and try to rebuild our relationship? It's all I've ever really wanted." She put her hands up to his face. "No man has ever excited me the way you do."

They had reached the end of the Mall. Amanda honestly did not know whether he would commit. She had agonised about how to approach him. Night after night, after the tears of frustration had dried themselves out, she had considered her options. She had made several attempts at writing a letter but she lacked Zach's literary talents. She thought of texting and wrote a number of emails, none of which she'd been able to send. She'd called the taxi in a rush of spontaneity, after remembering the single line text Oliver had sent her. She would recreate his fantasy; she would appeal to his romantic instinct. And when he'd responded immediately and opened the flat door, her morale had soared. But now, after walking down the Mall, Oliver was simply not reacting. She had nothing more to offer.

"Let's find a bench in the park," he said.

They did not have to walk far and were soon sitting beside each other on a hard wooden seat. A few people milled around.

Oliver turned to Amanda and gazed upon her face. Even now her beauty dazzled him as her face caught the rays of the early morning sun.

"Would you like to know something?" he asked.

"What?"

"There was no need to walk down the Mall – although I've enjoyed it."

"Why? Why was there no need?"

"Because I had already made up my mind as we went under the Arch."

"Made up your mind?"

Oliver stood and lifted Amanda to her feet. The dress hung naturally over her hips and he looked at her and saw only her lips. He put his arms around her and pressed her towards him. She immediately responded and he felt her fingers probing his back. They stayed there for some moments. He then stepped back and put his hands tenderly to the sides of her face.

Slowly he moved towards her and brought his lips down upon hers. She responded and he felt her tongue slowly enter his mouth. They stayed together for several minutes, getting closer and closer.

Oliver pulled back, holding both her hands.

"Time to make a life together at last," he said.

Amanda looked at him and gave a half smile.

"I've made a mess of this." She wiped her eyes. "I've been lying in my flat wondering if you'd ever take me back." Tears continued to well, threatening to spill onto her cheeks. "I've been hurting, Oliver. Do you believe me?"

"You are the most beautiful woman I've ever seen," he said. "And I want to make you the happiest too. I want us to share our lives."

"You really mean that?"

"Yes, Amanda. I really mean what I'm saying. We're together now and this time, that is how it's going to stay."

"Because we love each other."

"Right," said Oliver, "but there's another reason."

"What?" she asked. "What other reason could there possibly be?"

"Amanda, a deal's a deal!" he laughed, as he threw his arms around her.

The End

Postscript

A week later, when Amanda was showering after another night spent at his flat, Oliver received the following text message:

"You English have an expression: 'a bitch.' Well, Oliver, I am not a bitch. The music was composed by Shostakovich and is called 'The Assault on Beautiful Gorky'. Did you find her? Love Christina."

About the author

Tony Drury is a corporate financier based in the City of London. He is a Fellow of the Institute of Bankers and a Member of the Securities Institute.

Tony has written extensively over the years and is particularly well known for his financial and political books. He blogs weekly for www.enterprisebritain.com - both in his name and that of his alter ego Mr Angry. He writes for 'The Freedom Association' on City matters and broadcasts every Tuesday on the Hardman Video Channel which reaches a range of financial institutions.

He is chairman of Axiom Capital Limited, a London based corporate finance house, and chairman of Ford Eagle Group, a business advisory company, which is based in Hong Kong.

He lives in Bedfordshire with his wife, and they have a son and daughter, both now married.

He published his first work of fiction *Megan's Game* in May 2012 to critical acclaim. *The Deal* continues his romantic thriller theme as does his third book *Cholesterol*, which will be published in Spring 2013.

For more information about Tony please go to
www.tonydrury.com

You can follow Tony on Twitter @mrtonydrury

Coming next...

Cholesterol

Adrian Dexter is a corporate financier struggling through the turbulence of recession in 2012. Far away from the City of London, the love of his life waits for him in Johannesburg - as does his mortal enemy and notorious South African fraudster, Nigel de Groute. As if that wasn't enough, he is also about to turn sixty.

When Adrian meets the beautiful Helen Greenwood and they embark on a passionate affair, he begins to feel young again. But his newfound happiness is about to be rudely interrupted…

A business merger; an unplanned pregnancy; a kidnapping; a royal ambush – suddenly Adrian's life is spiralling out of control. Can he get a grip before it's too late? Can DI Sarah Rudd continue to triumph in her fight against evil and corruption? And don't forget about those nasty fatty deposits lurking beneath the surface…

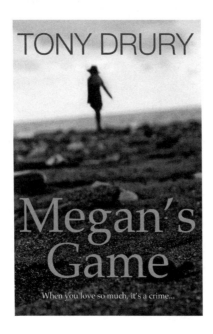

City veteran has scheming broker's story to tell *Daily Telegraph*

Tony enjoys success story *Leighton Buzzard Observer*

I have just finished reading Fifty Shades of Grey and it isn't a patch on 'Megan's Game'....I look forward to your next book *Lizzie Lee*

As good as John Grisham *Judy Constantine*

It's a very, very good book *Austra Laukyte*

A thoroughly enjoyable read and very moving *Roger Chapman*